DEEP SLEEPERS

DEEP
SLEEPERS

BALMUIR
BOOK
PUBLISHING
LTD.

JOHN STARNES

Cover design based on an oil painting of a
troika copied by the author from an example
of Palekh art on a lacquer box dated 1878.

© 1981
Balmuir Book Publishing Ltd.
302-150 Wellington Street
Ottawa, Canada K1P 5A4   ISBN 0-919511-03-1

For Helen Gordon Robinson

ONE

S.S. Hauptsturmführer Franz Vogel flicked an imaginary speck of dust from the front of his well tailored black uniform trimmed with silver braid, as he walked briskly to the large black Mercedes parked outside.

"Heil Hitler."

Vogel's response to his chauffeur's salute was automatic, as he flipped his right forearm from the elbow.

"Any messages, Karl?"

"Jawohl, Herr Hauptsturmführer. A telegram."

Vogel quickly broke the seal and read the message, which, he noted, had been dispatched from S.S. Headquarters, Berlin, at 0515 hours. The date was Thursday, July 16, 1942.

S.S. Haupsturmführer Vogel. Köln Abteilung. Text begins: Regret today's meeting cancelled, due Führer's decision to move headquarters immediately from Wolfsschanz to Werewolf, Vinnitsa. Will advise soonest new time, date and place. Signed, Horst Bruggman. S.S. Ober-führer. S.S.

"Plans have changed Karl. I will not be flying to Berlin. Instead, we will drive to Düsseldorf. We do not need to hurry."

As they made their way slowly along the Rhine road from Cologne to Düsseldorf, Vogel mused that if Hitler was moving his headquarters to the Ukraine, it meant he was closing in for the kill. Good. Soon all of Russia would be in German hands. He glanced out the window at the blue sky through the high clouds, and thought himself fortunate. It was probably raining in Berlin.

Vogel was not to know that the 16th of July, 1942 which had begun so pleasantly along the middle Rhine, was the last day of his life. He and his driver were killed instantly by the blast from a bomb dropped during the first R.A.F. daylight raid on the Ruhr. Elsewhere, in Cologne, many others died that day, including Heide Prager; schoolgirl.

Heide Prager's Hitlermadschen membership card was still gripped tightly in the right hand of the severed arm. She had felt nothing as blood spurted from her gaping wrist. A piece of concrete torn loose by the direct hit on the Severins Tor shelter in Cologne had smashed into the top of her skull, bringing the release of unconsciousness before death.

A jackboot gently kicked the card loose. It was picked up and examined. The man bent over the girl's body, wiped the card against a dry part of her blouse to remove the still wet blood, then carefully removed the thin gold chain and cross from her neck. He placed the two items in the side pocket of his field-grey tunic before turning to examine the next of the ten bodies in the devastated shelter.

A sparrow hopped among the rubble where Anton Prager lay, face up, less than a kilometre from the scene of his daughter's mutilation. He was half-conscious, his left leg pinned beneath the twisted mass of joists and beams. The July sun was hot on his face, when it cut through the clouds and smoke drifting across Cologne. He angrily wiped the sweat and the flies from his mouth and eyes. Christ, how long had he been like this? It seemed hours since the 'all-clear' had sounded. The daylight raid had caught the bloody Nazis by surprise. It had not lasted long but it had been heavy. It must have caused a lot of damage along the Rhine.

Anton groaned as he tried to shift his body slightly. His whole left side throbbed. Where in hell were the rescue squads? He could smell burning rubber but he could see nothing for the rubble around him. He hoped that Maria and Heide had managed to reach shelter.

"Karl. Komme hier, noch ein."

A search party member turned under the broken arch of the stone gateway leading from the Koblenzer strasse and climbed over the debris to join his mate. They worked quickly with shovels and crowbars. Using a broken cross-beam as a lever they dragged Anton free. The sudden release of pressure from the twisted leg brought him back to consciousness with a scream of pain.

"Hold him still Joachim, I'll look for the stretcher party."

Karl scrambled back towards the Koblenzer strasse. It was getting dark. Anton lost consciousness again. His was a release that Maria Prager would have welcomed. She and Heide had parted only minutes before the sirens began their ululating sound . The shelter in which she took refuge had been untouched. But as she sat in it listening to the dull thud of explosives, the conviction grew deep inside her that the Prager family was in trouble. By the time the 'all clear' sounded, Maria was in a state of near-panic. As she rushed from the dark shelter into the opaque daylight her eyes were blinded. She stopped. Desolation was everywhere. She crossed herself and muttered, "In namen Vater, Sohn und Heilige Geist."

Maria Prager, like Anton, was a secret member of the German Communist Party. They had joined together in 1928. While Anton had moved over the years from the benevolent agnosticism of his youth to the atheism that the Party preferred, Maria had held tenaciously to her Roman Catholic belief. It had not hindered her work for the Party. And now, alone, convinced that her family was destroyed she clung to her faith as she had never done before.

Maria set off in the direction her daughter had gone when they parted an hour before. Others were in the streets now searching for family and friends. At one nearby shelter that had been hit Maria searched for Heide while an old woman, bleeding from her forehead and arm, hysterically pulled free the battered corpse of her husband. At another a uniformed policeman stopped her from going in. He assured her that he had checked the bodies and there were no children amongst them. Late in the day, about the time that the workmen Karl and Joachim were prying Anton loose, Maria was outside the remains of the house they rented. It had been demolished. She cared nothing for the house and little for its contents, but the sight of the ruin together with her inability to find any trace of her husband and daughter, was too much. She recalled the terror and the despair she had experienced two years earlier when Heide had nearly died from acute peritonitis. Only an emergency appendectomy performed by a skilled surgeon had saved her life. This was far worse. Tears she had fought back all afternoon poured down her cheeks. She fell to the pavement, sobbing.

It was dark before she struggled to her feet. Through the endless hours of the night she wandered the streets. Several times her search took her to the smouldering ruins of the Bayerische Analien und Soda Fabrik laboratory where Anton worked. He was not there. As dawn broke a nurse going off duty at a temporary hospital persuaded her to take a sedative and took her to an emergency shelter that had been set up to provide beds for the homeless.

Maria slept fitfully through the next day and night. When her head cleared, she was torn between a desire to remain burrowed under the rough grey blanket and an urge to renew her search.

It was the pain of those around her that finally drove Maria Prager back onto the street. The clean-up had begun. Streets were being repaired and cleared for traffic. Unsafe walls, the only remains of a thousand structures, were being demolished. Bodies were being buried in special cemeteries. Maria filed reports on both Heide and Anton. Then she waited.

It was two weeks after the raid before police located her to tell her that Anton was alive in a temporary hospital set up in Bad Godesberg. When she reached him, she learned that although the doctors had been able successfully to reset his leg, there was little they could do about his smashed kneecap. He would be permanently lame. It mattered nothing to Maria. She had all but given up hope, when she was told that her husband had survived. Her prayers had been answered, at least in part.

While Anton was in hospital, Maria was allowed to remain in Cologne and continue her search for Heide. But on the day he was released they were told they had to move to Tützing in Bavaria where a new job and accommodation awaited them.

They begged and pleaded with the billetting authorities to let them stay longer in Cologne. For a few days they were successful.

Maria used the precious time to scour the city for some trace of her daughter. On the wet Wednesday following Anton's release from hospital, they got in touch with the Communist Party to enlist its help in the search, and to report their impending transfer to Tützing.

The meeting with their contact took place in Cologne's Sud Parc, in the rain. The water streaming down her face felt good to Maria. It felt like tears. Her own tears had dried up a week before. She wanted so much to cry, but there was nothing left with which she could.

"We will keep looking for Heide," their contact promised. "As soon as you can, go to Munich. There your contact will be Fritz. He is a waiter in the Hofbraühaus and is well known there. If we have word of Heide, he will tell you."

Next morning when they reported to the Cologne billetting office a faceless official refused to let them remain any longer.

"Your daughter is a missing person, she may even be dead. You cannot stay here looking for her forever. If she is alive she will turn up and you will be contacted. Your report is on file. In the meantime, Herr Prager, there is much work to be done in Munich and a billet has been arranged for you and your wife in Tützing."

Maria tried to summon up tears to assist in her plea. They would not come. They would have done no good. The would-be Gestapo man handed them their transit papers and dismissed them with a military click of his heels.

"Heil Hitler," sneered Anton to himself and hoped that the day would come when the bastard had to be dug out from under a pile of rubble.

Tützing was very different from Cologne. It remained undamaged by war, unchanged from what it must have been like a century earlier. The architecture was distinctively Bavarian with steep roof-tops overhanging large, carved wooden balconies. Life size bucolic scenes were painted in a baroque style on both ends of many of the barns. The main street ran for three or four kilometres, skirting the west side of the lake. Off it ran small side streets crossed by streams which were carefully dyked to provide irrigation for the gardens. It took Anton and Maria months to adjust to village life and even longer to be accepted by the villagers. Anton's job at the Bayerishche Analien und Soda Fabrik laboratory differed little from his former job in Cologne. He was still a technician with special knowledge of dye stuffs and film emulsions. He had, however, been given a promotion, mainly because he could not stand for long periods, and now had three employees working under him.

They were allocated a small apartment over a bakery. It had only two rooms, a small bedroom and a combination living room, dining room, kitchen. There was cold running water. A coal fire which heated both the oven and the apartment and could also be used for bringing pots of water to the boil. One part of the stove was constructed of green glazed ceramic tile and must have been at least a hundred years old. In the first weeks there, they were able to make three trips to Munich: once to fill out more forms and twice to buy furniture. On their second trip they made contact with Fritz. He turned out to be a beefy, middle-aged waiter in the Hofbraühaus whose specialty was Nazi marching songs and sentimental Bavarian lieder. His heartiness was a tonic for Maria. It made her smile for the first time since she said goodbye to Heide a thousand years before. It did nothing for Anton.

Fritz had no news of Heide, but promised that they would be contacted if anything came to light. The local authorities at Tutzing were sympathetic and helpful. They kept up a flow of enquiries to the Cologne city administration. The replies were unchanged: Heide was listed as 'missing.' Months went by. Summer turned to autumn and autumn to winter. They continued to hope that she might be alive, but slowly the void in their lives was being filled by new routines. They were getting used to Heide not being there, but Maria still could not cry and she was feeling older than her forty-two years.

* *

"Herr Prager?"

Snow clung to the hood of the loden coat of the woman standing at the door. Her face was half in shadow.

"Jah. I am Anton Prager."

"Fritz suggested I come to see you. I have news of your daughter."

Anton opened the door and stood back.

"Come in. This is not a night to be walking. Have you come far?"

"From Pahl. I am the school teacher there. My name is Schneider. Lotte Schneider."

Without her overcoat she seemed thin, almost frail, an impression that was heightened by the streaks of grey in her hair. Piercing blue eyes, high cheek bones and a deeply lined face belied any weakness. Anton found it hard to guess her age. Somewhere around fifty which could mean that she had probably joined the German Communist party before he had.

"Would you like coffee and something to eat?"

"I would prefer something stronger if you have it. Nothing to eat."

Anton brought out from the corner cupboard a small bottle of local pear brandy, a half-empty bottle of Slivovitz and an unopened bottle of Steinhager they had brought with them from Cologne.

"Not much choice, I'm afraid."

"I would prefer the Steinhager. I can't stand these Southern German drinks."

Anton broke the heavy seal on the stone bottle and poured three glasses. He raised his glass.

"To us."

Lotte Schneider stared at her glass. Maria, standing, gazed at the visitor.

"I am afraid I have bad news about your daughter. We have established that she was killed during the British air raid. Her body was discovered with a number of others when they were searching through the debris around the Severins Tor. She was the only child among them. This was found on her."

Lotte Schneider handed Anton the thin gold chain and discoloured cross.

Anton let the chain run through his fingers. On the cross the letter 'H' was inscribed with the date of her first communion. He handed it to Maria. They didn't look at one another.

"We are sorry. I am also sorry that we were unable to tell you sooner. Not long after you left Cologne, we knew that she had been killed."

Anton and Maria both started to speak at once.

"I know. You ask why? The Party had good reason. By chance the person to find the gold chain was a Party member. He concealed his discovery and there turned out to be no other way of identifiying the body. Only two of the ten bodies discovered were eventually identified. The unidentified bodies, including that of Heide, were given a decent burial in a new cemetery on the outskirts. Here is a photograph of Heide's grave."

Anton passed the photograph to Maria.

"We had intended to tell you shortly after her death was known, but the matter was taken out of our hands at a higher level and we were asked to delay informing you. It seemed that by doing so Party interests could be furthered. We are sorry that we have had to add to the months of anguish and uncertainty. We hope that you will be willing to help the Party and make Heide's unfortunate death serve a good cause?"

Anton looked quickly at Maria. Her eyes were fixed on the photograph, her face expressionless. He passed a hand through his hair and poured another drink for all of them.

"I suppose there is no mistake?"

"No. We are quite certain that Heide was killed. However, the official records still list her as 'Missing'."

Anton grunted. Maria blew her nose.

"What do you want us to do?"

Lotte looked from one to the other and slowly finished her drink.

"What we ask of you may be particularly difficult. We want you to drop all your other activities for the Party and accept a replacement for Heide. We want you to pretend that she is Heide. All the details will be attended to. What you have to do is accept this person as Heide; bring her up as your own daughter and present her to the world as your daughter."

Anton could not think of anything to say. Maria whose gaze had not lifted from the gold chain since it was handed to her, passed it and the photograph back to Anton. She looked steadily at Lotte. Her grey eyes, which had lost all their sparkle in the months since she and Heide parted, were expressionless.

"That will not be easy," she said.

"I know."

"We may not like her."

"That is possible. We all do many things with people we do not like in serving the cause. But you probably will not dislike her. Certainly she will not be as a daughter to you. She has a difficult, even dangerous assignment to prepare for. She will need all the help you can give her, particularly in the early years. No, I don't think you will dislike her."

Anton said nothing. Lotte got up and pushed aside the heavy curtains. She waited for their reply. It was Maria who finally spoke, ending minutes of silence.

"We will do it," she said quietly.

"Good."

There was another, longer silence. Finally, Lotte Schneider spoke again.

"The snow has stopped." Then, "I will come back in about ten days when our plans are completed. In the meantime go on with your lives as before. You should continue your inquiries about Heide. I am sorry I cannot leave the photograph with you and I must have the gold cross back; 'Heide' will be wearing it when you are reunited."

Anton helped her into her loden coat and opened the door. The wind had shifted from the east to the south. The snow would soon melt. Lotte quickly walked away from the bakery without a backwards glance.

Anton and Maria sat up all night. They did not drink any more of the Steinhager. For long periods they sat quiet and motionless. When they spoke it was of Heide as she had been, not of Lotte Schneider and the news that she had brought or of the task they had accepted. They did not speculate on the new 'Heide'. Before dawn they heard the bakery being opened beneath them in preparation for making the first batches of bread. Maria rose and cleared the bottles from the table. She carried the glasses to the sink and washed them. As she carefully dried them, a solitary tear at last rolled down each cheek. She had buried her daughter. Now she would have to let Heide live.

The days that followed were difficult for both Anton and Maria, but more so for him. Neither had wavered in their support for the Party since they joined it in 1928 when they lived in Berlin. Their conversion to Communism had been gradual and had arisen out of a genuine search for solutions to the seemingly insoluble social problems that plagued their country in the aftermath of World War I. When they reached their road to Damascus, they had wanted to proclaim their good news from the roof tops. Hans Weber, himself an openly proclaimed Party member, had dissuaded them. He foresaw troubled days ahead when Party members would be rounded up and jailed. In that day it would be essential that fertile seed remain undetected from which new roots could spring and the work continue. They belonged to a small cell of about a dozen people which Weber led. In addition, they each, separately, belonged to another cell where they were known only by their first names.

In 1933 when the Nazis, now in power, decided to smash the German Communist Party and the S.S. methodically set about the task, Weber's precautions paid off. Weber himself was hunted but escaped through Switzerland, Italy and Greece to the Soviet Union. En route he used the Prager home as a safehouse for several nights. Two other couples in Weber's cell were picked up and never seen again. They had been briefly active in the 1920s before going underground but the long tentacles of the Gestapo had sought them out and found them. They apparently did not divulge their more recent contacts for the others in the cell remained untouched. They could never be sure, however, that they were not part of the remnant that the Nazis deliberately left behind to monitor for any resurgence. Only the fact that they remained unharmed throughout the search for Weber suggested that in fact they were undetected and their arrested comrades had not broken under interrogation. The other two cells suffered still heavier casualties and only their self-imposed security measures prevented complete chaos.

The dual dimensions which Party membership had given to each of their lives since the events of 1933 had long since become an accepted feature. Both of them carried out difficult, sometimes hazardous assignments; acting as couriers, providing a safehouse, laundering secret Party funds. The most difficult times were the months, sometimes years, of almost total inaction. The decimation of the Party and the strictly enforced separation of Soviet espionage from local and national Party activities had left little room for manoeuvre. The uncovering of the Schulze-Boysen spy ring by the Gestapo on August 31, 1942, ended all of that. Overnight the Red Orchestra, the Soviet espionage network in Western Europe, was bereft of its Berlin string section. At the 'Centre', the building on Znamensky Street in Moscow which was the home of the Soviet Military Intelligence, the Director was forced to break his self-imposed embargo and approach the Central Committee for permission to use its contacts with the German Communist Party to help fill the void while he sought to replace the Berlin strings.

The Pragers in far off Cologne knew nothing of the Schulze-Boysens in Berlin or the aristocratic network they masterminded. They did, however, notice a decided upswing in the number of assignments they were given by the Party in the fall of 1942, and they were grateful for it. It presented them simultaneously with an opportunity to advance an ideal and a cause in which they fervently believed and to help eradicate the canker that was destroying Germany. Lotte Schneider had warned them that their new mission would mean an end to these activities. From here on nothing would be asked of them that would endanger the establishment of the new identity of the girl who would replace their daughter. The years of inaction would be returning.

The real Heide had brought much joy to their lives. She had inherited not only Maria's beauty but much of her even temperament and love of books and music. She was a good student but school had brought problems. Education was being used by the Nazis to instill loyalty to the regime as the highest good. The Pragers had been forced to conceal their political loyalties from the child lest she betray them either accidentally or under duress. When Heide was of age to join the Hitler Jugende, Anton was beside himself with rage, but did not try to stop her. Except for whispered conversations with Maria at night he kept it bottled up inside, but his sullenness against the 'bloody Nazis' increased. They relied on Maria's guiding the child's reading to counteract the propaganda of Goebbels' machine. The relationship with the new Heide would be easier in that respect. But in everything else it would be difficult. Anton worried as they waited that it would be too much for Maria. She and her daughter had a special love. He need not have worried. Maria had buried her child.

In both their minds, however, was the question of what the new Heide would be like and what the task would be that she was to perform. There was no use speculating. The full answer to the second part they might never know. The first they would find out in time.

It was five weeks before Lotte Schneider appeared again. Maria and Anton found the time long.

"I am sorry for the delay. The Gestapo discovered a courier network. We have had to re-arrange matters."

Lotte accepted Anton's offer of a glass of Steinhager. She noticed that he had to break open a new bottle. She wondered how many he had opened since last they met. His bloodshot eyes suggested there had been quite a few.

"You will receive word, probably through the local police, that a girl answering the description of your daughter has been tentatively identified. You will be asked to travel to Cologne to identify her, which you will do. She resembles Heide in certain respects although you will find her somewhat more developed since she is older. She speaks fluent German but has a north German rather than the Rhineland accent that Heide probably developed in school. You will find her well briefed on her family background but you will have to coach her to fill in the gaps. When your identification has been formalized and the necessary papers signed, you will bring her back here where you will continue to live."

"How was she discovered?" asked Anton.

"It seems she was found in the field of a farmer in Wesseling, south of Cologne. She appeared to be in a state of shock with numerous small cuts over her body. The farmer and his wife took her in and restored her to health, although she obviously suffered from severe amnesia. Their son had been drafted into the army and had been killed on the Russian front. They kept the girl and she helped them work the farm. Recently, following an accident in which she was knocked on the head, her memory began to return and she remembered her name. You will have no trouble recognizing her. She will be wearing the gold chain she was given at her first communion and both her hands will be bandaged, for they were hurt in the accident."

"Will the Cologne authorities not be suspicious?" asked Anton.

"No there is no reason for them to suspect anything. This will be only one of thousands of cases involving missing persons. A number of similar cases have occurred since the British began their heavy bombing. The girl is well briefed and the farmer was carefully chosen. He and his wife have also been secret members of the Party for many years. The girl has been living with them for some time and the authorities are already checking out their report that she is Heide Prager. Your recognition of her will confirm the matter. The only danger is that you might know too much and let something slip. To avoid that it is best that I tell you no more now. You must continue to live as usual until the Cologne authorities contact you. I will be in touch again in a few months. I don't think you will require money now. If you do, or if you want to contact me for any reason, do so through Fritz, not directly."

Lotte went as unobtrusively as she had appeared. Anton poured himself another drink and threw it back. Maria watched him in silence. He was drinking more than she had ever known him to do. She said nothing but resolved to watch carefully lest it continue and start to loosen his tongue.

TWO

The Boeing 747 from Tokyo touched down at Vancouver International airport as lightly as a feather. When the huge aircraft had been locked onto the unloading ramp and the doors opened, the passengers slowly emerged, making their way towards the customs and passport control area.

Lines quickly formed before the half dozen booths where immigration officers were stationed. When his turn came the man stepped forward and presented his Canadian passport with his gloved left hand. The immigration officer leafed through the pages of the passport and glanced briefly at the holder.

Name: Thomas Rolf Volker
Birthplace: Kitchener, Ontario, Canada
Birthdate: 16 July 1921
Sex: M
Height: 173 cm
Hair: Black
Eyes: Brown
Distinguishing marks: None.

The officer glanced at the passport. The first few pages were filled with entry and exit stamps from different countries.

"How long have you been out of Canada?"

"About three weeks."

"Have you anything to declare?"

"I bought a bottle of Suntory in Tokyo. That's all."

The immigration officer stamped the passport and returned it to him. He turned towards the next traveller. Had he been able to read the inscription on a tombstone erected some fifty years ago in a Lutheran churchyard near St. Jacob's, on the outskirts of Waterloo, he would have ordered the man detained for questioning. The faded etching read: 'Thomas Rolf Volker. Beloved son of Wolfgang and Cornelia Volker. Born July 16, 1921. Died January 10, 1927. His soul lives on.'

It seemed more than his soul lived on. Once through customs the reincarnation of Thomas Volker walked purposefully to the nearest bank of pay telephones. He thumbed through the yellow pages for the listing of Sheraton Hotels, dialed the toll-free number for the Sheraton Mount Royal in Montreal and booked a room. From there he walked over to the Pan-Am desk and bought a return ticket on the next flight to Los Angeles.

"Will that be cash, sir."

"No, I would like to use my American Express card."

When the transaction was finished he found a men's washroom. Before entering it he scrutinized the usual array of weary travellers, bustling air crew and haggard businessmen in the lounge area. Inside he slowly and methodically washed and shaved before changing his shirt, tie and jacket. He stowed his raincoat in the suitcase, extracted a pair of glasses from it, adjusted them on his face and returned to the lounge. Once again he checked the crowd before moving briskly to the Air Canada counter and purchasing a one-way ticket to Toronto.

"Your name, sir."

"James Rawlins."

"Will that be cash or charge, sir?"

"Cash please."

He paid for the ticket in crisp twenty dollar bills and hurried to the departure lounge as they called the flight for boarding. On board the plane he kept his eyes fixed on the door until it was closed. No one boarded after him and as they taxied onto the runway the man's face visibly relaxed.

Thomas Volker alias James Rawlins made a point of being last to leave the plane after it arrived at Toronto. He was alert as he walked through the terminal, after having picked up his suitcase at the baggage carousel, to the limousine stand where he hailed a car and instructed the driver to take him to the Royal York Hotel. At the hotel he crossed the road to the railway station and descended to the subway line where he caught the Yonge Street train. At Bloor Street he got off and went into the bustling Hudson's Bay Company store through the direct access route from the subway system. After ten minutes ascending and descending the escalators he left the store. He went back down to the subway line and caught the west bound train, getting off at the next stop. No one else got off the train. Satisfied that he had not been followed he walked the couple of hundred yards to the Park Plaza Hotel.

"Do you have a reservation, sir."

"No, I'm afraid I do not, I do hope you have a vacancy," he replied in a very English accent.

"Yes, I'm sure we have. Would you like to complete the registration card Mr. uh? Mr?"

"Finlayson, Roger Finlayson."

* * * * * * * * * *   * * * * * * * * *

At every level of government in every belligerent country, the war brought new strains. The city of Cologne was no exception. The old Rathaus quickly proved inadequate to house the burgeoning bureaucracy that war demanded. Whole departments moved out into office blocks, some to old and spaciously incongruous leftovers of a more gracious age, others to hastily constructed temporary buildings. Anton Prager was nervous as he climbed the stairs of the building that housed the department established to deal with the problems of dispossessed and missing persons. Suppose something had gone wrong? What if some neighbour had told the Gestapo that Heide had only recently come to live on the farm? What if their links with the Party had been uncovered?

In the end it was ridiculously simple. He and Heide met in the sparsely furnished office of a junior official of the Cologne government. Anton was surprised at the emotion he was able to put into his performance, considerably aided by the warmth with which his 'daughter' greeted him. Her hugs and kisses and her tears seemed genuine. She did resemble Heide. Her eyes were almost a sapphire blue and wider spaced, her cheek bones slightly more prominent but the other features remarkably similar. Although dressed as a girl, to Anton she felt like a woman. This was no child and certainly not his. Their excited talk was interrupted by the tired looking administrator.

"Herr Prager, we had better get on with the paper work."

Anton and Heide sat on hard wooden chairs on the other side of the desk.

"If you will just sign here and here and over the page, at the bottom."

Anton Prager displayed none of his usual contempt for the government and its forms.

"I also have your daughter's new identity card and ration card for which you must sign. You will also need this form so that she can attend school in Bavaria. And you must not forget to sign this form concerning proof of age and take it with you. A new birth certificate will be issued and sent to you in a few weeks."

At last they were finished. As the official showed them out, Heide resumed her chatter, asking how her mother was and telling of the new family she had found at Wesseling, of how kind they had been to her and how sad she had been to say goodbye but happy too for she knew she would soon be seeing him and Mutti.

She kept up the constant stream of small talk until they were out on the street and beyond the first corner, then fell silent. Anton did not speak either. There was much for them to discuss but it would be better if they waited until they were with Maria. The journey to Tützing took a long time. Their passenger train was left standing on sidings several times to make way for trains carrying troops and the material of war. Once they waited while no fewer than three trains passed. Heide had a tattered book that she read from time to time. Anton had only the envelope containing the papers given to them in Cologne. He had read every rule and exception printed on the back of each sheet no fewer than four times by the time they arrived home.

"I could become an expert and write a treatise on the forms of the Third Reich," he thought to himself.

Maria was waiting in the apartment. Without the need for emotional dramatization that had existed when Anton had met her in Cologne, Heide somewhat coldly proferred her hand to her new mother. Maria took it. She asked no questions. Instead she told her new daughter of the plans for the next few days. Tomorrow night the baker and his asistant and the few other villagers with whom she and Anton had made friends would be dropping in to welcome Heide home. Tonight only the village priest would come by.

"I have no need for a priest," the girl said with more than a little contempt in her voice.

"Perhaps not," replied Maria icily, "but Heide Prager does."

Heide accepted the rebuke. Long after, when she was leaving the Prager household, she thanked Maria for it. By then Maria knew that it had been an uncharacteristic slip. The girl had a deep contempt for all religion and a special contempt for Roman Catholicism. Maria was puzzled and hurt by this attitude but concealed her feelings. Heide did the same and carefully acted out her part in Maria's church. Even Anton was not aware of the chasm between the two women in this area.

In everything else the relationship between them grew with the passage of time. It was not easy at first but as the pattern of their lives settled a healthy respect developed. They became, not as mother and daughter, but as older and younger sister, a facet they were careful to conceal from outsiders. Heide carried out her role with skill and sensitivity, forming friendships at school and in the village. Maria for her part never asked the younger woman questions she might not want to answer. It was apparent that she was at least a year or two older than their daughter and, although her German was flawless, Maria knew that it was not her mother tongue. Her intelligence was evident from the ease with which she achieved consistently high marks in school. They shared a love for books and music which did much to compensate for the differences over religion. They also shared a mutual interest in the real Heide. The woman was happy to have someone with whom to share every minute memory of her only child. The girl was delighted to add to the depth of her new identity by vicariously reliving the younger girl's life through her mother's words.

Easier at first, Anton's relationship with her never developed the closeness of Maria's. For one thing, unknown to the Pragers, the girl had no need for a substitute father. She had a father with whom she had shared her childhood and early adolescence. Even now, facing the prospect of years of separation, she felt close to him. She was following in his footsteps in an exacting trade. Her mother on the other hand had died at her birth and Maria was the first woman with whom circumstances had ever permitted her to share her life. An assumed mother, in an assumed life, touched a deep human need. The relationship of Anton to the girl was also complicated by their living arrangements. The rooms over the bakery meant living at close quarters, a problem for all of them, but most particularly for Anton. Heide's replacement obviously was no longer a girl. He could not help but feel the natural urges aroused by close contact. Yet, although the taboos against incest did not really apply, the masquerade they were living not only required that such taboos be maintained but aroused deep inside Anton, a feeling that physical contact with the girl was forbidden. For Heide's part, she was only vaguely aware of the feeling she aroused in Anton. Instinctively, however, she maintained a certain cold professionalism to the relationship. It was made easier for her by the fact that the physical attraction was purely one-sided. The balding, podgy, middle-aged, lame, German chemist who had a constant smell of formaldehyde about him, aroused no passion in her.

Although none of them voiced their satisfaction as the Nazi forces suffered defeat after defeat following the Allied landings in Europe, there was a shared pleasure that the end was in sight for Hitler. By April of 1945 with the Russian armies pushing from the east and the Allied armies and air forces victorious in the west they knew it was only a matter of time before the complete collapse of the Third Reich. Tützing was far removed from the Gotterdämmerung being enacted in Berlin and elsewhere in Germany. Only fragments of news of these events reached the villagers, and that slowly.

Even the unconditional surrender in May had little impact on their lives. The shortages of food and fuel were the most immediate effects. The bakery opened only on Tuesdays and Saturdays. Meat was unobtainable, as was coal. Happily the warmer weather eased their heating needs, fish and poultry were relatively plentiful and winter stocks of potatoes, swedes and beetroot lasted until garden produce again became available. With the surrender all work at the BASF was suspended and Anton was laid off. His period of idleness, however, lasted only a few weeks. Early in June he was recalled and sent to work in a new laboratory, the construction of which had begun months before the war ended. With his new job, Anton was able to enlist the help of the BASF in securing more spacious, self-contained accommodation. The new house eased the strain within the family, especially for Heide who that autumn graduated to Hochschule where she had to work harder in the evenings if she was to continue to excel.

Occasionally, Allied troops of the Occupation passed through, but except for these, the villagers rarely saw an American soldier. The exception was when they made one of their infrequent visits to Munich. There the streets bustled with American soldiers and airmen. They were rich and affable. Although the brashness of some threatened to sour relations with the local population, for the most part their generous love of life made them a welcome relief after six years of war and twelve years of dictatorship.

In April, Heide went alone to Munich to have some teeth filled. She did not relish the thought. But she had waited more than six months for the appointment and, once it was over, the relief, mixed with the smell of early spring that hung in the air left her in a buoyant mood. She decided to take advantage of her day off to stroll through the centre of the city.

"Cigarette?"

She pulled herself up ready to repulse the unsought approach. Her instructions before arriving in Tützing had been to avoid romantic attachments. She realized the wisdom of those instructions and had generally followed them. Only once had she let her guard down. For a brief period around Christmas 1944 she had found herself responding to the puppy-love advances of the baker's son. She kept a tight rein on herself, however, and in January the boy turned eighteen, was called up and disappeared into the bloodbath of the eastern front. After a week of moping around the apartment, she unburdened herself to Maria and quickly recovered.

"Thank you. No."

The tall handsome American in the uniform of a U.S. Army Captain, smiled.

"Then how about a coffee?."

He was obviously older than she was. Probably in his mid-twenties. His white teeth glittered and his eyes sparkled. Before she knew what she was doing, Heide had accepted the invitation.

"We'll go to the railroad station."

Three hours later Heide was infatuated by Captain Frank Delacourt, U.S. Army of Occupation, Munich, and the last bus to Tützing had left. It was the first time since she had entered the training camp for espionage six years before that she had allowed the discipline in her life to slip away. She did not stop to ask what it was about him that appealed to her.

"I can get a jeep and take you home," he volunteered when he heard of her plight.

She agreed, and, an hour later was huddled against him for protection against the cool wind. There was no warmth escaping through his leather jacket, but she imagined there was. Anyway, her own young body felt warmer than it ever had before. She invited him in to meet her parents. He refused. He suggested she come out with him again on Saturday. Heide glowed at the suggestion and quickly agreed. Frank cupped her chin gently in his right hand and kissed her on the lips. She pressed towards him and he responded warmly before pulling away.

Anton Prager watched them from the darkened window of his bedroom. Before Heide turned towards the house after the Captain had disappeared towards Munich, Anton had gone to the kitchen and told Maria of what he had seen.

"Don't worry about it," said Maria. " We can trust Heide."

But, knowing the feelings the girl had aroused in him, Anton did worry about it.

The passage of time from Wednesday to Saturday took seven eternities. In bed at night the heat generated by her body and trapped by the down-filled comforter became the closeness of Frank as she drifted into the twilight of sleep. On the street, in the morning, the snap of fresh air on her cheek became the tingle of his caress. At the supper table the hot chocolate on her upper lip became the softness of his kiss. At the same table afterwards the words on the page of the school notebook became the words of a love letter.

She was not inexperienced in sexual encounters. She had had two men before she became Heide Prager. This time was different. Her precious encounters had been occasions for her to dominate males who loomed large in her life. This time she did not want to dominate but to be dominated. It was different in another way too, she was totally inexperienced in affairs of the heart and suddenly she was head over heels in love. She could not control the emotion or the desire, and she did not care.

Frank Delacourt's experience was the opposite. He was married and he had been in and out of love dozens of times.

At last Thursday passed into Friday, and Friday into Saturday. Shortly after nine o'clock Frank Delacourt appeared in his jeep. Anton let him in with bad grace, but Maria intervened right away to make him welcome. He had brought some coffee and chocolate from the PX which he presented to the mother. It had been a long time since they had had coffee. When Heide came in, Maria dragged Anton to the kitchen with her to boil some water and brew a pot of it.

"Damned Yankees think they can buy anything with their lousy coffee."

Maria fixed him with an icy glower.

"You have nothing to sell," she told him. "This is a gift, and you would do well to accept it as generously as he gave it."

The rich aroma of the coffee as it brewed softened Anton's mood. Even if it had not, the clear indication that he risked Maria's wrath would have kept him quiet. She had never lost her sense of romance and he knew better than to cross her in that area of her life.

"Don't worry, I will talk to Heide about her instructions and remind her of her assignment."

After the second cup of hot coffee had removed the last of the early morning chill from Frank's bones, he and Heide went off to hike through the forested hills that lay to the south of the lake. Frank slung a haversack over his shoulder. In it was a picnic lunch that Maria had packed for them and an old blanket that Heide had added as an afterthought. Maria had prepared some of the local butcher's summer sausage, some home made dill pickles, farmer's bread, hard boiled eggs and a slender bottle of white wine from the Nahe which she must have gone to considerable trouble to acquire.

The spring run-off was still not completed. Much of the old wood-cutter's trail and all of the low lying ground was muddy. But high on a ridge of hills they found a dry clearing in the woods. There, Heide spread the blanket, and in the middle of it set the lunch. The noon sun was winning its battle against the cold ground in warming the spring air. Heide untied and slipped out of her mud encased hiking shoes and socks before sitting on the blanket. Frank did the same before sprawling out opposite her. Throughout the meal they kept up the easy flow of conversation that had gone on uninterrupted all morning.

In many ways it was Heide's first real test of her new identity and she passed it easily. The girl she revealed to him was the Heide born to Maria and Anton Prager, in Berlin in 1929, raised in Cologne and Tützing, and soon to graduate from Hochschule. She felt at ease in the role.

The wine and the exercise had made her sleepy. She fell asleep to be awakened as Frank Delacourt tried to cover her with the blanket.

"Sorry. I thought you might catch cold. The sun has gone behind some clouds."

She smiled and reached her arms to his shoulders as he leaned over her.

"That was kind Frank. One kind deed deserves another."

She pulled him towards her until her hands were able to feel the hair at the back of his neck. He dropped beside her. Their lips met, she opened her mouth, her tongue probing. Her hands dropped, loosening his belt and shirt. She ran her hands under his shirt. Her fingers dug into the muscles of his back. Their love-making was passionate and prolonged. Frank Delacourt was no novice. She felt deep satisfaction.

Later, the increasing cold drew them together again. This time the rhythm of their love-making was more measured, the pleasure more intense.

When they had returned to the house, Maria lavished on him a home-cooked German dinner of sausages and sauerkraut. He left with a promise from Heide that she would meet him in Munich, the following Saturday. Even Anton agreed to the arrangement. Maria was surprised at her husband's ready response.

Late that night, after Frank had left and Anton had gone to bed, the two women sat by the fire and talked.

"You know", said the older one, "you have really become Heide to me. You are not my daughter, and you cannot be, but you are Heide."

The younger woman understood exactly what the other meant.

"Thank you. For the first time I really feel like Heide. I no longer have to pretend."

Maria grew serious.

"I have never pried into your background or your instructions, you know that, but I must now. Is there anything in them that should stop you from becoming too close with this American?'

Heide was silent for a long time.

"I am some day to go to America."

Maria was both relieved and saddened at this news.

"Perhaps knowing Frank will make that easier for you when the time comes."

"I was also told to avoid romantic involvements." She paused. "I think I am falling in love."

"Perhaps it was falling in love with a German and putting down roots here that they were afraid of."

"I hope so."

Heide tried to put Frank out of her mind for the next week. She could not. The days once more dragged past, but there were more of them. When Saturday finally came she was awake before dawn. She and Anton caught the first bus to the city where she went off to meet Frank while Anton busied himself in the shops until the Hofbraühaus opened its doors.

"Good day my old friend, it has been a long time since I last saw you."

The jovial waiter slapped Anton on the back. In fact this was the first time Anton had called on Fritz since he had made contact on first moving to Tützing. It had taken the waiter a few minutes to recall the stranger who so obviously wanted to attract his attention.

"Can you get in touch with Lotte Schneider?" Anton asked quietly as soon as the people had turned away from the sound of the waiter's noisy greeting.

"Jah, one stein of dünkel coming up."

As he put the beer on the table Fritz said, "She will come to your house after eleven o'clock on one of the next three evenings."

Having nothing to do until he met Heide, Anton spent the rest of the afternoon and the early evening in the Hofbraühaus. His continued presence put a strain on Fritz. Having greeted the stranger so warmly, he had to continue to put on a show for the other waiters and customers. It was not easy. Anton did not really like the man and tended to reject his jocular and boisterous approaches. In addition, Fritz wondered whether the little man was staying because he had information to pass on. He tried several times to give him an opening to speak confidentially, but the other did not take up the opportunity. Finally, about eight o'clock, the lame chemist made his way through the tables and out to the street.

Only Anton was awake when Lotte Schneider appeared. It was

his second night of waiting for her visit. She saw the light in the front room window and knocked lightly on the door. Anton let her in quietly so as not to disturb the others. It was the first time they had met since Heide came to stay. As he helped her off with her coat he was shocked at the change in her appearance. She had lost several kilos and her complexion was sallow. She looked tired.

"Can I give you some Steinhager?" he asked.

"No, thank you. I cannot touch alcohol. If you have milk I would like a glass."

When he returned from the kitchen she took the glass and said, "I want to talk to you about your drinking habits. In future you must use the Hofbraühaus in Munich only for making contact with Fritz. If you want to continue drinking, find some other place."

She was much harsher than she had been before. Even the pitch of her voice had an edge to it. Anton did not demur from her rebuke.

"Now, why did you want to see me?"

Anton quickly told her of the young American soldier.

"Is she sleeping now?."

"Yes."

"Awaken her, and tell her I would like to see her."

When Heide came into the room, she was still drowsy. She and Lotte had never met and for a few minutes, after the introductions, they took the measure of each other before either spoke.

"You are as I imagined you would be. Perhaps taller, more beautiful and less gemütlich."

Heide said nothing.

"We think that you should be contemplating higher education. I am informed that your marks at Hochschule are excellent and probably good enough to earn you a scholarship to the University of Munich. You should apply now. Write to Profesor Scheel in the Department of History and ask him to arrange to have the forms sent to you. When you have completed them return them to Professor Scheel. He is a friend and will facilitate your admission although he cannot guarantee a scholarship. He has no standing on the scholarship screening committee but he has some influence. In any event, if money is needed we will arrange financing through Anton."

Maria, who had heard her husband awakening Heide, joined them in the living room. At first, when she saw Lotte she assumed she was there in connection with Frank. She was relieved to hear the instructions concerning the university. Her relief was short-lived.

"You have been seeing an American?"

Heide made no reply.

"You will break off the relationship. What is his name?"

"But. . . ."

"There are no 'buts'. You must stop seeing him immediately. You know your instructions. If you continue seeing him you will be disobeying a direct order. That will not be permitted. What is his name?"

"Frank Delacourt. He is a Captain in the U.S. Army."

"Good. I will make inquiries about him."

Heide fought back.

"I understood my instructions to mean that I was to avoid involvement with any German men. If you knew my assignment you would know that the American is not in any way a detriment to my being able to fulfill my mission. Indeed, it could be a great help."

"I know what your assignment is, Galena Nadya."

The sound of her real name came as a shock to Heide. It had been a long time since she had heard it spoken. Lotte's use of it now was a clear sign that she spoke with authority. Heide soon regained her composure, however, and continued to argue.

"Then you know that I am destined to go to America. Frank could help me get there."

"You are indeed destined for America, but your Frank cannot help you get there, for you will not be going to the United States. You will be going to Canada."

Heide was speechless.

"When the time comes you will be given instructions about how to get there. In the meantime, you are to go to the University of Munich, Comrade Galena Nadya."

Five days later Lotte appeared again at the house in Tützing. She demanded to see Heide alone.

"Well, your boyfriend is not what he seems. He is a member of the U.S. Army Counter Intellingence Corps. Did you know that?."

"No. He said he was on general duties assigned to a supply headquarters."

"Huh, likely story. We had his rooms searched and found his diary. Quite a ladies' man. Did you know he was married? His diary shows that he is curious about you. Seems you used your mother tongue in your extremes of passion. Evidently he understands Russian. He is curious about why a German girl is able to speak Russian. You silly little bitch."

"I'm sorry."

"Too late for that. He will have to be liquidated."

The blood drained from Heide's face.

"Liquidated?"

"Yes. Liquidated. I'm not taking any chances of your cover being blown. You represent years of investment. Now, this is what I want you to do."

Acting on Lotte's instructions Heide got in touch with Frank Delacourt and persuaded him to take her to the Hofbräuhaus. Being a Saturday night it was crowded and noisy; most of the noise being made by the G.I's who filled half the huge hall. Heide sought seats at one of the tables served by Fritz. He took their orders. Heide drank slowly. After his second litre of Dunkel, Frank headed for the washroom.

"Be right back, honey. Keep my seat."

The door leading to the urinals was crammed. Frank Delacourt joined the line-up. As he was about to gain entry, Fritz went by with a tray full of empty steins.

"Way. Make way."

Fritz shoved through the crowd. He pushed past Frank Delacourt with his free hand. Heide saw Frank disappear through the swing doors.

In a moment there was a commotion at the door through which Frank had disappeared.

"Help, help. Call a doctor. One of the Americans has fainted."

"Get out now. Quickly."

Startled she grabbed her purse and rose. She could see a large crowd around the lavatory door, through which a policeman was trying to force his way. She made her way quickly to the door. She headed directly on foot to the railway station and caught the next train for Tützing.

The next day the Munich paper carried a brief story about a U.S. Army Captain who had died of a heart attack in the Hofbraühaus. His name had been withheld at the request of the U.S. Army authorities. Heide felt no other emotion than fear.

* * * * * * * * * * * * * * * * * * *

About the same time that the man calling himself Thomas Volker was making his way through immigration procedures in Vancouver, 2,400 miles away Jack Patterson was mingling with the throng of sailors entering Montreal's Pier 11. He was excited.

He had not had so much stimulation since the old days when he and his fellow students travelled from Berkeley to Kent State to Chicago to Washington protesting the war in Vietnam. He was in his mid-thirties now and most of his friends had disappeared into the woodwork of the establishment. Their protest had only been skin deep but his had been for real. He never did fully trust the Soviet Union. As a super-power it was only too willing to abandon the doctrine of Marx and the Revolution of the Proletariat for international and domestic political advantage. Even so the Party did have its uses, and now as he waited to board the *M.S. Alexandr Pushkin* he was wondering whether he had perhaps allowed his ideological purity to stand in the way of greater challenges. Be that as it may. He at last had an opportunity for greater involvement.

He had not gone looking for the job. At a party meeting two week's ago he had been approached to see whether he would like a three week cruise on the *Pushkin* when it sailed from Montreal. He had jumped at the chance and, even when it was explained to him that he would have to board the ship disguised as a Russian sailor and carrying false papers he had not balked at the idea. Having his hair bleached blonde and cut short had been a bit more traumatic, but he accepted that he had to resemble the photograph in the passport he would be carrying.

The customs man at Pier 11 could not possibly handle the crowd of sailors individually. He was content to herd them into a holding room, collect their passports, do a head count to see that the 187 who had got off the boat was the same number as were boarding it again and that there were an identical number of passports. After all who would want to defect to the Soviet Union? And, if someone did want to they were welcome to it. The numbers tallied and Jack Patterson found himself climbing the gang plank disguised as Anatoli Ablavski.

At that moment the other Anatoli Ablavski who had disembarked ten hours earlier was sitting in a piano bar in Hull, Quebec, across the river from Ottawa. He was supposed to keep out of public places but it had been three weeks since he had boarded the *Alexandr Pushkin* and he was as horny as the crowd of real sailors had been when they set out for a night on the town in Montreal. Now, after the two hour bus ride from Montreal to Ottawa and having checked into the grubby hotel that was his lot, he was eyeing the slim, dark-haired girl at the other side of the bar. He had already caught her eye and let her know that he was interested. Now he was waiting impatiently for her to respond.

THREE

INTERNAL MEMORANDUM

SECURITY CLASSIFICATION:
Top Secret
DISTRIBUTION:
Opal Indoctrinated
Only

FROM: Director-General
TO: Inspector Randall
SUBJECT: Opal.

This memorandum will confirm your authority to proceed with preparation for the next phase of Operation Opal. Implementation will only be carried out upon explicit orders from me.
J.B.

* * * * * * * * * * * * * * * * * * *

"Good morning, inspector."
"Good morning."
Brad Randall's response was automatic as he passed the corporal in the long corridor on the top floor of RCMP headquarters in Ottawa. At a quarter to six in the morning the building was empty except for security patrols and the few unfortunates who manned the watch. The mass of concrete was as grey and forbidding on the inside as it was outside on Alta Vista Drive.

At the end of the corridor a thick steel door blocked his way. On it was a notice with large black lettering on a red background: 'Restricted Area Authorized Personnel Only Admittance by Positive Identification.'

The inspector pushed a sequence of numbered buttons on a panel to the right of the door. A metallic voice crackled from a speaker above the panel:
"Identify."

"Randall, James Bradley, Inspector. Regimental Number 8493207. Reporting code: forty-seven. File, Opal."

After a brief interval, Brad heard the bolts in the door being electronically activated. It swung open and he entered a small foyer to face another door into which was set a bullet proof window measuring twelve by eighteen inches. Beneath the window was a small drawer like the night deposit box outside a bank. The steel door swung closed behind him and its bolts clanged into position. He felt a fleeting claustrophobia. Above, on each side of the inner door, two television cameras swung back and forth scanning him. The metallic voice instructed him to deposit any firearms he was carrying in the receptacle beneath the window.

"I am unarmed."

"Stand on the white tiles in the centre of the floor."

He did as he was told and waited for the automatic metal detector to pass over him. He heard the tell-tale beep through the wall and was already searching in his pockets to see what had caused it when a familiar red face peered at him through the tiny window.

"Caper, you old son-of-a-bitch, would you open that door before they have me stripped to the skin."

The disembodied face grinned like a Cheshire cat before disappearing. The door opened to reveal Staff Sergeant Jack Caper still grinning.

"What's the matter? Did the robots decide your ugly mug wasn't kosher?"

They were old friends. Caper had been a member of the staff at Regina training camp when Brad joined the force. Although Caper was ten years his senior, they had hit it off from the beginning. In fact it had been largely due to the older man that Brad had gone into intelligence and security work. Caper recognized that Brad's knowledge of Ukrainian, learned from his mother, was an asset to be exploited. He also knew that the Security Service was desparate for men with a decent command of Eastern European languages and that promotion there would be fast. He had been right on both counts.

"Let's go to my office. I've got the Opal file ready for you — and a pot of hot coffee."

"Thanks. I need it."

The eldest son of James Connors Randall and Helena Ludova Mikhailov, Brad was only a year old when his father was killed while serving as an RCAF gunner attached to an RAF bomber squadron. His mother had tried at first to raise her two sons on her pension. It was an impossible task and within a year she moved to Regina from the small town in which Brad had been born. There she got a job as a secretary at the RCMP's divisional headquarters. That decision affected the rest of Brad's life. He could not remember a time when he did not want to be a Mountie. As soon as he was eligible he submitted his application. He was only eighteen and had just finished grade 12 when he was accepted into the force. Three years later, after he had finished basic training, had done his probationary work in Winnipeg and Toronto and had served an apprenticeship in intelligence and security work in Ottawa, he was posted to Germany. His title there was Visa Control Officer in Cologne. His job was intelligence liaison with the Bundesverfaschungschutz.

As he went into Cap's office and saw the stack of Opal files on the desk memories of Germany and Gwenneth flooded back. It was in Germany that he first stumbled on Opal and began to suspect a spy in the higher echelons of the Canadian government.

He had married Gwenneth MacLeod a few weeks before leaving for Europe. Cap, who had also been posted to Ottawa, was the best man at the wedding. Germany was a happy time for both of them. It was the only happy time in their brief marriage. They took advantage of the opportunities Europe afforded. For Brad the experience was the equivalent of undergraduate studies. He worked hard to fill the enormous gaps in his education, and he succeeded. Among other things he became reasonably fluent in German. There was time to do all this without the pressures that were so much a part of the job in Canada. Germany was, for the most part, nine-to-five with weekends free.

After their return to Ottawa the marriage soured. His work meant late hours and numerous absences. Since they had no children and Gwenneth had no job, she was bored. She simply could not understand why he kept such irregular hours and why he refused to discuss his work with her. She compared their lifestyle with that of their neighbours, and found it wanting. In her eyes, everyone else lived a better life. Brad's determination to get a university education did not help matters. Eventually he received his B.A., without financial help from the Force. He was proud of the accomplishment and was deeply hurt when Gwenneth did not bother to come to his graduation ceremony. Not long after, they split up. Again it was Caper who stood by him through the trauma of separation and divorce.

"Looks as if you may have hit the jackpot, me boy."

"Yeah, Cap. It looks that way. We'll have to see. There are still a hell of a lot of question marks. Guess I'd better get at the files. J.B. said he would be in early."

"Okay, Brad. Why don't you use the conference room. You can spread yourself out there and nobody will bother you."

Brad went through the files systematically. The earlier papers related entirely to the field investigations carried out when 'Opal' first joined the Canadian foreign service. Her name at that time had been Heide Hlinka, née Prager. The investigation had been thorough and time-consuming. It turned up nothing to suggest that Heide Hlinka was not what she appeared to be: a German-born immigrant of ten year's standing, the widow of a Czech refugee who had come to Canada after the war. To the contrary the investigations by the German and British authorities in Berlin gave her a clean bill of health. It was only many years later, during a routine up-date of her Top Secret security clearance, that doubts were raised. Brad raised them. By that time she had remarried and was now Heide Latour. The request for a security up-date eventually was referred to the Visa Control office in Cologne. Brad had been given the case and had been on the point of giving it only the most cursory attention. He noted that on the last check it was reported that the official records on Heide Prager had been destroyed during the Allied bombing of Cologne. As a last ditch effort he decided it might be wise to check out the Allied Documents Centre in Berlin. It had been checked before to no avail, but there was an off chance that something had been added to the documentation. It would also give him an opportunity to visit Berlin and he was not averse to getting out of the office for a day or two. He may have liked the idea but his boss did not. He had a hell of a time convincing the Staff Sergeant in charge of the Cologne office to let him go.

"Okay, Randall, but I don't want any complaints from Headquarters about unnecessary expenses. The last time I let someone go to Berlin I got shit over the size of the claim for hotel and meal expenses. I can live without that kind of hassle. If you have to go to Berlin, you can can go on the early morning flight and come back the same night. And you can eat at the British canteen at Olympic Stadium. It's no hell, but it's cheap."

The ruse may have backfired as a paid vacation but it paid off in information. New material had indeed been placed on the file since the initial investigation. The French, in their inimitable fashion had suddenly turned over to the Documents Centre, masses of paper captured in their Zone immediately after the war. Why they had not done so earlier nobody seemed to know. Among the documents were records from the Cologne area which the Nazis had shipped south for safekeeping when Allied bombing of the Ruhr intensified. Included among these were SS files containing reports on persons the Nazis suspected of working for the German Communist Party. Among the names listed, were Anton and Maria Prager.

Brad had been surprised and excited to discover the cross-reference, which some diligent researcher had inserted into the Prager file. He requested the original documentation and copied everything that appeared to be relevant to take back to Cologne. A careful study of the documentation assisted by a German speaking member of the Cologne office showed that Anton and Maria Prager had been among suspected members of the German Communist Party whom the Gestapo kept on a string after the Shulze-Boysen network had been destroyed in 1942. The difficulty had been to convince the Staff Sergeant that the matter should be reported to Ottawa.

"I'm not saying that you aren't right, Randall. What I do know is that such a report will cause Headquarters to come back with all kinds of questions. It's trouble, and with a year to go before my retirement it's something I can do without. Jesus, when you've been in half as long as I have you'll learn that it doesn't pay to rock the boat."

In the end, it was only by convincing the Staff Sergeant that failing to report the matter could lead to even more trouble, that Brad had been allowed to go ahead. To the surprise of both of them there was no reaction from headquarters. Nothing!

It was only months later, after his return to Ottawa and his assignment to the counter-espionage section that Brad was able to pursue the matter. He found that his report had simply been filed. He studied Heide Latour's file with care, but beyond the possibility that her parents were secret members of the Communist Party, there was nothing in her background to arouse suspicion. She had a clean record and a long and successful career to her credit. However, she was the acting Secretary of the Cabinet Committee on Security and Intelligence and it was common gossip that she was the mistress of a Cabinet Minister. Although in itself not suspicious, Brad noted that she was a skilled amateur photographer. If she was not what she appeared to be she certainly was in a position to do damage.

Brad's nagging doubts continued but repeated reviews of the file shed no new light on the case. He could find no way to test her bona fides until he decided to request translations of every last scrap of the material he had obtained from the Allied Documentation Centre in Berlin. His German was reasonably good but he found difficulty in deciphering the German script used in some of the documents. In a translation of a brief hand-written medical record, made when Heide Prager was inducted into the Hitlermadschen, he found what he had been looking for. Heide Prager had had her appendix removed.

He asked for surveillance photography of the subject — in the nude. At first, his requests met with skepticism and ribald comments.

"Christ, Brad, simply because you have an eye for this broad you want us to collect filthy pictures for you. Forget it. We have more important things to do."

It was not until his obsession came to J.B.'s attention that Brad was taken seriously.

"Okay, Brad. Its a very long shot. I'll agree, if only to put you out of your misery."

Brad remembered his satisfaction when the almost portrait-size colour photographs of Heide Latour in the nude, taken from different angles with a powerful telephoto lens, had revealed a smooth, flat belly without a blemish or scar from her pubic hairs to her well formed breasts.

Eventually the suspicions, together with the reasoning and the evidence which led to them were communicated to the Security Officer in the Privy Council.

Brad grinned as he read notes describing the very different reactions of the Privy Council Office and the counter-espionage branch. The Privy Council Office had been in a real lather. The counter-espionage people had been like bird-dogs flushing a partridge.

"Thought you might need a refill."

Cap appeared at the door with a steaming coffee-pot. Brad looked at his watch. It was almost seven-thirty.

"Great idea, Cap. Thanks."

"George McCain called to let you know he's in. It's all set to pick her up when you get the green light. He will have a car at the back door."

"Good. Let me know as soon as J.B. comes in."

"Okay, Brad. I'll leave you to it."

Brad's reading brought him to the period when he and two other members of the counter-espionage branch had been assigned full-time to the case. From that point on, the file contained many of his own memoranda. One of the last papers on the file was not his, however. It was a note from the Force's top analyst. Brad read it with care;

INTERNAL MEMORANDUM

SECURITY CLASSIFICATION:
Top Secret
DISTRIBUTION:
Opal Indoctrinated
Only

FROM: Special Analysis Group(Merrivale)
TO: Director-General
SUBJECT: Opal

You asked the SAG to provide you with an appreciation of the short and long-term risks and advantages associated with seeking a direct confrontation with Opal with the object of 'turning' her. You asked for such an appreciation to assist your discussion with the Prime Minister and others on whether and when to make the attempt.

To date surveillance has revealed little we did not already know, and it has done nothing to resolve our doubts about her identity.

Given the key and sensitive position she occupies in the Privy Council Office, and her intimate relationship with a Minister of the Crown, it is only prudent to assume that Opal is not the person she pretends to be and that she probably is the agent of a foreign power, who has been deliberately infiltrated into the government.

Logic suggests that if she is an enemy agent she has been active for many years and that the damage she has done is considerable.

It seems obvious that we should salvage whatever we can from a bad situation. The only way we can derive any political and professional advantage is to attempt to get her to work for us and against her present masters (probably the Russians). To 'turn' her, however, involves risks, some of which, given our ignorance of her real identity, her modus operandi and her motivation, might produce results quite different from those we would be seeking. In fact, because we know so little about her, the biggest risk we run is that she could lead us into thinking she is under our control when in reality she continues to work against us.

It is a gamble, but in the circumstances perhaps it is one the government would be justified in taking and especially since the alternatives are so limited. For example, she could be left in her present job under close surveillance, but increasingly such a course would become politically risky to defend and to control. We could attempt to get the Justice Department to agree that she should be arrested and charged under the Official Secrets Act; unlikely unless more incriminating evidence can be produced.

If a decision in principle is taken to 'double' Opal, the following steps could be taken to reduce the risks associated with the operation;

(a) Surveillance be intensified immediately, including full electronic coverage and Level II searches of her house, which, so far has only been done at Level I. Among other things, of course, this would involve arranging her absence and that of her son and his governess for at least a 24 hour period. Should she agree to work for us it is important that intensive surveillance be maintained — especially during the initial period of interrogation — to satisfy us that there are no unrevealed channels of communication.

(b) Elimination, or at least neutralization, of the many problems inherent in her relationship with a Cabinet Minister. Normally this might involve bringing the Minister in question into the picture. However, we gather the Prime Minister, for reasons of his own, probably would not permit this. Should Opal cooperate and agree to break off the relationship, under some pretext, the potential problems inherent in the situation would be overcome.

(c) The placing of a woman operative in Opal's house under some plausible cover to provide essential inside coverage from the moment she is 'doubled'. This would be an important complement to outside surveillance.

(d) Special arrangements (overnight shifts) to deal expeditiously with documentation identified by the 'damage report', and to examine it carefully to detect any inconsistencies in her interrogation statements.

(e) Immediate compilation of a full inventory of all classified documentation to which she had access during her assignment to the Privy Council Office.

(f) Detailed comparison of this inventory with her interrogation statements in an effort to know whether she has sought to conceal information she might have passed to her handlers. A chronology of Opal's attendance at all meetings of the Cabinet Committee on Security and Intelligence, together with a list of all the documentation circulated, would assist this process.

(g) The country house, now being used in connection with Operation Thumb Tack, should be cleared for its immediate use for intensive interrogation of Opal.

(h) The immediate establishment of a Double Cross (XX) Committee of Ministers and senior officials to provide an expeditious way of feeding material to Opal's handlers (presumably the KGB). One important task of such a committee would be the selection of material, the transmission of which would cause minimum damage to Canada's interests. It also would provide protection in the event that Opal is able to trick us into thinking she is working for us while in reality continuing to work for her present masters.

When the Security Service explained to the Privy Council office their doubts about Heide Latour's *bona fides*, the initial reaction of the Secretary to the Cabinet was utter disbelief. When he and the handful of officials involved were finally convinced that Heide Latour might be a spy, they immediately wanted to suspend her from duty. It took a great deal of patient argument to calm them, and enlist their help in persuading the Prime Minister that no steps should be taken that might alert her to their suspicions.

Heide was placed under continuous surveillance and all her communications were intercepted. Surreptitious searches of her house yielded nothing. These were only Level I searches of short duration, usually by a lone agent, and carried out as opportunity permitted. They needed the thoroughness of a Level II search. Various schemes were drawn up to get Heide, her son Paul and his governess, out of the house for a long enough period. None succeeded. Eventually, Grandpre, the Minister involved, unwittingly came to the rescue. Telephone interception revealed that Grandpre was driving to a two day conference at a resort in Eastern Canada, and was taking Heide, Paul and the governess with him. They planned to be absent for at least three nights. Plans were hastily laid for a full-scale Level II search.

To everyone's relief the trip took place as planned and the house in Sandy Hill stood empty. The search paid off handsomely. A few scraps of film were found in the darkroom which she used for her hobby. They contained fragments of highly classified Cabinet documents. Her Hasselblad camera was taken apart in the RCMP laboratory and found to be cunningly fitted with equipment for the production of microdots. The case against her was nailed down. That had been two days earlier. Now Brad was waiting to hear whether J.B. had succeeded in persuading the Prime Minister that Heide should be confronted and, if possible, recruited as a double agent. Brad pushed the files away. He had finished reading them, except for the voluminous surveillance reports, with which he was already more than familiar. He opened an envelope affixed to one of the file folders and shook out a number of photographs, black and white and colour, in various sizes, all of Heide. Brad placed them on the table. On top were passport photographs and those that had accompanied the Personal History form she had completed when her first security clearance had been sought.

The more recent photographs, taken by the surveillance team, were in colour. Some had been enlarged to portrait size. Among these were several excellent shots of Heide in the nude, taken while she was in her bedroom. Given the circumstances, the detail was quite extraordinary. She was a very beautiful woman, and there could be no doubt that she never had an appendectomy. Brad reluctantly shuffled the photographs together and replaced them in the envelope.

He shoved his chair back and put his feet on the table. There was no clue to her real identity. What was her nationality? Certainly she was not German, although she had emigrated to Canada from Germany in 1948, as the wife of a former prisoner of war and a displaced person. Her husband, Jan Hlinka, had been a Czech, born in Lidice, or at least that is what his immigration file showed. The copy of the marriage certificate on the file showed that they had had a civil wedding in Tützing, Bavaria, on November 8, 1947. Her name was shown as Heide Hoettel Prager, born in Berlin August 3, 1929. Brad doubted that she was of Czech origin. She was more likely Russian. The KGB seldom used non-Russians as deep sleepers.

What could have motivated her? She must have been stunningly beautiful when they first recruited her. What could have caused such a young, attractive girl to take on so difficult, lonely and dangerous an assignment? Some form of coercion? Patriotism? Perhaps a combination of both. God knows how much damage she had done. Interrogation might provide at least a preliminary guess. To some extent it would depend on how long she had been activated. Brad guessed this might have been after she joined the foreign service. At least ten years. The damage report could run to thousands of pages.

The files reflected a brilliant career. She had made her mark as a junior foreign service officer, working first in Ottawa in the division dealing with European affairs. Her boss, Armand Latour, had certainly been impressed by her attributes, for within a year he had married her. That was before the days when husband and wife teams were common in government departments, but she had already demonstrated her skills to the point where the hierarchy went out of their way to keep her on staff. When Latour was posted to Bonn as number two at the Canadian embassy, arrangements were made to find a spot for her at the same post so that her career could continue uninterrupted. Subsequently when Latour was moved to the Canadian Delegation to the United Nations, she was given responsibility for following the work of the Specialized Agencies. After the marriage broke up, apparently largely because Latour was playing around, she returned to Ottawa and was seconded to the Privy Council Office. Brad wondered what she had seen in that separatist bastard Latour. His file suggested he probably had been leaking material to various separatist movements for a long time.

Whatever her identity and background, she was a remarkable woman. It must have taken a great deal of courage — a special kind of courage — and determination to persevere in the role she had been given. To live out a life which was not her own, in alien surroundings, required a dedication and strength of character quite out of the ordinary. Brad could only guess at her age. From the photographs he judged she was in her forties. She must have been recruited in her teens.

It was clear from the files that her son, Paul Latour, was a very important part of her life. This might be a key factor in getting her to co-operate. It would have to be played with care. Brad guessed that a heavy-handed approach would fail. Cap's cheerful face appeared at the door.

"JB called. He would like to see you. Leave the files, I'll put them away."

"Thanks, Cap."

"Good luck, me boy."

JB wasted no time. He seldom did.

"Okay, Brad. This is it. We have the green light from the PM. Is it all set for this morning?"

"Yes, everything's ready. We'll pick her up when she leaves the house and take her to the suite in the Skyline Hotel. If she admits to espionage and agrees to work for us we'll move tomorrow to the country house. In the meantime we'll go for the information we will need immediately to control her. Communications methods and schedules, identity of her handlers and dates for future 'meets', current operational tasks and tombstone data. We'll have to deal later with damage reports. If she has been working for as long as I think she has it will be a real horror story."

"Okay. Phone me as soon as you know if she'll play. The PM is pretty twitchy. There's a lot riding on this, given her relationship with one of his cabinet ministers. Let's agree that if she admits to being an agent it will be 'green'. If not, 'red'. If she agrees to co-operate, 'white'. If not, 'black'. Let's hope it's 'green and white'. Good luck, Brad."

* * * * * * * * * * * * * * * * * * *

Thomas Volker, James Rawlins and Roger Finlayson had enjoyed his own company in the Park Plaza Hotel in Toronto for two days before emerging into the light of day. He was by now convinced that he was not being followed and abandoned the counter-surveillance tactics that had marked his every move from the time he landed at Vancouver Airport until he settled in his Toronto hotel room. It was a conscious decision. He remembered the story of the agent in Washington who had been caught because of the counter-surveillance techniques he had employed. The man had been tailed as part of a routine operation. On the surface he was perfectly clean and would have gone undetected. But in the process of doubling back on his tracks and going down blind alleys, he alerted his pursuers to the fact that he was trained in avoiding pursuit. That alone had betrayed him. Thomas Volker would not make the same mistake.

After walking down University Avenue to the Museum Station, he took the subway to Union Station and bought a coach ticket on the afternoon train to Ottawa. He spent the hour and a half until he could board the train sitting in the cavernous waiting room reading a Toronto newspaper. He was not impressed by the quality of Canadian journalism. The front page was filled with stories of local thuggery and swindling that confirmed his own belief in the decadence of the society.

By the time he boarded the Ottawa train he had had enough of the news. As he settled back into his seat he emptied all thoughts from his mind and sank into a semi-comatose state. Long experience in the field had taught him that when an operation began there was often no time for rest. Only with total relaxation before-hand could he force his body and mind to endure the torture of the event that might last a hundred hours or more. He knew the theory was scientifically unsound, but it worked for him. There was another advantage to the technique. An empty mind was incapable of worry. Too many good operatives failed in their mission because they dwelt too long on the dangers and difficulties that lay ahead. To survive in 'mockroye dylelo' required immediate response while on your feet, not long hours of nagging doubt.

FOUR

Brad climbed into the waiting car. It was one of those beautiful, clear days that come to Ottawa in September, when the promise of winter is softened by the warmth of Indian summer. They drove to Sandy Hill and parked about a block from Heide Latour's house. She emerged twenty minutes later. Brad and George McCain waited until she passed before getting out of the car. Within two blocks they caught up to her, one on either side.

"Mrs Latour. We are from the RCMP Security Service. Here is my identification. My name is Randall, Inspector Randall. Staff Sergeant McCain is on your left. We would like to have a word with you."

Heide could feel her heart pounding. She struggled to maintain her composure. She had often wondered what it would be like. Now she knew. She felt frightened but, at the same time, relieved.

"I assume you have a warrant for my arrest?"

She handed back the identification that Brad had given her.

"No, Mrs. Latour. We hope that won't be necessary. We can, of course, get one. We thought you might be willing to talk to us unofficially, as it were, without any of the publicity that would accompany your arrest. No doubt scandal is something you will want to avoid — at least for your son's sake."

At the mention of Paul she stopped in her tracks and faced Brad. For a moment he thought she was going to hit him. Her nostrils flared and her eyes stabbed into his.

"You bastard. Touch my son — in any way — and I'll rip your balls off. I mean it."

Brad knew she meant it. From the corner of his eye he saw George McCain getting ready to pounce. Before he could, and before Brad could consider how to retrieve his fumble, her anger subsided. She held his gaze a moment longer, shrugged and said,

"What do you want?"

"We have a suite booked at the Skyline Hotel, where we can talk without interruption. The car following us will take us there."

"But, I'm expected at the office."

"Arrangements have been made to deal with your absence."

"What about Paul?"

"There is no problem. We understand the nurse will be with him all day. You can phone from the hotel to arrange when you will be back. We'll have one of our operatives stay with you tonight. You can introduce her as an old friend who will be visiting for a few days. A precaution for your safety."

"I have a lunch date with Norman Glass"

"The reporter?"

"Yes."

"Okay, we can fix that when we get to the hotel."

They drove to the hotel in silence. Brad took her through the lobby to the elevators and up to the nineteenth floor where he let her into a large suite looking north to the Gatineau Hills. Brad introduced her to the two technicians from the Security Service who were already in the room. It was their job to operate the electronic counter-surveillance equipment which they had brought with them and the Uher tape recorder that sat on the table in front of the two comfortable looking couches set at right angles to one another. Brad handed her the telephone.

"Phone Norman Glass. Keep it simple. Tell him something urgent has come up and you are sorry you can't keep the date. Do you know his number?"

"Yes. It's the press gallery."

George McCain came in while she was talking to Glass. When she finished he offered her coffee. Still standing she sipped the warm brew and eyed her captors. Brad could not tell what was passing through her mind. Her face was blank, but not vacant. Whatever her thoughts were he let her finish them in silence. At last she settled into one of the sofas, McCain began.

"Mrs. Latour, we have good reason to believe you are not Heide Prager, born in Berlin in 1929, but someone quite different. We know you came to Canada under a false name. We have concrete proof that you are not who you pretend to be. We also have proof, from a search of your house, that you have photographed highly classified documents, which you were not entitled to have in your possession."

Heide remained silent.

"We examined your Hassleblad camera. We photographed the equipment fitted into it for making microdots. Here, see for yourself."

McCain spread about a dozen colour photographs on the table. Heide merely glanced at them as she reached for the pack of cigarettes that lay beside them. Brad leaned forward to help her. On a sudden hunch he said,

"We are sorry they are probably not the brand you like."

Heide accepted the cigarette with a smile and lit it from the lighter Brad held for her.

"You're right, Inspector. These are not my favourite brand. The tobacco I crave grows only in a special region of my own country."

"Mrs. Latour, we need your co-operation. We have ample

evidence to lay charges under the Official Secrets Act. I think we would get a conviction without much difficulty. However, that would cause you a great deal of trouble. And, I know you won't like this, but you have to face the fact that it will also cause your son a great deal of trouble. A lifetime of trouble."

Heide smoked in silence. McCain moved as if to speak but Brad motioned him to silence. She butted her cigarette and shifted her position on the sofa to face them directly.

"Very well, I will help you, but I will do nothing explicit to harm my homeland. I will help you to put down those bastards in the KGB. They murdered my father. They have also threatened Paul. The pigs."

Brad and George McCain exchanged a quick look of triumph.

"What do you want me to do?"

"Well, we would like you to continue in your present job as if nothing had happened. We will monitor all your communications and screen all material you pass to the KGB. In this way you will be working against the KGB. I will not pretend that what we are asking will be easy. It will be difficult and it could be dangerous. We will do everything we can to minimize the risks but there will be aspects of the job over which we will have no control. For example, outside Canada you would be largely on your own."

'I understand what you mean. My only concern is Paul. What can you do for him if they discover I am working for you?"

"If you are caught and unable to return, Paul will be looked after until he reaches maturity. We would find good foster-parents for him and give him an entirely new identity. We would provide funds for his upkeep and see him through university. If you are able to return to Canada, we will do the same for you during your lifetime. The secrecy of your identity and that of Paul will be assured. Believe me, we are not without some experience in such matters, and some success."

"I understand. What do you want me to do?"

"Well, in time we will want you to do many things. For the present we have a great deal of hard work ahead of us before you can do anything. There is much we must know right away. Your communications methods and schedules, your assignments and any current operational matters you know about. We want to know about your handlers. Where and when you meet them. You will have to be patient. We will have many questions. But first George McCain will take your fingerprints. Messy but necessary."

"Fingerprints? Don't you at least have those already?"

"Yes, we do. But we require a full set. What we have is one set of thumb-prints."

Heide looked startled. She muttered something in Russian.

"I beg your pardon?"

"Oh, nothing."

McCain had set up the roller and the inking pads. As he started taking impressions of each finger of Heide's left hand, Brad Randall went into the adjoining room of the suite and phoned headquarters.

"Rosemary, it's Brad. Can I speak to him? Okay, I'll hold."

He could hear a jackhammer on the street outside, the sound muffled by the heavy double-glazed windows. Seemed as if they no sooner paved a street in Ottawa than they were digging it up again.

The girl's melodic voice came back on the line.

"I'll put you through now, Inspector."

"Yes, Brad?."

"Green and white."

There was a sigh at the other end of the line.

"Okay. Come and see me here as soon as you have more. I need all the ammunition I can get."

Brad put the phone down and walked to the window. He lit a cigarette. He wondered where it would lead and how it might end. There was no way of knowing. He hoped to God it wouldn't be another Pavlov case. Two years of painstaking work, only to have the stupid bastard have a stroke when the operation was about to pay off. He knew from experience what lay ahead. Reel after reel of tape which would have to be transcribed, typed by special teams working through the night, edited, summarized, checked and cross-checked. Small points became very important. The least detail overlooked could blow the case sky high. And what if she were only pretending to co-operate? What if she walked out of the hotel tonight and in some way got word to her handlers that she had been compromised? At first it would be easy. All she had to do was start talking. But as the volume of transcipts grew, he would have to pour over the ever fattening files, night after night, looking for the contradictions that might give a clue that she was tricking them. The thought of what lay ahead was like a preview of a nightmare. The only way to handle nightmares was to stop dreaming and come face to face with reality. He butted the cigarette and returned to the room where McCain was cleaning up. For a minute Brad thought his worst fears had come true. Heide was no place to be seen. McCain noticed the startled look on his superior's face.

"It's okay, Brad. She's in the washroom. I got two good sets. Guess we can get down to business as soon as she returns. Found out she likes seafood and Russian vodka. I asked Withers to pick up a bottle of the best Russian stuff they have at the liquor store. It might help later on."

"Good thinking, George."

They both rose when Heide returned. She sat between them on the sofa. One of the technicians set the tape recorder rolling.

"Let's start at the beginning. Your name, place and date of birth, family and early life."

She put her head back and closed her eyes.

"My name is Galena Nadya Gribanov. I was born in the village of

Noginsk near Moscow, on April the fifth 1927. My father was Anatoli Ivanovich Gribanov. My mother's name was Larissa Kiselnikova Belinkov. She died giving birth to me. My father was a colonel in the NKVD. He brought me up. I went with him to Berlin and to Stockholm when he served there as an attache at the Soviet Embassy."

Brad interrupted. She was at the first checkpoint.

"Did your father use other names?"

"In those days no, at least not as far as I knew. Later, I don't know, but I should think so. He would have to in his work. Most senior NKVD officers did. He was always careful to tell me as little as possible about his work, even after I was recruited. He joined the State Security organization when he was very young. He once told me he had been in the State Political Directorate when it was only a Division of the NKVD. Later the Division became a part of the OGPU. Later still, when the Committee of Information was formed by Stalin and absorbed much of the work of the NKVD, he was transferred to work abroad. I last saw him in 1943 at the training camp I was in, near Moscow. He was then a colonel."

Galena stopped and asked for a cigarette. Brad lit it for her. He sensed a tension in her voice and waited while she drew deeply on the cigarette before asking what was the last she had heard of her father.

"He's dead!"

Her voice was flat.

"Dead?"

"Yes. The bastards killed him — slaughtered him."

"Who?"

"The KGB. Well not really the KGB. It was before the change over when it was still the NKVD."

"How did you find out about it?"

"They told me he had been killed in an action by the CIA. For years I believed them — Oh God how I hated the Americans during those years. But recently I found out it wasn't the CIA who had killed him. It was my own people."

"How do you know?"

"From you — or at least from your people. I learned it from a report dealing with espionage in Canada that your people circulated to the Cabinet Committee on Security and Intelligence. It was contained in an annex about the NKVD-KGB, quoting a recent defector who claimed first-hand knowledge of the great purge of the NKVD carried out by Stalin. He told you that over a hundred NKVD officers had been liquidated at the time — General Sukilov, head of the Directorate, and his deputy, Nicolai Ignatiev were among those he named — so was my father'.

Brad made a mental note of this as the second checkpoint. A copy of the document she had seen should be in the files, if it was real.

"Presumably that was one document you did not pass to your masters?"

"No. That would have been foolish. I made up my mind to confront my handler with the information it contained. The son-of-a-bitch was the first one to tell me of my father's death. I remember it well. The bare-faced liar told me he had been killed in an intelligence operation in Northern Turkey, probably by an American agent. I believed him. Later he even showed me a medal which he said had been conferred on my father posthumously, in recognition of his great service to the fatherland."

"Confronting him was a dangerous thing to do. How did . . . .what is his name?"

"Lavrov. Viktor Aleksandrovich Lavrov, SOB and bar."

Brad ignored the display of emotion. There would be time enough later to have empathy for her if her story checked out.

"How did Lavrov react to your accusation?"

"We had a fight. I cut his face with the glass of a broken test tube before he pulled a gun. I'm sure I scarred him for life. I daresay if we had been meeting in East Berlin, which we used to do when I was posted to Bonn he would have used the gun on me. But we were in the West, so instead of shooting me, the pig threatened Paul. In the end I let him think he had got the better of me. I told him I would continue working for the Centre. In fact I have been trying to think of ways of safely approaching the Canadian authorities ever since. I didn't see how I could do it without risking Paul. You appear to have solved the problem for me, but", she hesitated, "this morning you brought Paul into the discussion. If you try to use my son in any way you will never get my co-operation. Worse, you will win my undying enmity just as surely as Comrade Lavrov has done."

There was a smile on her face as she crossed her shapely legs, but her eyes were unsmiling. Brad appreciated the friendly gesture but he knew her threat was no gesture. She meant it. Their reverie was interrupted by the telephone. McCain answered.

"That was Withers. He's bringing up the supplies I asked him to get."

"Good, let's take a break. George tells me you like Russian vodka and we have some coming up. We can order some lunch from room service while we have a drink. You can turn off the recorder for a while, fellows."

One of the technicians pushed a button on the Uher. The other removed the microphone from the table, wrapped its cord around it and placed the bundle beside the machine. In the next room from which Brad had called JB the reel on another Uher continued turning. Three hidden microphones in the sitting room picked up every word of their conversation. They were all highly sensitive and extremely well disguised. Two masqueraded for cloth buttons on the armchairs. They were identical to the other dozen or so buttons that decorated the backs of the chairs. The third was hidden in the telephone just in case both chairs were accidentally occupied at the same time.

Withers arrived and was introduced to Galena. After the drinks were poured he sat and talked with her while McCain and Randall went into the adjoining room.

"Quite a gal. Story sounds a bit fishy but it could be true. Some of it at least can be checked. If we can track down the report referring to the death of her father — if he was her father — it will help. We should check our name index for Gribanov. If we haven't any dope on him the Brits or the Yanks should be able to help. Certainly if he was in Berlin and Stockholm and used the name Gribanov we should be able to find out if her story fits.

"We can change the tape next door at this point and get Withers to take it back to headquarters to let the computer boys and the typists get to work on them. Give Withers a note to get anything he can on Viktor Aleksandrovich Lavrov. He sounds like a nasty bit of work. I'm surprised he didn't shoot her.

"Can I leave you with all that, George? Oh, yes, I nearly forgot. Ask Patricia Haley to join us some time after lunch. She's about to become Galena's long lost friend."

Brad returned to the room where Peter Withers and Galena were chatting. He had the technicians change the tape.

"Peter, could you take the tape back with you? I think George would like a word with you before you go."

FIVE

In Ottawa, Thomas Volker, alias James Rawlins and Roger Finlayson made his way to the Lord Elgin Hotel where he registered as Clive Ardrey, Salesman.

Once in his room he unpacked and had a shower. Later he ordered a selection of newspapers, a couple of drinks and a steak dinner from room service. When his order came, he tipped the waiter generously, concealing his left hand in the pocket of his dressing gown.

When he had finished his meal, he put the tray outside, hung the 'Do not Disturb' sign on the handle and locked the door. He spread a large-scale map of the Ottawa area, on the bed and studied it with care and especially the areas around Parliament Hill, the Governor-General's residence and the U.S. Ambassador's residence. By the time he went to sleep there was little about the street layout of these areas which he could not remember; it was as if he had been born in the city.

* * * * * * * * * * * * * * * * * * * *

"Okay, Galena, feel like continuing, while we wait for lunch to arrive?"

Only she, Randall and the two technicians were in the room. Peter Withers had set off with the first tape a half hour before and George McCain had not yet emerged from the other room. Brad found himself wishing the technicians were not there either and that the hotel room rendezvous had been under more pleasant circumstances. When next he spoke, he was surprised by the bruskness of his own voice.

"Let's deal with your methods of communication?"

"What do you want to know about them?"

His voice softened.

"Well, how did you communicate, how often and with whom?"

"Apart from oral reports to Lavrov, made when we met, all documentation was sent by microdots. You found the equipment. I used my darkroom for the reduction work."

"How were they sent?"

"Through normal postal channels. Lavrov gave me a list of

addresses of convenience from time to time. I committed them to memory. They didn't change very much. It was left to me to choose which addresses to use. I tried to vary them. If I had a heavy volume of material to send I might use them all."

"I would like you to write out for me the current addresses and as many of the old addresses as you can remember."

"I can remember all of them."

"Were the addresses those of individuals or business firms?"

"Both."

"Where did you post them?"

"At different mail boxes around town. I always used street boxes. Never the boxes at post offices."

"Why?"

"You know why. Security. Lavrov insisted on it, but even if he hadn't I would have done so anyway. I am my father's daughter."

Brad ignored the rebuke. He had deserved it for he already knew he was dealing with a professional.

"Did you work to a time schedule?"

"No. What I sent and when I sent it was at my discretion."

"How many microdot messages would you send each month?"

"It varied greatly. Sometimes I might send ten or twenty. Other months I might send nothing."

"How frequent were your meetings with Lavrov?"

"Again, it varied. When I was at the Canadian Embassy in Bonn we met several times. When I was in New York, not at all. Since I have been back in Canada I have met Lavrov twice."

"When was your next meeting with Lavrov to be?"

"Nothing was scheduled. The last meeting was not a success."

"So I gather." They both smiled.

"Was Lavrov your only handler?"

"No. Once when Lavrov was sick I met another handler in Austria."

"What was his name?"

"Molev. Fedor Nikolaivich."

"Did you only meet him once?"

"Yes, only on that occasion."

"Were there other handlers?"

"Well there was one other, in New York. He wasn't a handler. More of a contact."

"His name"

"I don't know his real name. I knew him as Flaherty. Terence Sean Flaherty. He was a member of the UN Secretariat. He was caught by the FBI. We never exchanged information before he was arrested."

"Did you use any other means of communication?"

Galena leaned forward for a cigarette. Brad lit it.

"No"

"Radio?"

"No."

"Tell me about Lavrov. Viktor Aleksandrovich, I think you said?"

"That's the bastard's name. I first met him in 1941 before going to the training camp."

"You said your last meeting was in West Berlin. That would have been recently, when you went to see Maria Prager."

"Yes, but how did you know I had gone to see her?"

"We have been intercepting your communications since you came under suspicion. Incidentally, Maria is not your mother is she?"

"No, of course not. I told you my mother was Larissa Kiselnikova. She died giving birth to me."

"Stupid of me. I forgot what you said."

He knew she would not believe that, but he said it anyway. She ignored him and continued.

"I have become very fond of Maria. She has been as a mother to me all the time I have known her. I hope she will not get into trouble. She has had a tough life."

"That's a question only the West Germans can answer. Perhaps we can help when the time comes. Obviously I can make no promises."

"Could I have some of the vodka."

"Sure."

Brad poured some of the vodka into two tumblers from the bathroom. Her timing had been perfect. As Brad handed her one of the glasses a knock on the door announced the arrival of the food he had ordered from the next room.

Galena tossed back the vodka.

"More?"

"No thanks."

"Okay. Let's take a break. George said you like seafood, so I ordered some lobster and a salad."

The tape recorder was turned off while she and Brad ate their lunch. In the course of the conversation she talked a little about her last meeting with Lavrov in West Berlin.

"When I got to West Berlin, Viktor Aleksandrovich had left instructions for me to meet him in a doctor's office there. It would have been difficult for me to go to East Berlin without arousing the curiosity of members of the Canadian Military Mission, who would have had to arrange to get me through Check Point Charlie. Since I was no longer accredited in Germany it would have required special arrangements. I came to use the excuse of visiting the East Berlin comic opera when I needed to make contact with Aleksandrovich."

Following the meal McCain rejoined them, and after they had coffee he took over where Brad had left off.

"Let me see. Where were we? You were talking about your last meeting with Lavrov in West Berlin, in a Doctor's office."

Galena did not respond at first. She merely looked at McCain, her blue eyes dark and intense.

"How clever of you, Staff Sargeant. I didn't know you were clairvoyant."

George McCain cursed silently. He decided to ignore the jibe. He stared back at her. Galena smiled sweetly, crossing her legs and answered him.

"Yes. Lavrov asked me to meet him in the medical centre off the Kurfurstendam, room 602. It is a large building, where Maria normally goes to see her doctor. I went with Maria and she did go to see her doctor. Viktor Aleksandrovich was waiting for me in 602."

"Was it a doctor's office?"

"Oh, yes. I think so. We met in the dispensary at the rear of the office where Viktor Aleksandrovich had set up counter-surveillance equipment. Rather like yours."

She pointed to the electronic box in the corner beside the technicians.

"He started by congratulating me on the material I had been sending back and the new job I had in the Privy Council Office. I guess he sensed I wasn't responsive. He asked me if there was something the matter. I lost my temper and accused him of lying to me about my father's death. He didn't answer but I could see in his eyes that it was true. I slapped him and when he hit me back I grabbed a glass test-tube off the table and ground it into his face. He bled like a stuck pig, but before I could do any more damage to him he pulled a gun on me."

"Would he have used it?"

"I don't know. In East Berlin, I don't think he would have hesitated. West Berlin. That's another question. I recognized the revolver. A Kaba 9mm Special with a silencer. Capable of doing the job. We used them in training. In any event he didn't use it but he did force me to sit down. There wasn't anything else I could do."

"Did he deny the story about your father's murder?"

"No. When we talked he told me that Anatoli Ivanovich had been among those purged by Stalin for alleged plots against his life. He even agreed that the accusation was baseless. He said they had kept the real story from me for fear that it would upset me and endanger my mission."

"Do you think he told you the truth?"

"I don't know. As far as it goes what he said probably is true. I will never know. In any event we ended the meeting with my saying that I no longer wanted to work for the bastard and him saying that if I didn't Paul would be in danger. Oh, he didn't put it quite so bluntly, but the meaning was plain. My last word was that I would carry on. What else could I do? No doubt he will be suspicious of me now."

"Unfortunate for us, but it can't be helped. There are ways perhaps in which we can allay Lavrov's suspicions to some extent.

Certainly the Centre will have marked you down as a doubtful. Hmm. We will have to think about this aspect carefully."

Galena asked for another cigarette, which Brad handed to her and lit. McCain got up and walked to the window. Brad took up the questioning.

"During your last meeting with Lavrov, did you receive any new instructions, any new assignments?"

"No. After my fight with him very little was said. It was left that I would continue to send material as before."

"Were you involved in any intelligence operations. Do you know of any specific operations."

"My only contacts have been Lavrov, Molev and Flaherty. All of our meetings were outside Canada. I had strict instructions never to deal with anyone else. In particular I was told never to attempt to contact the Rezidentura in Ottawa or Montreal. My job has been the collection of documents and information about people, and, to a limited extent, to act as an agent of influence. Lavrov referred to operations in Canada only once. On other occasions, by putting two and two together, I was able to learn a bit about two additional operations. Quite by chance."

"What was the operation mentioned to you by Lavrov?"

"Well, he asked me to be on the lookout for any indication that the Canadian authorities were worried by the circulation of counterfeit Canada Savings Bonds."

"Did Lavrov say why he thought there might be such counterfeits in circulation?"

"No, he didn't say much. Something about an East German experiment using laser optics for copying such documents. I had the impression the Rezidentura in Ottawa was involved."

"When was this?"

"I can't be certain, but I think it was while I was still in New York with the Canadian Delegation to the United Nations. No, I'm wrong. It was after my marriage to Armand broke up. I can remember Viktor Aleksandrovich's satisfaction. The Centre were never happy about my marriage to Armand Latour. Yes, it must have been after I returned to Ottawa and had been seconded to the Privy Council Office."

"Jesus. Can't you be more specific?"

"Perhaps if I have time to think . . . ."

"Okay. Let's leave it for now. Can you remember the other two operations?"

"While I was still in Bonn at the Embassy, on one of the occasions I met Viktor Aleksandrovich in East Berlin, he asked me to obtain information about the layout of the communications centre. He wanted dimensions, location of different equipment and power inlets, telephones, height of the rooms. Things like that. I was able to provide him with pretty accurate sketches. I had the impression our technicians may have developed a means of detecting electronic emanations at a distance and of reading in plain text material being cyphered and de-cyphered. From something he said I gathered the Rezidentura in Ottawa might be using a similar technique against electronic targets in the area."

Brad and McCain exchanged a quick look.

"And the other operation?"

"Well, it isn't an operation exactly. It involves a man. When I last saw my father, in 1943, he had come to my training camp on business. It was a large camp. We were in older buildings. To the east, in the compound, there were two recently constructed cantonments, which were surrounded by high barbed wire fences, guarded by Red Army units. In the school we never asked questions, but there were rumours the cantonments were for the training of specialized sabotage and assassination squads. My father spent most of his time there."

"What kind of rumours?"

"Well, I'm not certain. I was told they were used by 'spetsnaz' units."

"Spetsnaz units?"

"Yes. They sometimes also are called osnaz."

"Osnaz?"

"Yes. Standing for 'Otryad Osobogo Naznacheniya.' In English, roughly, Detachments of Special Designation."

"Do you know what they are used for?"

"Not really. I believe Osnaz provides communications support for special operations overseas carried out by other spetsnaz units."

Galena asked for coffee. Brad telephoned room service.

"Before he left we had an evening together. He pulled his rank to get us a half decent meal served in his room. During the evening we were interrupted. I answered the door. A man asked to see my father. He said he had papers for him. I offered to take them. He pushed by me and handed an envelope to my father. They spoke together for a few minutes, then the man left without speaking to me. I was annoyed. My father chided me when I asked him what it was all about. He said that those who worked in 'mokroye dylelo', as he called them, had to keep their business secret."

"Mokrie dela?"

"Yes, 'Mokroye dylelo'. The trade name for what is now referred to in the KGB as Executive Action — Department V. It literally means, 'wet affairs'. Perhaps 'Krovavoye dyelo' might be more accurate — bloody affairs. Needless to say I didn't ask any more questions. However, I remember the man. He was powerfully built. His eyes were set close together. He looked Mongolian and he had a finger missing on his left hand."

There was a knock on the door. McCain went into one of the adjoining rooms and had their tray of coffee delivered there. He brought it into the sitting room when the waiter had gone. Galena sipped her coffee and continued.

"I next saw the same man, years later, during one of my visits to East Berlin to see Viktor Aleksandrovich. Our meeting place was the office of the manager of the East Berlin comic opera house. On this particular day, the British army driver and car delivered me to the theatre a bit early. For some reason there were not the usual delays at Check Point Charlie. We were through in a few minutes."

Galena lit another cigarette.

"When we got to the opera I went straight up to the manager's office, on the second floor. In the hall leading up to the office I saw the man I had first met in my training camp. He didn't recognize me but I recognized him. He was heavier, nearly bald but the same man. His eyes were close set and a finger was missing on his left hand. I waited for a few minutes before knocking on the door. I didn't mention the matter to Viktor Aleksandrovich and he didn't say anything about his visitor. I assumed the man also was assigned to North America, since this was Viktor Aleksandrovich's area of responsibility."

"Was that the last time you saw him?"

"No. I saw him, or at least I could swear it was the same man, last night."

"Last night?" McCain and Brad said at the same time.

"Yes. Last night."

"Here? In Ottawa?"

"Yes. Marc . . .Marc . . ." she hesitated.

"We know all about your relationship with the Minister."

"I thought you would. Well, Marc and I went to the restaurant in the National Arts Centre and then to the opera. At the end of the evening we waited by the escalator to go down to the garage. You know how people line up along the stone balustrade looking down on the descending escalator? Suddenly I saw the same man again. He did not see me since he was talking to a younger man on the step below, who looked Chinese. I saw his face , the bald head and the close set eyes. His left hand was on rubber rail. A finger was missing."

Randall and McCain exchanged looks.

"You are sure it was last night?"

"Yes. Absolutely — though it seems a long time ago."

"You are sure he was with another man — a Chinese?"

"I don't know if they were together, if that's what you mean. They were talking to one another. Certainly he was Chinese, or at least an oriental."

They were interrupted by the arrival of Patricia Haley. Brad introduced her to Heide.

"Mrs. Latour, this is Mrs. Haley, Patricia Haley, who will go home with you tonight. We would like her to stay in the house with you for at least the next few days."

The two women greeted one another warily. Although they were about the same age they were very different in appearance. Patricia Haley was small of build, seemingly fragile, very blonde, with wide-spaced eyes which were seldom without a smile in them. Her delicate appearance was belied by the firm set of her well-shaped jaw and an indefinable air of quiet self-assurance. One would hardly credit her with a black belt in judo, but some of the larger male members in her judo class could attest ruefully to her extraordinary skill and ruthlessness. Brad wondered how they would get along. Despite the apparent differences between them they were quite similar in many respects. Both were intelligent, resourceful, attractive and very determined.

The two interrogators had intended ending the session when Patricia Haley arrived. They could not do so now given the obvious urgency of what she had just told them. For the next hour they took her over the same ground again and again. When precisely had she seen the man? What was he wearing? How could she be sure it was him when she only saw him from above? What height was he? Weight? Hair? Eyes? Shoes? Why had she not mentioned it earlier? Did she point him out to the Minister? What was her reaction? What height was he? Weight? Hair? At last she exploded.

"Look, I don't mind going over every detail, but once ought to be sufficient. I've already told you all I know. If I remember anything else I'll tell you tomorrow."

"Okay. Let's call it quits for today. But if you remember anything more about him don't leave it until tomorrow. Tell Constable Haley tonight. She will know how to get in touch with us. If we don't hear from you we'll pick up where we left off tomorrow. We will be moving to a new location — outside Ottawa but will pick you up as we did today, a block or so from your house. If its raining hard you and Patricia can drive, in your car, to the small parking lot in the park on Range Road. Patricia knows the place. We'll pick you up there and Patricia can return your car to the garage. Any questions?"

"No. I think you have asked enough questions for both of us."

For the first time in years Heide had been Galena Gribanov again. As she and Patricia Haley put on their coats and made their way to the elevators, she shed her old identity and once more became Mrs. Latour. Patricia carried a small, brown leather suitcase. Heide went first into the lobby. Patricia said,

"The car is parked around the corner to the right."

They pushed their way through a crowd of new arrivals in the hotel lobby. Suddenly Heide found herself face to face with Norman Glass. She could not avoid him. Patricia Haley hurried past.

"Well, well, well. Not often I get stood up."

Galena braced herself. There could be no doubt how he had spent his afternoon. He smelled like a distillery. Sober he could be delightful. Drunk, he was an unpleasant nuisance.

"Sorry I had to cancel out, Norman. You know how it is."

"Yeah, I know," he sneered.

"Something urgent came up."

"Like a big spy story?"

Heide panicked.

"What do you mean?"

"Why else would you be with that woman snoop?"

"I don't know what you're talking about."

"I'm talking about that woman you got off the elevator with. She lives on my street. She's a spook chaser."

"I have no idea who she is or what she is."

"Bullshit."

"She was on the elevator when I got on it. She was complaining that when she pushed the button to go down, it had gone up instead. We had a few words about the unreliability of elevators. You're drunk again."

"Drunk I may be — but stupid I am not!"

"Goodbye, Norman."

She left him standing unsteadily in the lobby. She walked quickly through the doors and down the ramp onto the street below. She could see Norman Glass still in the lobby. She hurried to the waiting car. They quickly drove off.

"Damn. He lives on our street. I'm afraid he suspects I work for the RCMP."

"He does: he said something about you being a snoop. I tried to put him off. I said that you had got on at another floor and that we have exchanged a few words about the unreliability of elevators. I didn't succeed. He was drunk but he's no fool."

They drove to Sandy Hill in silence. Heide introduced Patricia to Paul's Scottish nurse, Janet, and showed her to the guest room. Later Patricia telephoned Brad and explained briefly their unfortunate encounter with Norman Glass.

"You were right to let me know. I'm seeing J.B. in a few minutes. I'll fill him in. Perhaps I can persuade him to instruct section K to mount a disinformation operation on Glass. See you tomorrow."

* * * * * * * * * * * * * * * * * * *

INTERNAL MEMORANDUM

SECURITY CLASSIFICATION:
Top Secret
DISTRIBUTION
Opal indoctrinated
Only

FROM: Special Analysis Group
(Merrivale)
TO: Director-General
SUBJECT: Opal.

We have only had time to listen to the tapes of Opal's initial interrogation during the morning. A more detailed analysis will have to await transcription of the tapes and the results of voice modulation tests with the oscilloscope. These latter tests should indicate those parts of Opal's interrogation which induce undue strain.

In the meantime the following steps appear to be called for:
(a) Name indices search for Gribanov and Lavrov. If, as may well be the case, we draw a blank we can request the British and the Americans to run the names through their computer records. This could be done in a routine manner without having to reveal our reasons for the request.
(b) Further Level II searches of Opal's house seem essential, although it may take time to arrange to have the house empty for the period required. The Level II search which led to discovery of incriminating evidence of her espionage activities did not extend to the entire house. Only a cursory search of the attic and the basement was possible.
(c) An intensive effort is needed to identify the memorandum she alleges referred to her father's execution on Stalin's orders.
(d) Interrogation should continue immediately at the country house, where a more sophisticated mix of interrogation techniques can be employed.
(e) A difficult and increasingly urgent problem concerns the question of informing our allies about the case. In essence, which of our allies should be informed about Opal, when, and how much should they be told? As with any such problem there are pros and cons, some of which extend far beyond the professional interests of the Security Service. From the point of view of the Security Service the following points would appear to be important:
(i)The greater the number of those persons in Canada

and abroad who are aware of our efforts to 'double' Opal,
the greater the chances that the operation will be
compromised. For example, we should avoid informing
foreign agencies, who, we suspect may have been
penetrated by the KGB.

(ii) At the present stage there appears to be no overiding
need for corroborative information from foreign agencies
(other than a name index check on Gribanov and
Lavrov). This situation may change rather quickly as
interrogation proceeds.

(iii) It goes without saying that if and when we decide to
inform our principal allies we should seek to exact a quid
pro quo from them, just as they always attempt to do
with us. The difficulty is that, at the moment, we are
rather heavily in debt to the British and the Americans in
connection with the uranium affair.

SIX

SECURITY CLASSIFICATION:
Top Secret
DISTRIBUTION:
Opal Indoctrinated
Only
FROM: Special Analysis Group(Merrivale)
TO: Director-General
SUBJECT: Opal.

Opal's revelations, during the first day of interogation, change radically the nature and the urgency of the problems associated with 'doubling' her. The possibility that a 'V for Victor' agent may be present in Ottawa calls for immediate action. Past experience suggests the despatch of such an agent means an assassination is planned.

The following are some of the measures which might be taken immediately;

(a) Compilation of a list of Canadians and foreigners in the Ottawa area who might be candidates for such an assassination attempt. This probably should include distinguished visitors. Since the XX Committee already is in being it might be charged with the task.

(b) Standing security measures for the protection of the Prime Minister and others be reviewed urgently, and augmented where necessary.

(c) Agreement should be sought to inform the British and the Americans of the possibility that a 'Victor' agent is in Ottawa, and to seek their assistance. Since this would involve a full disclosure of the Opal case, you may think a personal briefing by you of your counterparts in Washington and London would be the most satisfactory and secure way of doing this.

(d) The suggestion of some Chinese connection is puzzling and disturbing. If the Chinese male, seen by Opal in the presence of the 'Victor' agent with the missing finger was there by chance, there would seem to be no cause for concern.

If, however, he was a mainland Chinese acting as an accomplice, that would have important implications. The possibility that the Chinese Intelligence Service and the KGB are secretly co-operating, while their respective governments are seeking to give the appearance of being bitterly opposed to one another, would require us and our principal allies to reassess our appreciations of Chinese and Russian relationships and intentions. In the circumstances, perhaps a direct telephone call from you to your counterpart in Hong Kong might give us a better idea about the possibility that the Chinese Intelligence Service are involved. For example, he probably can say whether their coverage has detected anything in the last two months which might suggest unusual activity directed against North America.

Once the immediate problem has been tackled, and assuming we are to continue with our attempt to 'turn' Opal, we should examine how a 'V for Victor' operation could have been mounted in Canada without our having received some warning from our usual sources of intelligence.

In particular, we will have to evaluate the assurances we have had from the Americans that they have penetrated the KGB's Executive Action Department, which controls 'Victor' agents. Either the U.S. penetration is not as thorough as we have been led to believe, or they have held back information which, in this case, is of the utmost importance to Canada.

While realizing full well the difficulties facing Opal's interrogators, and the strain, both physical and mental, which is involved for them, SAG considers it important that they be on their guard against making the kind of mistakes revealed by a study of the transcripts. It is quite clear that Opal is intelligent, tough, ruthless and quite capable of taking advantage of every opportunity she may be offered. For example, it was unfortunate that Inspector Randall attempted to test Opal's credibility by asking her whether Maria Prager was her real mother. Similarly, Staff-Sergeant McCain should not have let slip that he was aware of what she had said during lunch, since this may have alerted Opal to the fact that her conversation was being recorded even after the recording equipment ostensibly had been turned off.

* * * * * * * * *   * * * * * * * * * *

The unmarked Security Service car crossed the McDonald-Cartier bridge over the Ottawa river and sped North. The South bound lanes were full of traffic. The North bound lanes were almost free of other cars.

As if by mutual agreement, Brad, Heide and McCain said little during the three quarters of an hour it took them to reach their destination; a stone and white clap board house overlooking a small lake. Set back from the lake and reached by a long winding drive, the house was secluded from neighbours and passersby. It turned out to be a good deal larger that at first appeared.

Heide was surprised to find that Patricia Haley and the technicians with their equipment were already there. Patricia greeted them with large mugs of steaming coffee. Heide gratefully accepted hers. Brad started the interrogation.

"Okay, Heide. Before we move on from where we left off yesterday, were there other agents in the training camp that stood out or that you've seen since?"

"No. None I've seen. We were organized in such a way that our training did not bring us in contact with agents going into the same area unless we were going to work with them in the field. Early in my training I was teamed up with one boy — Oleg. I think we were destined to work together, but something went wrong."

"What?"

"I don't know — unless . . . ."

"Go on"

She hesitated.

"We worked very closely. I think we were perhaps being considered for a husband and wife act. Well — we jumped the gun."

"You think that's why they changed the plan?"

"I don't know. It may have been."

"You said his name was Oleg. Oleg what?"

"I don't know. I never knew. I don't think Oleg was his real name. He told me he had the given name of Yuri."

"Last name?"

"I think it was Smirnov. But I don't know why I think so. I don't remember ever being told."

"Can you describe him?"

"It was so long ago. No — no I can't. All I can remember about him now were his eyes. They were deep. Very deep. Brown eyes with a touch of green."

"Was he sent to North America?"

"I don't know."

"Tell us about the period when you were at school and university in Bavaria."

Heide found it difficult to concentrate. Oleg was still in her mind but she had to jump six or seven years to her life in Bavaria and a different love affair. Also, her training was proving inadequate. Espionage school had prepared her well for the kind of interrogation she might have experienced in wartime. It had not prepared her for a situation in which she was expected to work in partnership with those questioning her. She found the experience unnerving.

As the tapes turned, her mind slipped back to the period when she had masqueraded as Heide Prager, university-student.

The cancer that ravaged Lotte Schneider's body finally destroyed it. Her death came three months after her last visit to the Pragers. Anton and Maria never saw her again after she instructed Heide to apply for admission to the University of Munich. Heide, however, met her one more time. The encounter was in Munich during the girl's first few days when she was looking for lodgings. They met by arrangement in a quadrangle of the University. Lotte's physical condition had deteriorated; mind not at all.

"You read about your American boyfriend?"

"Yes. I saw that he is dead."

"Good. Let that be a lesson to you. You should know that the diary has been destroyed. Now let us look for accomodation for you."

Together they found a room in the Schawbing district of Munich in the pension run by Frau Hostrup. The room itself was large and airy and looked onto a small garden at the back of the house. The meals were uniformly bad. The cooking was done by a bad-tempered Sudeten German who had been a cook in a mental hospital before it had been bombed. He used dumplings in everything, including the watery soups. The ten roomers were students. Although Heide joined in the life of the pension, she was careful to avoid close friendships. She had not been cowed by Lotte, but she was not anxious for a repeat performance.

Professor Scheel, her academic mentor, she liked from the outset.

"Heide Prager. Welcome to Munich. Your application for entrance to the university has been accepted and I am hopeful that the scholarship committee will grant at least a bursary on the strength of your academic record. Come sit down."

Professor Scheel ran a thin hand through his white hair and started to clear a pile of books and papers from one of the chairs, all of which were similarly covered. Heide helped him.

"I am sorry. Since my wife died I don't seem to be able to keep things tidy. I have a woman who comes in to clean but I don't let her into my study since the time she threw out a manuscript on which I was working."

She found it hard to judge his age. Probably about seventy. Although they were quite dissimilar she could picture her father looking like Professor Scheel in twenty years time.

"Well my dear I am sure you will like Munich despite what the war and the Nazis did to it. It probably is the most civilized of German cities. I understand we have mutual friends and they have asked me to assist you whenever you may need help and I can provide it."

When Heide started to speak he held up his hand.

"Better that we leave it like that my dear. We only need to talk when it is absolutely necessary. We both have our roles. Of more immediate interest — what have you decided about your studies? I wouldn't recommend my Medieval History courses. History has a limited usefulness, although in the Nazi period it was much in fashion. Perhaps it offered escape from the dogma of National Socialism."

She took his advice and avoided Medieval History. Through her friendship with him, however, and by helping him with his work, she learned at least as much as if she had attended his lectures. With his guidance, the courses she took were oriented more towards international affairs, with special emphasis on the activities of the newly formed United Nations.

As always, her ability to apply herself and her ready intelligence stood her in good stead. And, as always, she welcomed the end of winter and the return of warm weather.

The spring of 1947 brought with it relief from the continuing privations and shortages of winter. Although many of the trees in Munich had been felled for fuel, those that remained blossomed in great abundance, filling the city with their varied perfumes. Like her fellow students the new season brought a restlessness to Heide. It also induced nostalgia. Once exams were over, the feeling became pervasive. Professor Scheel sensed it and tried to ease the pain.

"Well, my dear, I understand you were among the first in your class. I am not surprised. Professors Bormann and Lautcher tell me you are one of their star students. You must be gratified. Would you join me?"

The professor held out a slim glass into which he had poured wine, an effervescent Boxbeutel. Heide accepted and they sat enjoying its cool freshness.

"Frankenwein may not be comparable with a Mosel or a Nahe but it is dependable and, more important, it is still available. This one is from the vineyard of a friend in Thüngersheim, in the Ravensberg area."

Later, when he sensed the wine had relaxed the girl he had grown so fond of, he said;

'I have a message for you. A friend suggests you meet him in the Chineschese Garten by the small bridge near the pavilion next Tuesday afternoon at three. If the meeting fails, then the same time and day, a week later."

Heide nodded but said nothing.

At the gardens, a week later, a man was throwing scraps of food from a brown paper bag he had stuffed into his jacket pocket. The ducks milled around him, swimming this way and that, venturing ever closer, in response to his largesse.

"Viktor Aleksandrovich."

"Yes, Galena Nadya. Gunter Schmidt, machinist-repairman for the state railway. I will not waste time. It will be arranged for you to meet Jan Hlinka who is living in Stuttgart. He was taken prisoner by the German army in Czechoslovakia and, for most of the war, was forced to work in armaments factories. Upon his release by the Americans he was permitted to remain in Germany since he was unable to return to his home town; Lidice. As a former prisoner-of-war and a displaced person, he is eligible to emigrate to Canada. He has already approached the Canadian immigration authorities who operate out of United States Army camps. You will marry him. He is likely to be accepted, and, as his wife, despite your status as an enemy alien, you probably will succeed in accompanying him. It will take time that's all."

"I understand Viktor Aleksandrovich. But marriage?"

"What you make of the marriage, Galena Nadya, is your own affair. From our standpoint it is strictly a business arrangement. Jan Hlinka, which is the name he was born with, has a task to perform in Canada, as you will have. Your marriage to one another will make those tasks easier."

Galena said nothing, watching the ducks compete for the scraps that were thrown to them. Viktor Aleksandrovich shrugged.

"It is only a marriage. You don't have to love him, Galena Nadya."

"What am I to do when I get to Canada?"

"Ah. For the time being, continue your studies in Montreal, where your husband will get employment. Eventually we want you to get a job with the Canadian government. But that is far in the future. We will instruct you in greater detail when it becomes necessary. Continue your studies at university and make as many friends as possible. Over and above what he earns Jan Hlinka will receive any monies you may need in ways that do not attract the attention of the Canadian income tax authorities."

"I also have news from Moscow for you."

"About my father?"

"No. I know nothing about your father except that he is still on assignment outside the country."

"Oh." Her disappointment showed.

"You should not be sad, Galena Nadya. News that your father is 'outside' is good news. In recent times many of your father's rank and higher have been recalled to Moscow and it has not gone well for some of them. They had been away too long and had been contaminated by the bourgeoise capitalism they were supposed to be fighting. Your father is one of the lucky ones. He is still abroad."

"My father is not one of the lucky ones — he is one of the loyal ones. He is a true son of the Revolution."

"Be that as it may, there have been many changes in Moscow. The

Centre has been brought under the authority of the Committee of Information. The Director is now Lieutenant-General Viktor Semonovich Abakumov, the former head of SMERSH. He was appointed by Stalin personally and reports directly to him. You, and other agents in the field, however, will continue to hold your military ranks and entitlements although you are now controlled by the KI."

Galena nodded. She had decided long ago to follow the advice her father had given her when she had first considered joining the service; she avoided the labyrinthine politics of the Kremlin's espionage machinery. Her handler continued.

"As for you personally, comrade, I have good news. You have been promoted to the rank of lieutenant in recognition of the excellent job you have done on the first part of you assignment. Once you have completed the second stage and established yourself in the Canadian government you can expect to be promoted to Captain. That is no mean accomplishment for one so young. Congratulations."

"Thank you, Comrade Lavrov."

He sensed, accurately, that her coldness was the result of his lack of information about her father.

"Do not worry about Colonel Gribanov, my little one. He has a long record of faithful service in the Middle East and he is probably there now. No one in the service is more expert in working in that cockpit than he is. I promise you, when next we meet I will have word of him and how he fares."

"Thank you, Viktor Aleksandrovich." Her voice had lost its edge. "I will hold you to that promise."

"I will not fail you."

Viktor Aleksandrovich removed the empty brown paper bag from his pocket and shook the crumbs onto the water. He blew the bag like a balloon, smashed it between his hands and threw the paper into a wire basket nearby.

"You will be contacted soon. Goodbye, Galena Nadya."

He turned and quickly made his way over the small bridge. Heide stayed with the ducks. It was all so cold and emotionless. She had been well trained and knew that she must obey. It was one thing to challenge Lotte Schneider's orders about her sex life. It would be quite another matter to disobey Lavrov's instructions which obviously had the approval of the Centre and affected the whole structure of her mission. Still, there was in her personality a romantic streak, nurtured by the image of a handsome young Captain and a beautiful ballerina. She stayed by the water's edge long after the ducks gave up hope of receiving more food and drifted away. Later, in bed, an excitement grew in her. She had been so disturbed at the prospect of an arranged marriage to a man she did not know, that she had overlooked the obvious. Slowly it dawned on her that she would be taking a great leap forward in her assigned mission.

Almost three years had elapsed between her departure from the espionage training school and the meeting with Viktor Aleksandrovich. She had been warned that during her 'sleeping' period contact would be infrequent and only when absolutely necessary. Even so, she had hardly been prepared for so long a wait or so basic an instruction from her handler. The die having been cast, however, events moved rapidly. Within a week Jan Hlinka called on her in Munich. Exactly a week after that, they went together to Tützing to bring the Pragers up to date and to make arrangements for the wedding. Another month and they were married.

Jan was nicer than she had dared hope. The relationship between them was, from the first, a business arrangement and he conducted himself in a matter of fact and business-like manner. His physical appearance was quite unprepossessing. He was a full fifteen centimetres shorter than Heide and the thick glasses he wore magnified his very black eyes until they were out of proportion to the rest of his head. He had about him, however, an air of quiet determination. She found it difficult to judge his age. He was older than she was by several years but not, she guessed, by as many years as he appeared. The life of a prisoner-of-war obviously had taken a heavy physical toll. But his spirit was intact, made of tempered steel. In time friendship grew between them.

The wedding took place in the Rathaus in Tützing. Heide wore a dirndl, sewn for the occasion by Maria who did her best to turn it into a proper wedding. Although the older woman had said nothing Heide knew that she had hoped they would be married in a church. Whatever her own reaction to a church wedding might have been, she had been surprised at the finality with which Jan had declared they would have a civil ceremony. He had left no room for argument and Maria did not raise the subject a second time.

The ceremony was short, efficient and bureaucratic. Afterwards the party of six, the newly-weds, the Pragers, a friend of Jan's who had been a prisoner-of-war with him and a girl from the village who had gone to school with Heide, went back to the Prager house. Maria had baked a cake and Anton produced some wine. Professor Scheel had been invited but had excused himself.

"I am getting too old to attend weddings at a distance, my dear."

Heide suspected he had his own reasons for not coming. The celebration was as short and efficient, if not as bureaucratic as the wedding ceremony had been. By five o'clock Jan and his friend were on the train back to Stuttgart. Heide stayed a couple of days with Maria and Anton before returning to Munich, where she had a job in the university library until the autumn semester. The village girl may have thought the honeymoon arrangements strange, but she said nothing.

Heide did not see Jan Hlinka again until after she had resumed her studies in the autumn. Then, in short order, he came to see her twice. Each time he had a fresh batch of immigration forms that required her signature. On the first occasion, once the forms were signed, he left immediately. On the second occasion, he invited her to join him for a meal in a small Weinstube. Once served and alone at their table, Jan told her that he expected to receive word early in the new year that their applications for admission to Canada had been approved. He suggested that at the end of the semester Heide should abandon her studies and come to live with him in Stuttgart. He had a two-room flat which they would use as their base of departure for Canada.

Heide agreed. Early in the new year she called on Professor Scheel for the last time. He showed her to an empty seat in his study.

"I will miss you, my dear. It has been a long time since the chairs in this room were kept so clear of papers and books. Soon there will be no place to sit again."

Heide took the chair and the glass of wine he offered her. She would miss him, too, especially the wondrous hours when he had woven a spell of medieval history for her private consumption.

"The beauty of medieval studies," he used to say, "is the paucity of documentary evidence that the historian has to work with. Because the proofs are so meagre, the historian has to meld his art with that of the novelist. It is such a relief to be free of the rigours of von Ranke."

When she left the old man, she promised to write, but she knew that it would not be the same. They had shared their secret that she was on a mission and it had drawn them together, though they had never spoken of it. Their friendship was that of the old, rather eccentric academic, with the young student who pierced his eccentricities to reach the liberal arts scholarship which was the essence of his being. He had touched her deeply and, although life would be a little empty without the benefit of his company, she would ever after carry something of Professor Scheel in her own personality.

She moved into Jan Hlinka's flat during the first week in February, 1948. A month later they received notification that their admission to Canada had been approved, and that they had been granted a loan towards the cost of their train and boat fare from Stuttgart to Bremen to Quebec City, and then by train again to Montreal. Early in April, Heide visited Maria and Anton in Tützing. Her instructions were that she was to maintain a regular correspondence with Maria. Should she ever need to make personal contact with her controllers in Moscow she was to tell Maria in a letter about meeting a fellow German emigré named Hans who had once lived near Tützing. Maria would then inform Fritz who would pass the message along and a meeting would be arranged. Heide was glad that keeping in touch with her adoptive mother was part of her instructions for the two had grown close and the correspondence would make her feel less isolated during the third stage of the long apprenticeship for her assignment.

Montreal was a shock to both of them. Life there was opulent. There were no bombed-out buildings, no food rationing, no fuel shortages. There were no signs of the six years of bitter warfare and suffering which had touched all of Europe and much of the Middle East and Asia. It was difficult for them to comprehend how Canada, an active belligerent in the war, had managed to stay so aloof from the outside world. To them, life in Montreal was unreal. It was not just the lack of physical evidence of the war that unbalanced them, it was also the lack among the populace of any awareness of what was happening in the rest of the world. Only the returned servicemen whom Heide met at McGill University and Jan met at his job on the Montreal stock exchange seemed to be aware that another world existed beyond North America's ocean fastness. When they raised the question with the ex-servicemen, they would nod and assure them that if they thought Montreal was bad they should visit Toronto, Regina or Vancouver. By comparison to these places Montreal was a cosmopolitan haven of international awareness.

They found an apartment which pleased them both in an old stone building, high on McTavish Street above Sherbrooke Street. They liked the high-ceilinged rooms and tall window frames. There was enough space to make them independent of one another, to facilitate their platonic camaraderie and for each to begin nurturing the contacts that promised to be useful to their respective assignments.

Surprisingly, it was Jan who had qualms about using people. Heide had none. For the first few months she was too absorbed in a fight with the registrar of the university to afford the luxuries of a troubled conscience. She was readily accepted into the university, but the credits they were willing to allow for her work at the University of Munich would have forced her to take two years to finish a degree. Finally the dispute was resolved in the late summer after Professor Scheel intervened. The old man wrote to a former student who was now on the faculty at McGill, to plead her case. His intercession was successful, and late in the summer Heide was informed that she would be admitted to the final year of the bachelor of arts program. Early in the second term, once she had proven her academic ability, with a good showing in the Christmas exams, she applied for admission to the faculty of law and was accepted.

The winter was bitterly cold. The coal-fired furnace that heated the water for the apartment's radiators was not equal to keeping the building's four floors warm. The high ceilings that permitted ornate sculpted plaster friezes and the large windows that provided city-scape views, combined to create constant drafts. The couple took to wearing heavy clothing in the apartment. For Heide, perhaps because of her Russian childhood, that was enough to limit the effect to a minor discomfort that had to be endured. Jan did not fare so well. All winter long he suffered from a succession of colds which laid him up for days on end. In early March he appeared to succumb to yet another cold. After a week in bed she suggested he see a doctor but he refused. As the following week passed his condition deteriorated. A high fever and a severe cough were the outward symptoms, but it was the look on his face that worried Heide. The skin, which had always seemed old to her, was now lifeless. She decided to overrule him and called in a doctor who was recommended by a classmate. The doctor diagnosed an influenza virus that was doing the rounds that winter. He recommended lots of liquids, aspirin and rest.

Another week passed and the strength continued to ooze from Jan's body. Heide called the doctor again. When he came he merely looked at Jan and immediately ordered an ambulance to take him to the hospital. X-rays revealed pneumonia. Too late, massive doses of antibiotics were pumped into him. Weakened by the slave labour he had endured as a prisoner-of-war, his constitution was unable to respond. He died in the Western Division of the Montreal General Hospital on April 5th 1949.

"I am sorry Mrs. Hlinka. We did everything we could to save him. The will to live was there, but he seemed to lack the physical stamina. It was almost as if he had exhausted all his reserves of strength earlier in his life. I dislike mentioning such matters at a time like this but if you agree we would like to perform an autopsy."

Heide continued to gaze out the window at the crowd filing into the Montreal Forum to watch a hockey game. Jan had died at 6.30 in the evening and the streets already were dark. Rain mixed with snow had been falling all day and the traffic moved slowly.

"Quite a birthday present," she said.

"Was it your husband's birthday today?"

"No, it was mine."

As she spoke she knew that she had blundered. April 5th was not Heide's birthday. It was Galena's. The slip haunted her for days. Until after Jan's funeral she lived in constant fear that some document which the doctor had to sign would require her date of birth on it. Had she been more aware of Canadian procedures for burying the dead she would not have worried quite so much. She would, however, still have berated herself. She escaped unscathed but learned how easy it was to let her cover slip. She swore never to be so careless again.

The doctor broke into her reverie. If he noticed that she was more distraught after their brief exchange, he simply put it down to the fact, which he knew so well, that grief comes in surges.

"We did all we could."

"I know, doctor. He was still weak from his experiences in a slave labour factory. But he refused to take life easier."

"Will you agree to an autopsy?"

"Yes."

She took the pen he offered and quickly signed the forms. The doctor left her. Heide picked up her coat and hat from the chair. She gave a last glance at the indentations on the bed where Jan's body had been. She took one of the roses she had brought earlier in the week and placed it on the pillow. She walked into the corridor. As she stepped onto the slushy sidewalk she knew that she would miss Jan Hlinka. She did not realize how quickly his absence would be felt.

For three days the minutae of death occupied her every waking moment. By the time the autopsy was complete, she had chosen a coffin and arranged with an undertaker to pick up the body and prepare it for burial. Their landlady fussed over arranging for her own parish priest to officiate. Heide was touched by the irony of a priest at Jan's funeral, but he had brought it on himself. He had thought it would speed the processing of his application for immigrant status if he said he was a catholic on the application forms. Once in Canada he thought it best to keep up the pretence although he never attended church. In death, however, he had no say in the matter and Heide gladly left it in the landlady's hands. Delighted to be a part in the mourning the woman also volunteered to serve a lunch after the funeral.

While these preparations were being made Heide looked after buying a plot in Mount Royal cemetery. She was amazed at the bureaucracy of death and wondered how the truly bereaved managed to cope with it. It was a comfort to realize that not only in Russia were such matters surrounded by red tape. A college friend, Marie Claire Houle, helped greatly in leading her through the maze.

She also was amazed at the expense of death. As the charges mounted she wondered how she would meet them. She found herself using the letter to Maria and Anton in which she informed them of Jan's death to let them know of her need for money. They would pass the request along and her masters would look after her financial needs. But that would take time and she could not wait. On the morning of the funeral, she went to the bursar's office at the university and filled out an application for a student loan, then she walked across campus and managed to take out a further loan from the student credit union. At the funeral that afternoon the burden was lightened when Jan's superior at the stock exchange gave her a cheque for the equivalent of a month's pay.

* * * * * * * * * *   * * * * * * * * * *

One of the technicians turned off the tape recorder. She gratefully accepted the cup of coffee offered her. It had been a long day. Brad and McCain looked as tired as she felt. None of them said much later as they drove back to Sandy Hill. The car stopped a few blocks from her house as she and Patricia Haley got out.

"Pick you up in the morning Heide. Good night Patricia. Good luck."

SEVEN

MEMORANDUM

SECURITY
CLASSIFICATION:
Most Secret
DISTRIBUTION:
Dept. V 'Special'

TO: Director I.V. Zagorin
FROM: Dept V (Krivolapov)
SUBJECT: Operation Orestes.

Confirmation received V operatives are in place. Target arriving on schedule. Authority requested to instruct agent V90, now in control of operation, to proceed with plan and to report its execution immediately thereafter.

* * * * * * * * * * * * * * * * * * * *

The following day was wet and cold. She and Patricia drove in her car to the small parking lot by the park on Range Road. There they were picked up by Brad and McCain. By the time they reached the country house, Heide was cold. She found welcome the sight and sound of logs burning in the fireplace in the room in which they worked.

"Lets continue from where we left off yesterday. You mentioned a friendship with a French Canadian girl in Montreal."

Brad stopped to look at his notes.

"Yes, Marie-Claire Houle."

Brad nodded.

"Right. Take it from there."

Heide stared into the fire, her mind going back to Jan's death.

Marie-Claire Houle came to the fore during the days following Jan's death. She was a classmate of Heide's and the two had developed a nascent friendship that winter. They were as two strangers at McGill.

Heide, a German, was a rarity among the students. Marie-Claire, a French-speaking Canadian and a native of Rimouski, almost as much so in that English language institution. The two women were taking mostly the same courses and often met in class. Early in the winter when Heide had to miss occasional lectures to nurse one or another of Jan's bad colds, she had borrowed Marie-Claire's notes to catch up. Later she was able to reciprocate when Marie-Claire was snowbound for 36 hours on a train back from a week-end visit to her parents. Long before Jan's final illness they had taken to going for coffee after the last class of the week and in January had held a joint celebration when they received word on the same day that they had both been accepted into Law School for the next year. Heide genuinely liked Marie-Claire Houle. Nevertheless she had deliberately nurtured the friendship as the one good contact available with the French-Canadian community.

When Heide returned from the undertaker's the day after Jan's death, Marie-Claire was waiting on her doorstep.

"I'm sorry, Heide. I don't think you really loved Jan, but you will miss him."

The girl's forthrightness caught Heide off guard. She started to protest, but thought better of it.

"No I didn't love him. It was a marriage of convenience. It let me leave Germany and come here to build a new life. But he was good to me, and I shall miss him."

She had spoken the truth, as far as it went. It was a cardinal rule of her business, repeated endlessly at training school, that with the exception of those lies absolutely necessary to an agent's cover honesty should prevail at all times. She knew that if she had professed love for Jan, Marie-Claire would have known she was lying and might have wondered why. As she confessed the nature of her relationship with Jan, however, she wondered what the authorities would do if they knew of the artificiality of her marriage. She feared that she might not be permitted to stay in Canada now that Jan was dead. It was a risk she had to take, an inherent danger in her assignment. If she were to draw close to people like Marie-Claire and make friends with them and put down roots, she had to expose much of herself and thus become vulnerable. If she did not do so, she would be unable to fulfil her assignment. She had nothing to worry about with Marie-Claire Houle.

"Our final exams start in two weeks. It's going to be hard for you to study living here alone. Why don't you move in with me after the funeral?"

"Thanks."

In the days that followed the plan changed. Instead of Heide moving in to Marie-Claire's one-room apartment, the latter moved in with her and took over Jan's room. They shared the chores and the cooking, coached one another in the subjects they shared and blew off steam together after each exam and when the tension threatened to become unbearable.

The deepening friendship opened a new world for Heide. Until Jan's death her associates in Montreal were primarily English-speaking Canadians from the university and the stock exchange. Now, as she was included in Marie-Claire's circle of friends she discovered the duality of Canadian society. The differences between the two groups reminded Heide of those that existed between the Russians and the Ukrainians. The comparison came to her on a Friday night at a party in the apartment of Marie-Claire's cousin, Jacques Dumois. She was sitting on the floor with a glass of wine in one hand and a cigarette in the other. A middle aged man whom she had seen for the first time that night started into a step dance solo, on the bare wooden floor. Heide turned to Jacques Dumois who was sitting next to her.

"That reminds me of home when the . . . ."

She caught herself in mid-sentence. To distract attention from her unfinished statement she deliberately dropped her cigarette into the folds of her skirt. In the scramble to find it, she spilled her wine on Jacques' leg. The resulting confusion averted attention from her ill-considered comment. It was as well, for there was nothing Germanic in the footwork of the dance. For Heide, though, the slip was not forgotten. Twice in short order she had allowed the personality of Galena to show through. The mistakes made her jittery and she brooded on the danger of exposure. As the weeks passed she began to realize just how much Jan had meant to her. He had been a link with her real world. With him at least there had been no pretense. Now the isolation of her double life was all but unbearable.

Relief came at the end of April with a second letter from Maria and Anton. Their first had merely been to let her know that the news of Jan's death had been received and was being passed on. "All your friends will be so sorry when they hear of the tragedy." The second letter showed that they had been in touch with her handlers. Maria and Anton had been thinking of how lonely she must be without Jan and had decided, as a graduation present, to pay her fare to come home for a visit. They enclosed a bank draft to cover her return fare and suggested that she come once her exams were over.

As it turned out Heide had to delay her visit to Germany until late in May. On receipt of the money she booked passage to fly to Europe from Dorval airport three days after her final exams. Events intervened. When she arrived home from her last examination Marie-Claire told her that an Immigration officer had called and would call back the next day. The hours of that night dragged interminably and sleeplessly until dawn. The irritational fear that her cover had been blown gripped deep in her bowels.

The sounds of the birds awakening, and the red sky that promised a sunny start to the spring day did nothing to relieve the tension she felt. Fortunately Marie-Claire had an examination that morning and Heide was able to avoid being with her and perhaps revealing her nervousness. When the phone rang at 10:30 its sound almost paralysed her. On its fourth ring her shaking hand lifted the receiver from its cradle.

"Hello."

"Mrs Hlinka?"

"Yes."

"My name is George Irving. I'm with the Immigration Review Section."

Her worst fears were confirmed. But why were they contacting her by telephone? She knew that the 4 a.m. knock on the door was not in the best Canadian tradition, although it did happen. But this was ridiculous. His next words did nothing to allay her fears.

"We would like you to come down to the office in the next few days."

"Can you tell me what it is about?"

"We'd rather not discuss it on the phone. It is only a matter of a few questions that the RCMP would like to have cleared up. It shouldn't take long."

The RCMP! Her heart thumped.

"When would you like me to come in?"

"Would Thursday morning be O.K.?"

Her plane was scheduled to leave Thursday afternoon. She had to delay them long enough to get to Europe.

"Friday would be better."

"Friday? Friday morning at ten?"

"Yes."

"Very good."

He gave her directions for finding his office on St. James street, and rang off.

She quickly prepared to abort her mission. She could not pack a bag yet without arousing Marie-Claire's interest. Instead she cleared the top drawer of her dresser and then refilled it with everything she would need for the journey. On the top of the clothing she placed her tickets for the journey and her passport. In the second drawer she gathered every scrap of paper related to her in any way. University notes, cancelled cheque stubs and bank statements, the last two letters from Maria, the earlier correspondence about their immigration to Canada, the deed to the cemetery plot, Jan's death certificate and an emergency one-time cypher pad disguised as a book of cross-word puzzles. On Thursday morning she would use the cypher to send a telegram to Lavrov informing him that her cover had been blown and that she was en route to Germany. She would contact him through Professor Scheel to avoid the risk of being picked up by the German security authorities at Maria and Anton's. Once she had prepared the cable she would put the cypher pad and the other papers in the incinerator of the apartment building. The cable she could despatch from the airport. With her plans made and her belongings organized she went to the bank to withdraw what little money she kept there. She would need every cent until she could make contact with her handlers. She decided, however, to leave a dollar in each of the two accounts at the bank.

The oppressive darkness of the clouds hanging overhead matched her mood as she descended the steep hill of McTavish Street. A storm was brewing on the mountain that dominated the city. Waiting to be served in the bank she could hear the deep rumbling of thunder outside. Suddenly the rain started. It pounded against the large windows. She turned to look and as she did a flash of lightning broke the mid-morning dusk. Without knowing why, Heide left her place in line and went back to the writing table against the wall. She tore up the two cheques she had written. Instead she wrote out a deposit slip for the $100 she had in her purse, the remainder of the money order she had received from Maria and Anton. She returned to the line-up to make the deposit.

Out in the street with the rain beating against her face she walked down town to the Trans Canada Airlines office to change her reservation. That done she went to the telegraph office.

"Have delayed departure. Now leaving sixteenth on flight 479. Will make own way to Tützing by noon seventeenth."

The rain had soaked her to the skin long before she got back to the apartment. She filled the chipped, enamel bathtub with steaming water and, as her skin turned red from its scalding heat, she knew she had made the right decision. If the Mounties had uncovered her they would hardly have telephoned to set up an appointment. They would have picked her up for interrogation. Whatever they wanted to talk about was of a lesser order. At worst some suspicion had been aroused and they were sniffing around for more concrete evidence. Perhaps they were even watching to see if she would try to bolt. She would not. She would play out the hand she had been dealt and at least wait until after the interview on Friday before making a run for it. She wished she had taken her father's advice and arranged a safehouse.

Brad interrupted her story.

"You say the Immigration Review Section in Montreal got in touch with you?"

"Yes. As I have said a man called Irving — George Irving, phoned me."

"Did you see them? Did they interview you?"

Heide lit a cigarette and, crossing her legs, stared at Brad through the smoke she blew across the table.

"I was coming to that."

"Okay, go ahead."

Brad made a note to have her story checked when they broke for lunch.

"Mrs. Hlinka? Come in please."

George Irving was a nondescript civil servant, who would have looked at home in any government office, anywhere in the world. The dirty windows of the building across the well from his spartan office reflected some blue sky.

"This is Sergeant Roger of the RCMP."

The sergeant was a heavy set, middle-aged policeman who looked like a policeman. He remained seated uncomfortably on a wooden chair while Irving pointed to a chair for Heide to sit on. The muscles in her stomach worked uncontrollably. Her knees felt weak. Nothing of her concern showed in her face or her hands. She took the chair offered and sat as easily as she could and waited for one of them to speak. The policeman broke the silence.

"It was really your husband I wanted to see."

"He's dead."

"Yes. We know. Even so perhaps you can help clear up one or two points. When did you first meet him?"

"In 1946."

"Where?"

"In Munich."

"Did you know him at all before the war?"

"No."

"During?"

"No."

"Did he see active service?"

"He was arrested when the Germans overran Czechoslovakia in 1939. He was suspected of being part of the resistance."

She would have to watch that reference to the Germans as though she were not one.

"Was he in the resistance?"

"No. He would have been, but he was arrested before he could make contact. Why are you asking all this?"

"We have received information which suggests your husband may have been a Nazi collaborator."

Heide sat stunned for a minute. Then the tension she had been living under broke into peels of laughter. Tears streamed down her cheeks and she searched in her purse for a handkerchief. Her response threw the sergeant and the immigration official into confusion. At last she controlled herself.

"My husband a collaborator? He spent six years as a slave — not a prisoner — a slave. When the camp was liberated, his name was high on the list of the Nazis for execution. Do you know why he stayed in Germany? Do you? Because his home had been Lidice. Every member of his family was slaughtered in revenge for the death of Heydrich. Last month he died. The death certificate said it was from pneumonia. It wasn't. He died because the Nazis had sapped his strength and he had nothing left to fight with. Perhaps he did not emerge from the camp with virgin purity. No one who survived in those conditions did, but he was no collaborator."

Her passion was real. All the hatred of the Nazis for what they had done to her Russian homeland was poured into her words. It was also effective. The immigration officer fidgeted with a paperweight. The sergeant coughed before speaking again.

"We had to check it out Mrs Hlinka. I hope you will understand."

"I understand," said Heide, "but for God's sake let it drop. My husband deserves to lie in peace. He earned it."

As she walked home from the interview a new buoyancy was in Heide's step. She had come through a crisis unscathed and she had learned to tough out a threatening situation. She had almost blown her years of training and preparation, but at the last moment she had persevered and had won. Soon she would be in Germany.

The reunion with the Pragers was a happy one. She found them touchingly glad to see her. Maria, in particular, welcomed the companionship. The winter had been a bad one for Anton. Another operation on his left knee had left him more crippled than before and dependent upon a cane. They talked about Jan and they were eager for news of Canada and Heide's life in Montreal.

"We have decided to move. I have the offer of a better job in a laboratory in Berlin. We still have friends there. One of them has offered to rent us rooms in her house, part of which was damaged but is now rebuilt. The city government with the help of the Allied Control Commission is offering tax concessions to attract immigrants. Our mutual friends have encouraged us."

"When will you move?"

"We are not sure. We still have to have permission from the Americans since we will be in their sector of Berlin. We hope that we can go this summer. Ah, it will be good to breathe Berliner luft instead of the soft wet winds which blow off these mountains. No more Föhn, which seems to go right to my knee."

Anton waved his hand in the direction of the southern end of the lake and the invisible Bavarian alps.

After the second day Heide received a letter from Professor Scheel congratulating her on her scholastic achievements and suggesting that she come to Munich to visit him. This she arranged to do the next day, delighted to see her elderly mentor and to have tea with him. He was very frail and told her that he was planning to retire from the university. He found the increasing numbers of students and the consequent administrative work too much. The university had offered him a small office and had agreed to finance his continued research after he vacated the chair. He also gave her a message. A mutual friend would like to meet her tomorrow and, failing that, the following Saturday at the same time and place. He suggested the kiosk outside the railway station at Garmisch-Partenkirchen.

"Frau Hlinka." The voice from behind her caught her unawares. She recognized it was that of Viktor Aleksandrovich despite the German intonation he affected.

"Gunter. How nice to see you." She turned to greet him. They took the road leading from the Bahnhof up through the village and out into the countryside, past the Geiger hotel. Soon they were alone but continued to carry on their conversation in German.

"I brought some bread, sausage and cheese. We can get beer in bottles at the Stube up ahead. We have much to talk about. We can do it over something to eat."

A cow path led them to a bluff overlooking the highway and a view of the mountains to the south and east. They sat in the sun beneath a wooden cross on which there hung a rough-hewn figure of Christ. Viktor Aleksandrovich seemed not to notice as he hung his coat from the pegs holding the curved boards which formed a protective roof over the icon.

"We were sorry about Jan. Could it have been prevented?"

"No. I think he had the best medical help available. He had no physical reserves. It all happened so suddenly. He was in hospital only a few days before he died. Poor Jan, he seemed almost to shrink to nothing in the hospital bed." She told him of her encounter with the immigration official and the R.C.M.P. officer. Viktor Aleksandrovich nodded his head.

"They are thorough. Perhaps Jan's death was timely after all. He might have jeopardized your mission."

Heide was shocked.

"Was he a Nazi informer?"

"Only when it proved necessary."

She was glad she had known nothing of this at the interview. A feigned disbelief might have proved transparent. Viktor Aleksandrovich fell silent. He rose and pulled a long stalk of grass which he began to chew as he walked up and down. Galena felt a tenseness in him.

"Jan's death was a pity though. He was proving useful. Luckily we have others to take his place. His death will change little for you. You have legitimate credentials now. When the time is right you will seek employment with one of the federal government departments, in the capital. You are to regard this as a base from which to try to gain entry to the Canadian foreign service. It will take time — you have to have a minimum of ten years of residence. You should apply for Canadian citizenship as soon as you are eligible. We don't think this will prove too difficult, provided you retain your married name and status as a widow."

"Should I take any special instruction in foreign affairs in addition to my law courses?"

"No. Not for the present. Perhaps later. We have examples of past examinations set by the Civil Service Commission and the Department of External Affairs. There are broad choices offered. Apart from general knowledge they are chess type questions, apparently aimed at exploring the flexibility of the candidate's mind. The approach may change with time. Better wait."

"We also would like you to establish photography as a hobby. You had instruction in the basics during your training, as well as those special aspects having to do with micro-miniaturization and the use of micro-dot communications. We want you to establish yourself as an amateur photographer. Make no secret of your hobby. To the contrary, the more it is known and accepted by your friends and acquaintances, the better. This will mean purchasing equipment of all kinds. Good equipment is not cheap. You will need money."

He sat down beside her. For a while he said nothing, staring at the distant Alps. He lit a cigarette and offered her one.

"As to money. Jan's mother, who lived in Prague, died recently and left some money. Not a great fortune, but we have arranged to supplement it for your purposes. She left everything to Jan. She did not know of Jan's death, which occured shortly before her own. As his widow you will inherit it. The probate will take time. When you return to Canada you will find a letter from a lawyer in Prague, notifying you of the inheritance. You will place the matter in the hands of a Montreal lawyer. We will leave the choice of a lawyer to you. In due course you will receive the funds — about $40,000 Canadian. You will have no taxes to pay on it. Bank it in the normal way, and draw on it as you have need. Eventually you may wish to invest the bulk of it. In the meantime I have additional funds for you — $5,000 in large denomination Canadian bills. We have not been able to arrange a legitimate cover for these funds, so you will have to smuggle them into the country. It should not be difficult. The Canadian customs and immigration authorities normally do not search for currency carried by travellers returning to Canada."

Viktor Aleksandrovich threw his cigarette away and nervously got to his feet again. He lit another cigarette.

"Galena Nadya. I have bad news."

Galena felt her stomach tighten and the blood drain from her head.

"Oh, no, Viktor Aleksandrovich, not, not . . . ."

"Yes, Galena Nadya. I am sorry to have to tell you that Anatoli Ivanovich was killed in an operation in northern Turkey. We think his assassin was an American agent working with the Turkish secret police. He was trapped; how, we are not sure. He was alone at the time."

Galena had difficulty breathing. She got to her feet unthinking. Viktor Aleksandrovich tried to help her but she thrust his arm away and ran through the grain field, stumbling in the furrows hidden by the tall growth. He did not try to follow. Much later he found her lying where she had thrown herself.

"Why?" She turned on him. "Why did you send him alone?"

"We didn't Galena Nadya. The operation was well planned. There were others. We do not know how, but he was tricked into making a rendezvous alone. He was shot in the head. He cannot have known the moment of death. It would have been so sudden."

"When did this happen?"

"Two months ago, Galena Nadya."

"Two months ago! Why was I not told sooner?"

"There was no safe way of doing so. We decided to wait until I could tell you personally. He was dead. There was nothing you could do by knowing earlier. He died like the soldier he was. His bravery is to be recognized by the state."

"Okay, Heide. Let's call it quits. I have to cut it short this afternoon. Tomorrow I'd like to go back to the period immediately after you were recruited and went to the espionage school."

Heide was happy to stop. She found it tiring work. They drove back to Ottawa through a heavy rain storm.

EIGHT

INTERNAL MEMORANDUM

SECURITY
CLASSIFICATION:
Top Secret
DISTRIBUTION:
Opal indoctrinated
only

TO: Director General
(Copy, Inspector Randall)
FROM: Special analysis Group (Merrivale)
SUBJECT: Operation Opal

As requested by Inspector Randall we have done an analysis of suspected wireless communications traffic directed to eastern North America with special reference to the past fifteen days.
In fact we extended our examination to the previous sixty days to provide a suitable framework for comparison.
Of the intercepted messages designated as secret agent traffic using normally accepted criteria for identification (known call signs, Morse code signatures, etc.) we found no evidence of significant variations in volume of traffic, length of average messages or unusual use of new call signs (possibly denoting new agent activity).
One only unusual occurence was a 36 hour period, beginning on day 47, when trans-polar traffic on a broad SW spectrum (19 metre to 16 metre) appeared to have been suspended completely. Since the period coincided almost exactly with sun-spot activity which affected global communications the unusual radio silence detected would appear to be attributable to this event and not any action by Moscow Centre.

* * * * * * * * * * * * * * * * * * * *

The following day dawned bright and clear. Heide felt refreshed.

During the drive to the country house she noticed early signs of approaching winter. Some of the trees were already nearly bare. Yellow leaves on the ground beneath a stand of poplars filled her with nostalgia and reminded her of the countryside surrounding her training camp in Russia. As the reels on the tape recorder began turning she went back in her mind to those dark days in 1942 when Russia had seemed on the point of collapse.

The yellowed leaves of the poplars on the ridge above the old estate had been stripped from their branches by winds out of the northeast. The bad weather had come early to Russia in the autumn of 1941. Valentin Petrovich Krylov butted his cigarette on the stone sill of the window as he stared through its steamy panes at the driving rain. The fields and the dirt pathway winding through them had been turned into a sea of mud. He muttered angrily.

"Kakôye proklyatoye boloto."

The cursed mud made it impossible to carry out orders to evacuate the training camp and fall back to the new rallying point at Kuibyshev. Fortunately, it also made it impossible for von Kluge's panzers to continue their advance. The road to Moscow had been laid open to the Germans by their sudden attack of June 21. The Red Army had been helpless to stop the advance. All they could do was slow its progress by setting whole divisions in its path to be engulfed in a German pincer movement and annihilated. The only hope was to gain time until their last ally, Winter, had time to arrive. It seemed they had succeeded. For the first time in weeks a cautious optimism crept into the reports from the Red Army command. It would not be long before the rains turned to snow. Adolf Hitler would soon learn by experience what Napoleon Bonaparte failed to teach him by example.

There was a light knock at the door. Krylov turned.

"Come."

The young Galena entered. Her blonde hair was combed straight back, tight against her skull and pinned in a hard knot behind. The battledress uniform which had been cut rather than tailored from a length of rough-woven grey wool cloth combined with the hair style to conceal her beauty under a cloak of sterile severity.

"Ah, Galena Nadya. Come in. I wanted to talk about the future. Here, take a seat."

He waved her to a chair by a bare wooden table from which half the varnish had worn away. He dragged another chair to the opposite side of the table. She looked at the floor to see if the legs of the chair had marked it. The planks of fir were beyond being scraped or scarred. He moved a lighted field lantern from a shelf to the table. As he turned up its yellow light, the lamp hissed more loudly and the strong smell of kerosene intensified. He brought a dossier from the desk and sat opposite her. Galena watched him carefully as he opened the folder and silently read the first page.

"Galena Nadya Gribanov, born Moscow, April 5, 1927, only daughter of NKVD Colonel Anatoli Ivanovich Gribanov (alias Vladimir Fedorovich Chuckukin) and Larissa Kiselnikova Belinkov (deceased 1927). Accompanied father to Stockholm and Berlin where she attended schools during his assignments. Languages: German (fluent); English (fair); Swedish (fluent). Intelligence testing: above average. Medical characteristics: normal; heart murmur as child; Photographic memory; almost total recall; no addictions; sexually normal. Motivation: excellent. Father recommended for recognition of his contribution to espionage operations in Sweden. Mother's father sentenced to jail by czarist police for seditious writing. Psychological testing: Responded well to testing process; high degree of self-control; capable of withstanding stress; strong attachment to father. Note: Chief examiner believes a part of her personality remained untouched by psychoanalytical tests applied, perhaps denoting a degree of independence not commonly found in a person of her age. Physical appearance and fingerprints: see attached envelope."

Major Krylov turned the page and opened the envelope. He removed a number of black and white photographs, each measuring 15 by 20 centimetres, showing Galena in the nude, front, back and side views with various measurements marked in the margins. There were three sets of fingerprints. He laid the fingerprints aside and examined the photographs under the hissing light of the lamp. After a long minute closely scrutinizing each photograph he held them, one at a time, at arm's length comparing them with the young woman before him. They showed a beautifully proportioned body with the promise of an early maturity.

"Your uniform conceals much, Galena Nadya. Your assets for the tasks ahead seem quite unusual."

He replaced the photographs in the envelope. Galena flushed.

"I am glad you think I am fitted for whatever tasks I may be given, Comrade Krylov."

Major Krylov took out a cigarette and lit it. The harsh, cigar-like smell of cheap Georgian tobacco filled the room which was already stale with the stench of earlier cigarettes that clung to the curtains and furnishings. He offered one to Galena.

"No, thank you, I do not smoke," she said coldly through the haze. She found herself thinking of the rich aroma of the pipe full of English tobacco which her father used to relish after dinner when they lived in Stockholm.

"Yes you do," said the major.

Galena was surprised by his contradiction. He smiled.

"At least you are going to." He made a note in her dossier.

"You had better also make a notation that I will be smoking something less pungent than Georgian tobacco."

The chief examiner was right about her independent spirit, he thought to himself. Then, aloud, and still smiling,

"Whatever kind you smoke try never to grow to like it. It is not good for you, and we are spending too much on your training to have you die young from these things."

"Then why are you telling me to start doing it?" she asked.

"You will see. As to the task ahead, you will know from your weeks in the school's general programme that the second phase is your assignment to a geographic area and to specialized training in various units: photography, wireless telegraphy, languages, secret communications techniques, firearms, explosives and so on. Your general training has included something of the theoretical aspects of these. Now you will go into them all in more detail so that you will understand them more fully and also be able to practice the various crafts. In some you will become quite expert."

Galena nodded but said nothing. Valentin Petrovich Krylov drew heavily on the end of his cigarette, exhaled the smoke and butted the last of it. He drew a single sheet of paper from the dossier.

"You will start language training in German and English. I see from your records that your German is fluent so it will be largely a question of acquiring colloquial styles and current usage. We would like to give you a local accent but we do not yet know what you will require, so you will have to train your ear to detect the various regional accents of Germany and if possible learn to imitate them. Those languages will be your first priority. We also want you to acquire French, at least some knowledge of the language. For your technical courses you will specialize in photography and certain aspects of secret communications."

He fished in the breast pocket of his tunic and brought out a spectacles case. He opened it carefully, took out the glasses, put them on and snapped the case shut. He handed the case to her.

"I do not need glasses, Galena Nadya, but if I am to take photographs with the camera that I just handed you, I must wear them. That is why you must learn to smoke. We are working now on a miniature camera that will be hidden in a cigarette lighter. Someday you will probably be supplied with one and your use of it will be more natural and less likely to arouse suspicion if you have smoked for a long time. But, please, do not smoke too much."

As he spoke he reached for yet another cigarette. When its fumes reached the girl's nose, she swore again that she would adopt a different brand, but this time she kept her thoughts to herself. She examined the case in her hand. Now that she knew what she was looking for the lens was obvious, but it was well hidden from a casual examination.

"In the other technical areas," Krylov continued, "your training will be more basic. When you have finished the course you will know how to handle a gun with some assurance, how to make a bomb from kitchen supplies, the manufacture of miniature photographs, how to send a wireless message in cypher and so forth. But you will only need some of these skills in an extreme emergency and not for many years, if at all."

"As for your geographic area, Galena Nadya, you will be assigned to the North American Section. Your studies will include the political structures, culture, history and life of the United States and Canada. You will specialize in the North American economy and you will examine the potential for conflict between the ruling classes and the underprivileged groups in those countries."

Galena shifted in her seat.

"May I ask a question, Comrade Krylov?"

"Certainly, Galena Nadya," he said and puffed on his cigarette.

"Surely America is far from the battle front?"

"I understand your question. With so many square kilometres of our land in enemy hands and so many of our people killed, the battle is here and now. Yet we must plan for victory and for further battles beyond. The Soviet Union has many enemies and many potential enemies. We are locked now in a struggle to the death with Nazi Germany but it is too late to begin building entirely new networks in Germany and Occupied Europe. We must rely there on the foundations we built before the war. They are good foundations and Hitler already knows that we are his superiors in this area. He has ordered a full-scale effort to crush our networks but he will find that a difficult task. There will be casualties, heavy casualties, and we will constantly have to replenish our forces. We will probably lose whole networks from time to time and when that happens we have to try to build new ones from the ground up, despite the difficulties. Even so the Director has given us orders that the present war is not to consume all our energies. We are also to prepare now to deal with our future enemies."

He butted his cigarette and lit another one.

"When the Germans are beaten, and they will be beaten, the United States of America will be a new and powerful force with influence throughout the world. The Americans, although they are our friends now, are opposed to the Soviet Union and to Communism; they may be the enemy of tomorrow. We must be ready, in the chaos that follows this war, to build for the future. That is why you are being assigned to the North American section. Your work there will be very important."

For the first time since she had entered the room, Galena felt the tension waning.

"Thank you, comrade, I understand. I will do what is required of me."

"I know you will, Galena Nadya. You are made of the same stuff as your father."

The interview was at an end. She went out closing the door quietly behind her. She felt kindly towards him. Major Krylov gazed at the door for a few minutes before picking up a pen and scribbling the date and his initials, 'VPK', on the last sheet of paper he had removed from the folder. As he returned the page to the dossier, his eye fell on the envelope. He removed the photographs from it again and spread them on the table beneath the lamp. He lit yet another cigarete and slowly let its smoke drift over them.

"It is a pity," he thought, "that the light from the lamp is so dim, I would like to have my own copies of these."

He put the glasses that were lying on the table back in their case and returned it to his breast pocket, replaced the photographs in the enveloped and turned to the window. It was almost dark outside. The rain had turned to sleet. He blew smoke at the panes of glass that would soon be frosted.

"Kakoye proklyatoye boloto." It was a long hard winter.

Driving through the streets of Ottawa more than thirty years later Galena remembered how late Spring had come to Russia in 1942. It was the end of June, after the Germans had mounted a great new offensive, before the warm weather returned. Then everything had burst into life with northern suddenness. The countryside around the centre assumed the verdant colours of summer. Galena revelled in the season's change and in the knowledge that she was excelling in the tasks set her. It had not been easy. The intensity of the programme and the deliberate segregation of the trainees from one another had an oppressive effect, heightened by the harshness of the winter and the lack of adequate rations. She had overcome the difficulties by bending all her energies to mastering her studies.

She was glad, however, when the second phase of her training ended in early July. Now she had free days in which to enjoy the sun and its warmth. Much of her time was spent in walks through the surrounding countryside, mostly uncultivated forest. To the south of the camp she discovered a small lake set among stands of ash, elders, birch and pine. A 'Yasnaya Polyana' which would have delighted Tolstoy.

A narrow sandy beach on one side enabled her to swim and sunbathe observed only by the waterfowl, the occasional hare and a mud-turtle that shared the beach.

"Ah, Galena Nadya. As I thought, the photographs do not do you justice."

Galena turned where she stood with the water up to her buttocks. Her bronzed back and arms glistened in the sun. Her hair, darkened by the water, had copper and gold glints in it. Major Krylov stood on the beach beside her neatly folded uniform. He wore a loose white shirt, his field-grey trousers and high leather boots. In his hand he carried a long branch stripped of its leaves. Her mind went back two summers before she entered the training school. At the villa where she and the children of other officers on foreign service were vacationing there had been a boy, she could not even remember his name, who had sought to dominate her. She had turned the tables on him, seized the initiative and lost her virginity. For the rest of the summer she had been the master.

"What a coincidence Major Krylov. We seem to have taken the same path."

"Valentin, not Major Krylov."

"As you wish."

She walked on to the beach and stood before him squeezing the water from her hair. Refracted by the sun's rays, small drops of water on the skin of her well-rounded breasts and flat, unblemished belly glittered like diamonds.

"Well, Comrade Valentin?"

Galena was amused to see the flicker of surprise in his eyes, even hesitation. The blackness of his curly hair was set off by the open-neck white shirt. He was almost handsome. Only his short stature spoiled the effect. Even in her bare feet she was the same height. He smelled of shaving soap and his Georgian cigarettes. Perhaps it was the combination, perhaps it was the open air, or perhaps it was that she too now smoked, but Galena no longer found the smell offensive.

"Come, let us not talk." She started unbuttoning his shirt. She ran her hand down his chest to the waist band of his trousers.

"You are strong, Galena Nadya." He lay back and let the sun soak into his body. He reached into his clothes which lay in a heap beside them for a cigarette.

"Will you have one?"

"No, I will share yours."

They lay watching the changing shape of a small cloud drifting across the lake. Wisps of its vapour evaporated before their eyes but did not diminish its size. She leaned over and took the cigarette from his lips, inhaled a couple of times and threw the half-finished stub away. He started to protest. She silenced him with her lips and hands. This time the pleasures were more prolonged, the ending more intense. Almost instantly afterwards he turned onto his back and slept.

Galena arose and waded into the lake to wash and swim then stood by the shore looking into its clear water while the sun dried her body. Her hair was still damp when she slipped back into her clothes. She took a clasp from her pocket and expertly fastened the hair to the top of her head to save her blouse from getting wet. She looked down at the sleeping figure.

"Ah, Valentino, you are lucky I have no camera with me. Your uniform conceals so little now." She smiled, picked up the branch he had been carrying and broke it at the three-quarter mark. The short section she stuck in the sand at the top of his head, the long piece between his legs. She admired her handiwork and then, without a backward glance strode along the path towards the training centre. Once clear of the woods she took the clasp from her hair and let the gentle breeze finish drying it. She knew that it would take more than one bout on a deserted beach to become the master of Major Krylov. But she had no desire to dominate him, only to ensure that he did not dominate her.

As the cold weather returned the German advances were again slowed and, in places, reversed. By November the Russians launched a great counter-offensive, beginning near Serafinov, which eventually led to the German capitulation at Stalingrad. The military successes had a visible effect upon spirits in the training centre which had by then almost doubled in size. There were two large new cantonments to the east of the old compound. Around the perimeter of one ran a high, barbed wire fence, constantly patrolled by units of the Red Army. No personnel walked through its double gates and most vehicles concealed their occupants. It was believed by those in Galena's classes that this was a training school for sabotage squads who were to be deployed behind the German forward lines and for attacks on key installations deep inside enemy territory. No one knew for sure, and no one asked questions. Early in their training they were taught not to be inquisitive outside their immediate field of studies. They were also taught that future security depended greatly on discretion and they were to begin now by revealing nothing of themselves to their classmates. They were a group of people but in the midst of the group each individual was a lone and lonely being.

* * * * * * * * * *   * * * * * * * * * *

INTERNAL MEMORANDUM

SECURITY CLASSIFICATION:
Top Secret.
DISTRIBUTION:
Opal Indoctrinated
Only.

FROM: Special Analysis Group(Merrivale).
TO: Director-General.
SUBJECT: Opal.
You asked SAG, as a matter of urgency, to list those targets which are most likely to attract the attention of Department V of the KGB.
It seems likely that a 'Victor' operation mounted in Canada at this particular time would have assassination as its aim.
However, since Department V also specializes in kidnapping

and sabotage, these activities cannot be dismissed when considering targets.

The most likely targets for sabotage are Canadian nuclear facilities, hydro plants, the St. Lawrence Seaway, and defence and communications installations. We suggest the standing orders for the protection of all strategic points be increased immediately to Level III. Later, should we be able to corroborate Opal's information about the man with the missing finger, the state of readiness can be raised to Level IV, involving provincial and municipal police as well as the federal police and the military authorities. A Level IV alert also would automatically activate the government crisis centre.

Potential targets for assassination or kidnapping already have been identified in the lists of Canadian and foreigners drawn up by the XX Committee. These include a number of Ambassadors accredited to Canada and various distinguished visitors who are expected in Ottawa within the next fortnight.

The most obvious candidate on the list of distinguished visitors is the President of the United States when he comes here next week. It is important however that we do not overlook the OPEC ministers who are due here to conclude the strategic supply negotiations which have been going on for some time. Although the visit by ministers from certain OPEC countries and the discussions with them have been kept a closely guarded secret, it must be assumed that the KGB have learned of it either through Opal, other sources they have in place in Canada, or their agents elsewhere.

An attempt to assassinate in Ottawa a minister from one of the OPEC countries friendly to the West, even if it was unsuccessful, would have advantages for the Soviet Union. It would serve to publicize the negotiations and disrupt completely the strategic supply and reserve agreement which has been reached only after months of secret negotiations. However, an assassination attempt on the President of the United States, especially while he is a visitor to Canada, would have even more serious consequences. Clearly the United States authorities will have to be informed without delay that we consider such an attempt a possibility, although, at present, it is difficult to believe that the Soviet government would ever agree to such an operation. The attempt could only be regarded by the U.S. government as a cause for war. No doubt the Americans will wish to consider whether, in the circumstances, the visit should be cancelled. If it is decided to go ahead with the visit presumably the Americans will suggest ways in which the already considerable security measures contemplated for the visit should be strengthened. The most urgent tasks are:

(a) To attempt by all means to confirm Opal's information about the man with the missing finger.

(b) An analysis of all records of direct entries to Canada from the Soviet Union in the past six weeks. The recently installed computer program at ports of entry should facilitate such a search. Since this will involve an expenditure of additional man-hours by the Immigration department, your personal intervention probably will be required.

(c) Since there is a possibility that more "V for Victor' agents may attempt to enter Canada in the next short while we suggest you recommend that the Immigration authorities institute red alert procedures at all border points. Such activity may heighten the risk of a leak, but we think the situation warrants it.

NINE

The man who had entered Canada as Thomas Volker and registered into the Lord Elgin Hotel as Clive Ardrey parked the nondescript rented Chevrolet sedan off the narrow dirt road, on a small culvert leading to an abandoned farm, the roof of which had long since collapsed. He folded the map which was open on the seat beside him and placed it in the glove compartment. He locked the doors and made his way up the path, now heavily overgrown with weeds. At the rear of the farmhouse, he made his way to a well about twenty feet from the building.

Unfastening the wooden lid he raised it. The rusty hinges had recently been oiled and made no sound. Inside was a length of rope tied to a metal flange set into the stonework. He pulled up a heavy oilcloth bag tied to the end of the rope, carefully unwrapped it and extracted two packets. From one of these he took out two automobile license plates with white lettering on a red background of the type issued to the diplomatic corps. The numbers were in the range assigned to the American embassy. The second packet contained a U.S. embassy identity card, bearing his photograph. He was described as an attache by the name of J.D. Malling. Also in the second packet was a large, brown manila envelope. On the upper left-hand corner was the inscription; 'Embassy of the United States of America'. On the reverse side of the envelope the flap was affixed with a large, blue circular sticker, embossed with the seal of the United States.

As he returned to his car a small, yellow school bus pulled up fifty feet away, on the same side of the narrow country road. A group of children and a young woman, evidently their teacher, emerged from it carrying empty jam jars, shovels, cardboard boxes and the assorted paraphernalia of a nature study field trip. He cursed silently, hurriedly unlocked his car and sped off towards the city. He headed straight for one of the city's new high-rise hotels and drove the Chevrolet down the ramp into its underground parking garage. On the bottom level he selected an empty space in an ill-lit corner.

Working quickly with a screwdriver and a pair of flat-nosed pliers he removed the car's blue and white license plates and replaced them with the diplomatic plates. The old ones were neatly wrapped in newspaper and placed under the driver's seat. In the few minutes which it took to perform the operation the area remained deserted. He drove off, paid the attendant at the exit, and, turning towards the east end of the city, eased into the stream of traffic.

* * * * * * * * * * * * * * * * * * * *

J.B. walked quickly along the corridor to a door, to the right of which was a brass plate on which had been incised the words, 'Director-General's Office'. He opened the door and stepped into an ante-room with comfortable chairs, a sofa with a low table in front of it, and a desk behind which sat his secretary. The attractive, dark-haired, vivacious woman in her early thirties looked up. Except for her the ante-room was empty.

"Hi, Rosemary. Any calls?"

"Brad and the Minister."

"Okay. Brad I'll see, but not right away. Say in half an hour. The Minister I will call direct from the 'cubby hole.' God knows what he wants."

J.B. opened the door leading into his office. Although furnished with expensive looking leather upholstered furniture, a couple of armchairs, a large comfortable looking sofa, and an out-sized mahogany desk the office had a sparse, almost antiseptic air. A couple of silk screen paintings of Canada geese in flight lent the room its only touch of colour. J.B. noted with approval that but for a small tray of papers and files, the desk was clear.

He picked up the In tray and crossed the room to a door leading into a large, well appointed bathroom. Once inside, he shut the door and opened the large medicine cabinet. Inside the cabinet were the usual array of bottles and tubes as well as an electric razor and a Gillette. The cabinet had a lighted, opaque panel of glass. J.B. pressed his right hand firmly against the glass panel. Part of the bathroom wall slid noiselessly open to reveal a large, well-lit room, known affectionately to J.B. and those in the know, as the 'cubby hole'. At the same time as the mechanism for opening the door was activated, a small green light on his secretary's telephone lit up. J.B. stepped into the room and the wall closed behind him. One of J.B.'s predecessors had conceived the idea of a secure retreat, but he had given the project flesh and bones. As new and miraculous communications equipment and better counter-surveillance techniques were developed these had been incorporated into the room. It probably was as sophisticated a 'safe-speech' room and secure communications centre as existed in Canada or any other country. Apart from these attributes J.B. valued it for the peace and quiet it afforded; a welcome buffer against the constant pressures of the job.

On the end wall were five clocks showing the hour in five different time zones across the world. J.B. noted that in Moscow it was 5.35 a.m.; about time for the KGB's early watch to come off duty.

He was tempted to call Zagorin and tell him that his 'V for Victor' operation had been uncovered and he might as well back off. It would be nice to get the bastard out of bed so early in the morning and give him enough to worry about to prevent him from getting any more sleep. But that would be premature. Until the target was identified, Zagorin must not know that his activities had been uncovered. Overhead was a large screen and a variety of maps which could be quickly lowered by operating the array of coloured buttons on the panel on the right hand side. To the extreme left and right were Chubb filing cabinets with dual combination locks. The entire wall to the right of the entrance was given over to a small but carefully chosen library. Apart from the obvious reference works, the library contained a remarkable collection of books devoted to various aspects of the trade. His own contributions to the shelves were not inconsiderable. He was particularly proud of leather bound translations of rare Chinese and Russian books on espionage, which had been acquired, at considerable personal expense, from a wide variety of sources.

In the centre of the room was his desk, piled high with files and documents. At right angles to the desk was a small conference table with six comfortable chairs — one more than the number of people who knew of the existence of the 'cubby hole'. On the wall opposite the bookcases were a number of paintings; all of them J.B.'s personal property. Beneath the paintings was a long table on which had been installed the gadgets: an impressive array of radio equipment, television screens, video play-back equipment and a battery of telephones in different colours.

J.B. sat at his desk and quickly scanned all the material his secretary had placed in the 'in' tray. As he finished with each piece of paper he scrawled his initials on it and placed it in the 'out' tray. Only the analysis group memorandum dealt with Opal and none required action. He crossed to the bank of telephones and dialled a number on the red one.

"Director-General here. The Minister wanted to speak to me?"

"Yes, I'll put you through."

There was a momentary pause before the Minister's voice boomed in the earpiece of J.B.'s telephone.

"J.B. Have you seen the letter from McCracken, the member from P.E.I.? He keeps hearing 'queer noises' on his office telephone and wants assurances the RCMP aren't 'bugging' him. He threatens to raise the matter in the House unless I give him an answer immediately."

J.B. tried to keep irritation out of his voice. Jesus, who needed government backbenchers like McCracken? He was always raising some crack-pot question.

He wished to God the Prime Minister had agreed to have the Minister informed about Opal. The Prime Minister had been adamant, arguing that since Grandpre and J.B.'s Minister were personal friends, a friendship which extended to Heide, he was not yet prepared to have him brought into the picture. J.B. suspected the Prime Minister had additional reasons for his refusal, which he was unwilling to reveal. It was bloody awkward.

"No, Minister, I haven't seen McCracken's letter. We'll get on to it, and have a suggested reply prepared and brought to your office by hand as soon as posible. So far as I know there is absolutely no basis for McCracken's fears. You could point out to him that authority to intercept his telephone communications would have to come from you, and assure him that you have never given such an authority nor have you ever been asked to entertain the idea."

"I know J.B. He is being unreasonable. I tried to reassure him but it didn't seem to satisfy him. The kind of letter you have in mind may do the trick. I also would like to talk to you sometime about recruitment standards. I've had a couple of letters from constituents complaining about the ham-fisted way some of your people make their enquiries for security clearances. Surely, if we had higher admission standards we would be able to avoid some of this kind of criticism?"

"I have made a note of it Minister. I will have a memorandum prepared on the matter. In principle you are right, of course, but we are hamstrung by the kind of standards laid down by the Treasury Board."

"All right J.B. I look forward to discussing the matter when we next meet. Goodbye."

J.B. sat for a moment writing a note to Rosemary giving instructions about the McCracken affair and recruitment standards. He wondered if Zagorin had such problems. Probably, although the KGB sure as hell wouldn't have members of the Supreme Soviet complaining to the Council of Ministers that their telephones were being 'bugged'.

The chimes sounded on the intercom box beside his desk.

"Yes, Rosemary?"

"Brad is here J.B."

"Good, send him through."

In a moment the concealed door slid open and Brad stepped into the room.

J.B. had decided some time ago to include Brad among those admitted to the 'cubby hole', since he had marked him down as being a potential successor, if not immediately, at least in the foreseeable future.

"Sorry if I held you up Brad but the Minister had a couple of beefs he wanted to unload on me. Wish to God he could be brought in on the Opal case. It would make life a bit easier in so many ways. Every time we need authority to carry out electronic surveillance for anything connected with the Opal case I have to go to the Prime Minister for a signature. Enough of my problems. Anything new? What's your assessment of her?"

"Frankly, I can't make up my mind. She seems to have levelled with us, but I have a gut feeling she has held back important bits of her story. It is as if there is a part of her we have been unable to touch. We are checking out the vital statistics she has given us. I will be surprised if they don't check out. On current operations, she has told us precious little. She claims her principal tasks were, talent spotting, acting as an agent of influence as opportunity arose and the collection of all kinds of documentation for transmission to the Centre. Given the precedents we know about this could well be true. The counterfeit bond bit is being checked out with the Bank, but I guess it will take time. Her story about some new electronic penetration techniques squares with our own research in the area, and what little we've been able to find out about similar work in the U.S. The KGB are unlikely to have used something like that as a throw away. Mind if I smoke?"

Brad lit his cigarette, exhaling noisily.

"Her story about the man with the missing finger is a real poser. We can't afford to discount it. If a 'V for Victor' agent is in Ottawa, it has to be for a specific operation. They wouldn't waste such a valuable asset on an unimportant target. The problem is to identify the likely target. Rather like looking for a needle in a haystack. A tall order and we haven't much time if I am reading the situation aright."

"I agree Brad. Certainly we can't afford to wait while the rest of her story unfolds. We have to act at once on the asumption that the man with the missing finger is for real. You've seen SAG's latest memorandum which I asked Rosemary to show you?"

Before Brad could reply they were interrupted by the chimes of the intercom beside J.B.'s desk.

"Yes, Rosemary?"

"I have John Lee on the line from Hong Kong. The orange phone. You will remember, J.B., security on the lines to Asia may be compromised."

J.B. smiled. She never missed a trick.

"Thanks, Rosemary, I'll try to be discreet."

He picked up the telephone and seated himself at the long table.

"Johnnie. How are you, you old heathen? I'll bet you haven't had a decent meal since you were here last summer."

J.B. motioned Brad to stay.

"Look, Johnnie, sorry to bother you, but you will recall our discussions when you were here? Yes? Good. I was wondering if you could say if any of the merchandise has been shipped to Canada, say in the last month or six weeks?

"You're sure? Not even to the States? Well, that's a relief, since we are being flooded with almost the same kind of product from Eastern Europe, and the market has turned very soft.

"No, nothing more. My kindest regards to Meilan. I hope you can both come and see us again soon. Thanks for your help. Goodbye."

"Well, that's something positive. Johnnie Lee's people have detected no sign that Chinese Intelligence agents have come this way in recent weeks. If anyone would know they would. His coverage makes ours look like child's play. We can't be absolutely sure but it looks as if there is no particular significance to the Chinese seen by Heide talking to the man with the missing finger."

J.B. got up and moved back to his desk.

"We were talking about the latest SAG memorandum. They make some sensible suggestions. The criticism of you and McCain may seem a bit unfair, but I think you will agree we can't be too careful. Opal obviously is a very intelligent agent who will take advantage of any mistakes we make. More important our position vis-à-vis the government is even trickier than it usually is. There is a lot riding on this case, in political and other terms. If something goes wrong you can bet your bottom dollar that we'll be the ones to be left twisting in the wind while everyone else is scrambling to cover their ass. If the case gets tossed into the political arena anything could happen. With a minority government the outcome could well be another Royal Commission. God preserve us from that. A nightmare of hypothetical obfuscation."

J.B.'s grimace caused Brad to laugh.

"I know the pressure you're under. Just be as careful as possible."

Brad didn't attempt to answer. He had got the message. Sometimes he wondered why in hell he had ever gone into this kind of work. Lots of risks, little money, and hours that would put most union members on strike the first week after starting.

"Okay, Brad. Sorry about the lecture. You and McCain are doing a good job. Keep it up. You are continuing at the country house? Okay, come and see me when you get back."

Brad pressed his right-hand on the lighted glass panel beside the door and stepped back into the bathroom. The sliding door closed silently behind him. J.B. turned to look at the clocks at the end of the room. It was 1645 GMT. He would call London before Washington, since he would still be likely to catch his British counterpart in his office. He switched on the intercom.

"Rosemary. I may be placing calls directly to London and Washington, but before that I want to speak to the Prime Minister. Could you place a call to his office."

Ten minutes went by before the chimes sounded on the intercom.

"They had to get him out of the House. He will be coming on the line on the grey phone."

J.B. seated himself before the long table and picked up the receiver. He waited a couple of minutes.

"Yes, J.B.? "

"Sorry to get you out of the House, Prime Minister but things seem to be moving quickly. You have seen my note about the man with the missing finger? I think we must assume he is real and I think the time has come to tell our American and British friends. The other members of the XX Committee are in agreement. If you agree I propose to fly to London and Washington as soon as it can be arranged. It seems the most satisfactory and the securest way of doing it."

There was a grunt at the other end of the line.

"Okay, but make it short. Call me when you get back. Anything else?"

"Yes. I want a Level III alert."

The PM exploded.

"How the hell do I keep that secret?"

J.B.'s voice was icy.

"You can't. You'll have to tell Cabinet that it's being done on your orders. Publicly, if necessary, the increase in activity can be passed off as preparations for the presidential visit."

The PM's voice was equally cold.

"You've got it — but it had better be necessary. Call me when you get back."

The line went dead. Obviously the Prime Minister was not in a mood to chat. He replaced the grey receiver, picked up the red one and quickly pressed three numbers.

"Hello. Is that Mary? Yes, I'm calling from Ottawa. Bet it's raining. It isn't. How is that beautiful daughter of yours? Still at Manchester? Can I speak to him. In a meeting? That's all any of us seem to do. Yes, it is important. I'll hold."

After a short delay the line came alive.

"Harry, it's J.B. Sorry to drag you from a meeting. I have something urgent to discuss with you and I would prefer to do it in person. I also intend to have the same discussion with Silas in Washington. In view of the hour I thought I should call you first. How soon may I come?

"You're expecting Silas in London tomorrow? That's a piece of luck. Perhaps the three of us could get together over there? You have no objections? Okay, I'll call Silas now. If he agrees let us say I will plan to catch the Concorde from New York tomorrow morning. I would like to return the same day but that may not be possible. That is kind of you Harry. I accept with pleasure. Will it be the Daimler with Griffiths. Good I'll look for him at Passport Control. Thanks Harry. See you tomorrow unless you hear to the contrary."

Three digits on the same phone and he was in touch with

Washington. Silas wanted an explanation on the telephone. J.B. refused to be drawn.

"Better leave it until we meet. Not the kind of thing I want to discuss even on this so-called secure line. You and Marshall Teller leaving tonight on the company jet? In a couple of hours? That's a kind thought Silas, but there's no way I could make it tonight. I still have a hell of a lot to clean up here."

"Okay see you tomorrow."

J.B. replaced the phone. Kind of Silas to suggest he would divert to Ottawa to pick him up, but the last thing he wanted was a working trip across the Atlantic, especially with Marshall Teller. Old Silas he liked, although a trip anywhere with him involved drinking far more Bourbon and branch water than he cared to handle. Teller was another matter. As head of U.S. Counter Intelligence there was little he didn't know. His curiosity was insatiable and his domineering ego insufferable. The entire trip would be given over to attempting to fend off Teller's attempts to take over Operation Opal. Besides J.B. distrusted someone who drank nothing stronger than Seven Up and constantly sought to make a virtue of it.

He called Rosemary on the intercom.

"Could you crank up the Cessna for tomorrow to get me to New York in time to connect with the Concorde flight from J.F. Kennedy. If you have any problems about getting me a seat, the Concorde people will just have to get Whitehall to okay a Priority 1 reservation. Somebody gets bumped but I haven't any choice. Harry offered to send a car to pick me up at Heathrow. I would like to come back the same day but that may not be possible. You'll have to check the schedules. If I can't get back tomorrow, could you book me on the Concorde the next day and lay on the Cessna to get me back here. I leave the hotel to you. Not that bloody swank place I was in the last time. The service was terrible and the food was lousy."

J.B. spent the remainder of the evening persuading a reluctant Deputy-Minister of Immigration to institute red alert procedures at all border points and to put extra man-hours into a search of immigration records of direct entries into Canada from the Soviet Union. Eventually it was only after J.B. picked up the telephone and started to dial the Prime Minister that the deputy caved in. It also took a lot of arguing with officials in a number of departments to get Level III measures put into force to give additional protection to strategic points and to certain Ministers and senior officials.

By the time J.B. was airborne protective detachments across the country were receiving reinforcements, and travellers at ports of entry were experiencing unexpected and annoying delays. In Ottawa the only visible signs of Level III alert were increased numbers of uniformed RCMP at the airport, on Parliament Hill and around certain government buildings. Many of the reinforcements were experienced Security Service agents, wearing unaccustomed uniforms for the occasion. There also was a measurable increase in the number of door to door visits made by RCMP officers making discreet inquiries about a narcotics smuggling suspect, who they described as 'Caucasian male, with oriental features, close-set eyes, balding, with a finger missing on his left hand'.

The XX Committee found itself in almost continuous session, using for its work the special operations room in the Privy Council Office, which had been established principally to assist the government crisis centre should it become activitated. It had become quickly apparent that the increasing tempo required a full-time secretariat, capable of operating 24 hours a day. Three watches were set up to handle the flow of information and to co-ordinate the work of the various departments and agencies.

Initially the natural tendency to bureaucratic infighting threatened to undercut the purpose of the Committee. The Prime Minister's personal intervention quickly put a stop to the internecine behaviour. Largely at J.B.'s suggestion, the Prime Minister presided over a couple of the meetings, making it quite clear that he would brook no delays, and that the future prospects of all concerned depended upon the speed and efficiency with which the committee did its work. By the time J.B. was en route to London the committee was a smooth-running, reasonably efficient instrument for giving political direction to Operation Opal and for providing essential co-ordination to the government's efforts to deal with the threat posed by the presence of a 'V for Victor' agent.

The XX Committee were agreed that among the list of foreigners the most likely targets were the OPEC ministers and the President of the United States.

Various diplomatic representatives resident in Ottawa were possible candidates. However, all of these had been in Ottawa for some time and none were known to have been threatened in the past. It seemed more likely that the intended target was somebody not yet in Canada.

The venue of the meetings of the OPEC ministers and their accomodation was hastily switched from Ottawa to an old mansion on the grounds of the Chateau Montebello, about eighty miles from town. The house provided an 'island site' which could more easily be protected.

Within the assumed time frame the most likely target seemed to be the President of the United States, although nobody was able to explain why the Soviet Union would want to make such an attempt. To assassinate or to kidnap the President, given the state of relations between the USSR and the United States, simply did not make sense. No doubt, however, when the United States Secret Service learned of the possibility they would treat it with deadly seriousness. If the

President decided to go ahead with the visit the Secret Service probably would demand a massive involvement. Already the measures planned for the President's protection were extraordinary in Canadian terms. Additional measures could only add to the frictions created by having the U.S. Secret Service trying to call all the shots.

* * * * * * * * * * * * * * * * * * * *

INTERNAL MEMORANDUM

SECURITY CLASSIFICATION
Top Secret
DISTRIBUTION
Opal Indoctrinated
Only

FROM: Special Analysis Group (Merrivale)
TO: Director-General
SUBJECT: Opal

The information you acquired during your visit to London, concerning the identity of a Victor agent with a missing left finger, is convincing corroboration of Opal's story. Your memorandum on this score is most interesting and helpful. The identification of Nikolai Bodgan Okulov as a Victor agent with a finger missing on his left hand, who the British believe was responsible for assassinating a member of the Roumanian Embassy in London, helps narrow the kind of activity we are seeking to prevent. It suggests the man with the missing finger specializes in assassination rather than sabotage or kidnapping. Okulov's name does not appear in our indices, which is not surprising since, no doubt, he carries several identities.

While apprehension of the Victor agent, and identification of his target, clearly takes precedence over all other activities, SAG believes there is a danger that the 'doubling' of Opal may suffer in the process. You may think it useful to express some concern on this score to the XX Committee and perhaps to the Prime Minister. There would appear to be no magic solution since many of the resources needed to prevent an assassination are the same as those needed to manage Opal, and they are finite. However, a word from you might help to maintain some balance in allocation of those resources when the two quite different objectives are being considered.

We now have a preliminary analysis of the voice stress tests we have been running on Opal's interrogations. Without further analysis and a greater body of material from which to make useful comparisons, we cannot be definitive about our findings. However, it would appear that she showed the greatest stress when discussing her methods of communication and her father's death, suggesting she has tried to conceal something from us. Possibly she has some alternative method of communicating which she has sought to hide from us. Although our findings are still tentative SAG suggest that further Level II surreptitious entries of her house be conducted at the earliest opportunity.

TEN

* * * * * * * * * * * * * * * * * * * *

Heide lay quietly listening to the wind whistling outside her
bedroom window. The long hours of interrogation had sapped her
energy and she felt tired in a way that she had never felt before. She
knew she had little choice but to co-operate with the police. She had
been caught and they would piece together a picture of the damage she
had done in due course anyway. By making life a little easier for them
she could preserve for Paul something of the life they had known. Her
dependence on Paul, she knew, could be unhealthy for him in time.
Yet, she could not help herself. Perhaps he would be strong enough to
pry himself loose from the suffocating element of her devotion.

Recent events in their home had not been easy for the child. At
first he had been inquisitive about the sudden appearance of Patricia
Haley, but he soon sensed that his mother was drained. Eventually,
when the answers to his questions proved less than satisfactory, he had
gone to his room to play. Before going to bed herself Heide looked in

on him. He was asleep by then, snuggled under the warm blankets. Not for the first time she was struck by the resemblance he bore to her father. She loved this child with the same passionate devotion she had felt for Anatoli Gribanov when she herself was a child. Now, alone in her room, the sight of Paul and the events of the day triggered her memory and she was flooded with recollection of the last time she had seen Anatoli Ivanovich Gribanov.

It was early in the new year of 1943. She was still hard at work in the training camp near Moscow. It was becoming routine and she was feeling the first stabs of boredom, when suddenly events started coming together and she was rescued from the monotony of camp life. On the last day of January she was told she would be given a refresher course in Swedish and could expect to hear word of her assignment within a matter of weeks. Two days later her father came to the camp. He stayed only a few days and for most of the time was closeted in the sabotage compound. Whether he was receiving instruction or giving it, Galena never asked. The hours they spent together were filled with other, more important things. She wished her own specific assignment had been decided so that she could tell him in the hope of some future chance for a surreptitious reunion.

"No my little one, it is better that I know nothing. If ever I betrayed you, even by accident, I could not live. Perhaps, someday, in a crowded room we shall see each other. Even if we cannot speak, we will know that the other is there. And," he smiled, "with good fortune we will be together in Moscow someday when our foreign battles are fought and won. Perhaps then we will be able to do good things for the Revolution from within our own land."

"I hope so. It is good to hear someone still talk of the Revolution. I sometimes wonder if there is anyone left who is still motivated by ideals. I learn a great deal about the techniques of espionage but I, and most of the technical experts, especially the younger ones, have lost sight of the real cause we are fighting for."

Anatoli Ivanovich Gribanov nodded his head sadly.

"Let me give you one more piece of technical information. Wherever you are and whatever you're doing try always to have a safehouse known only to you that you never use twice. The Director will always want to know your facilities and so will your handler; you will have to compromise your safehouses one after another to keep various rendezvous or to shelter a comrade in distress; but you must always have a refuge known to no one but yourself where you can drop from everyone's sight."

His face had grown hard while he spoke. He added, "I tell you this because I know the technicians and the bureaucrats can lose sight of the Revolution. Sometimes the true revolutionaries have to escape their masters."

They never again talked of their work. His last night at the school was a memorable one for both of them. He used his rank as colonel to have a fine dinner sent to his room for the two of them. Galena put on her mother's gold ear-rings for the first time since coming to the camp more than eighteen months before. It was as though this was their first meeting since his arrival instead of their last.

"Galena Nadya, my little rose bud, you have blossomed since last we were together. How like your mother you are. Same eyes, same colouring. And you carry yourself as she did. You too could have been a ballerina."

Galena kissed him shyly on both cheeks, standing on her toes to reach his face.

"Oh, Papa, I have missed you. I wrote often but was never sure that you would receive my letters. Are you well? You seem so tired."

"Yes I am tired, but I am well. I have been out of the country and caught some foreign bug. I am over it now. And I did get your letters. All of them — in one big package — when I arrived back in Moscow last month. It was as if I was with you even though we were still far apart." He laughed, "You will have to be more concise in your secret dispatches, or your enemies will catch you with your pen in hand."

The thought of her being captured made him serious again.

"This has not been an easy time for any of us. But the tide is turning in our favour. We will yet see this war through and turn once again to building the Russia the people need. But what about you? Your commandant, Colonel Belov, is an old comrade in arms. He tells me you have been one of his best students and that you will soon be given an important assignment for which you are well equipped. Tell me of you. How has it been with you?"

Anatoli Ivanovich Gribanov wore his thirty seven years well. He was tall and, although nearly 100 kilograms, he carried no fat. His uniform fitted him extremely well. He limped slightly, the result of a bullet wound received in an operation abroad. His short-cropped hair, prematurely white at the temples, enhanced his military bearing. The ready smile in his grey eyes suggested a warmth and compassion belied by exterior appearances. It was the look in those eyes that told Galena he did not really want to talk about their common profession. He had already satisfied himself that his daughter was as well prepared as could be for the tasks ahead. She dealt with his question quickly.

"I have studied hard, father. The training has been a challenge but I have worked at it to be prepared for what lies ahead. The only thing I regret is that I will be going far away. Far away from Russia and from you, Papa."

She controlled the emotion. She knew what she wanted to talk about, and she suspected her father did too.

"Will you tell me about Mamma. I want to know all you can remember of her before I go away."

It had been years since father and daughter had met, and even longer years since they had talked of his wife. In fact he had never spoken to Galena as a woman, of the woman who had borne her.

"Your mother was beautiful, Galena Nadya." His face softened, "I think she must have passed her beauty directly to you when she died at your birth. It was a great shock. We were so much in love."

"Oh, Papa, you must have hated me. I was the cause of her dying."

"No, Galena Nadya, you must never think that. If there had been a doctor instead of a midwife in attendance she might have been saved. The nearest doctor was forty kilometres away and the roads that April were still quite impassable. It was not your fault. And, although I blamed her at the time, it really was not the fault of the old crone who acted as a midwife. The complications which set in were quite beyond her skills and knowledge. It was fate. But it took me years before I could even discuss her death."

He paused.

"I will tell you something I have never told anyone else. During the latter period of her pregnancy your mother and I talked much about naming the child she was to have. We agreed that if it was to be a boy he should be called Paul Thorvald. Her father's name was Paul and my mother had a Norse great grandfather, called Thorvald. The name Thorvald never came into use in the family in Russia. It does not appear in any official records. If it was to be a girl we agreed the name should be Galena Nadya. Galena after my mother and Nadya after her mother."

He stopped and smiled.

"Now, you and I are the only persons in the world to know this. Who knows my little one, that secret may be useful to us one day. In this trade it is useful always to have special secrets."

"Thank you Papa for telling me. I shall keep to myself what you have told me. When you and mother met it was in Leningrad?"

"Yes. Your mother was a member of a ballet company from Moscow which had come to Leningrad for a month of performances. I saw her on stage and fell in love at first sight. I was very young, she was a year older than me. It's funny, I've grown older and cynical, but whenever I think back to those days I know that there is a romantic streak still living inside me. At first, she avoided my attempts to meet her but I persevered. It was one of those things. We were naturally made for each other. We fell madly in love. She became pregnant and soon after we were married in Moscow. Her father was dead but her mother was very much alive and was scandalized. She opposed the marriage but her own father, a writer and a poet and a marvellous old fellow, encouraged us. It wasn't much of a wedding, a few of my colleagues, two dancers from the ballet company, my aunt who lived in Moscow and your grandmother and great-grandfather."

"Did you live in Leningrad after you were married?"

"No. I had joined the State Security as a trainee by then and they moved me to Moscow. We lived with your grandmother. Larissa Kiselnikova continued her dancing in Moscow. Ah, what a joy it was to watch her perform."

"I wish I could have seen her."

He smiled again. "Just look into a mirror, Galena Nadya. Your mother lives in your every move."

"I am glad you let me take her place, Father. My life would be very lonely without you. I have no aunts and uncles or cousins."

They talked through the night. They were interrupted only once by a knock on the door. Galena opened it to find a powerfully built man in uniform who demanded to see her father. He had papers for him to see. Galena offered to take the papers but the man pushed past her into the room and spoke with her father. Galena noticed his Mongolian appearance and that he had a finger missing on his left hand. As she lay in her bed in Ottawa some thirty years later she could still recall the man vividly. He impressed her as few others have ever done in such a short encounter. She remembered how he had left as abruptly as he had come. Galena could not disguise her anger.

"Rude brute."

"Now, now, Galena. He has his job to do. Not an easy one and one that he does well. A ruthless, dedicated man."

"What does he do?"

"Some questions deserve no answer, my little one. That is something you must know in this business. Those who deal in 'mokroye dylelo' don't advertise. Leave it. We have so much to catch up on and so little time."

When he smiled she could forgive him anything. They talked until dawn.

"Goodbye, my little one. May those who watch over the likes of us guard you. I know you will serve our country well. It is time for me to go now."

Father and daughter embraced warmly. He quickly got into a waiting car which sped off, its tires throwing up small fountains of mud and icy water. Spring was still far off and there was a bitter chill to the east wind. She shivered in its blast until the car was out of sight and then walked briskly to her quarters.

Tears filled her eyes as she remembered the warmth of that embrace of so long ago. She had never seen Anatoli Ivanovich again and while she still loved the land that he had loved, and still on occasion could feel a passion for the Revolution that would right all wrongs, she hated the men and the system that had destroyed so good a man. As suddenly as the emotion welled within her she cut it off abruptly. This was no time for tears. With an iron discipline she turned her thoughts to her last days in training camp when she was told what her assignment would be.

Valentin Petrovich Krylov and Viktor Aleksandrovich Lavrov

had been waiting for her in Krylov's office. Lavrov was a squat, heavy-set prototype of the later Hollywood parody of a Russian spy. His first job with the NKVD had been as the heavy on an interrogation team. He looked the part. Galena first met him shortly before she entered the school. They got along reasonably well, which had been essential for her acceptance into the training school although she had not known it at the time. Because the assignment as an illegal, for which she was being considered, involved going under deep cover in Germany the Centre found it necessary to co-ordinate her mission with the Central Committee of the Party. It was a strict rule of Soviet espionage that the local national Communist parties and the Centre's networks be kept in watertight compartments. The demands and casualties of war, however, had deprived the Centre of safe ways of providing deep cover for long-term sleepers. To implant this type of agent the Director had to rely on the services of the Central Committee. When the Centre approached the Committee concerning the operation, the general secretary had turned the matter over to State Security and Lavrov was assigned as co-ordinator.

The significance of Lavrov's presence in Krylov's office was lost on Galena. She assumed he was but the latest in a long line of watchdogs. Ever since their encounter by the lake, all discussions between Galena and Krylov had been in the presence of a third party. Galena was both amused and relieved by the precaution. Amused that either Krylov had a loose tongue or she and the mud turtle had not been as unobserved as they had thought; relieved that she did not have to make it clear to Krylov that theirs had been a one afternoon stand. It did not occur to her that perhaps it was the major who was taking the precaution of having a third party present at their meetings.

"Ah, Galena Nadya, come in." It was Viktor Aleksandrovich who spoke and moved a chair to the table for her. He seemed to have taken over the major's office but it was Krylov who began the briefing.

"The time has come. You will travel to Sweden in the next few days where you will be accredited as an Attache on the staff of the Embassy. All the necessary papers have been prepared. Once there our colleagues will furnish you with documentation for the next leg of the journey — to Germany."

"Germany?"

"Yes, for the time being. There you will establish the identity that you will later carry with you when you go to North America. In the meantime, you will travel to Germany as the Secretary of Dr. Lindemann of the Swedish Red Cross. He has made the journey many times. I need hardly say that he has often acted for us on such occasions. He is completely reliable — in any event, once in Germany you will take on a completely new identity which he will know nothing about. For the journey your appearance will have to be slightly altered to correspond to the travel documents you will be carrying. You will go via Denmark by car. The important border check will be at Flensburg on the frontier between Sweden and Denmark. The post there is manned by members of a Schutzstaffel unit of the Gestapo. Once through Flensburg, however, any check points will be military."

Major Krylov paused. "You wish to say something?"

"Later, Comrade Krylov."

"Dr. Lindemann has authority to proceed with his secretary to Cologne where he will be meeting with the Rhineland group of the German Red Cross. Once there you will make your way by nightfall to a farm in Wesseling on the southern outskirts of Cologne. You will be expected. Viktor Aleksandrovich will show you the exact location of the farm on a large-scale map."

"Yes, Galena Nadya?"

"Will my absence on the return journey not be noticed?"

"As soon as you arrive at Dr. Lindemann's hotel in Cologne you will go straight to your room. There you will find another woman. She will immediately take your place as Dr. Lindemann's secretary. You will stay in the hotel room until after dark when you are taken to Wesseling. As soon as you arrive at the farm you will hand over your papers to the farmer for destruction. Your substitute will have documentation to match her appearance which, although different from yours, is generally similar. She is older and not so pretty."

Galena wondered whether he had experience of her replacement in the flesh or was basing his judgment on photographic evidence. As though reading her thoughts, Krylov hurried on.

"The frontier posts have no facilities for copying travel documents. We have found that even considerable differences go unnoticed. They seem quite satisfied with head counts. So much for German efficiency."

Major Krylov rose from his chair and lit a cigarette. Lavrov took over the briefing. He unfolded a map on the table and showed her the exact location of the farm at Wesseling.

"The difficult part, and the most important part, will be to establish your credentials as a German. Not only will it be dangerous at the time, but the future of your mission will depend upon there being no doubt that you are who you claim to be. You have the necessary qualifications; you speak German fluently and, just as important, the circumstances exist to make it possible. A girl about your age has been listed as 'missing' in Cologne for some time. We have established that in fact she is dead. By good fortune her parents are long-standing members of the German Communist Party. They have agreed to accept you as their daughter."

"And her friends?"

"Her family has left Cologne, they now live in Bavaria, so there are no friends to worry about. Here is a full dossier on the parents, Anton and Maria Prager, and the circumstances under which they left

Cologne. You will see that you have nothing to fear from old friends and neighbours. You may keep the dossier for the few days you remain here at the school. In that time, you should memorize its contents."

Galena said nothing.

"After you arrive in Wesseling you will have a small 'accident', a blow to the head which will trigger your recovery from a severe bout of amnesia. The farmer will notify the Cologne authorities and your new father will travel to the city from the small village of Tützing in Bavaria where the family has lived since they were bombed-out. He will identify you as his daughter and take you home to your new mother. It will challenge your acting ability."

"What will my name be?"

"Heide. Heide Prager."

"The Prager I could do without, but Heide I like. What am I to do in Bavaria?"

Lavrov replied. "Nothing, nothing at all. For the time being your only purpose is to establish your new identity. You will become a member of the Prager family, attend school and become part of life in the village. You should make friends in the community but avoid deep relationships or entanglements. At a much later date when you are activated as an 'illegal' it is unlikely that the authorities will go any further into your past then your life in Tützing. Cologne is a shambles and the chances of finding any trace of Heide Prager will be slim indeed. We, for our part, will make every effort to see that the chance is made ever slimmer. In due course, you and the Pragers will receive instructions about the more distant future, but that is several years away. In the meantime there should be no need for you to contact us. Should you have to do so, the Pragers will pass word through their contact. In an extreme emergency, and only if there is good reason not to use the Pragers, you may telephone this number in Munich."

He handed her a slip of paper with a number written on it and continued.

"Memorize the number before you leave this office. Before making the call you should go to the telephone kiosk in the underground station by the Rathaus, in Munich. You will open the telephone directory at the page whose number corresponds to the day of the month on which you desire a meeting and count down the right-hand column the number of names till you reach the one that corresponds to the time of day at which you want the meeting to take place. Underline that name with a pencil. You must allow at least twelve hours to elapse between the time you place your call and the time you desire the meeting. When you place the call you should say simply, 'The bird has been injured', and hang up. At the time appointed for the meeting you will walk past the main front doors to the main railway station in Munich with a newspaper in your left hand. You will be checked for surveillance before contact is made with you.

If contact is not made, repeat the process on the two following days before calling the number again. Now, repeat those instructions, please."

When she had completed her recitation, Krylov spoke, "It is not an easy assignment, Galena Nadya, to be a 'sleeper'. It will be a long time before your talents are put to use. By then there will be no question of your identity. We are confident, however, that you can do it. All I can say now is that your eventual assignment to the North American sector should continue to be a guide to you. Viktor Aleksandrovich will be one of those to direct you in the future. You are fortunate. He has much experience in foreign operations."

Lavrov ignored Krylov's flattery. He walked over to Galena who, sensing the interview was over, rose from her chair. He grasped her in a subdued bearhug and kissed her on both cheeks.

"We will make a good team, Comrade."

It was the first time he had called her 'Comrade'. She knew he had accepted her as a colleague, not only in the Party but also in the work of the Service.

* * * * * * * * * * * * * * * * * * *

The man who had entered Canada as Thomas Volker and the sailor who had slipped ashore in Montreal, met briefly at the newstand in the lobby of the Chateau Laurier Hotel in Ottawa. Standing beside one another before the crowded magazine shelves, they exchanged messages, according to a pre-arranged plan, with skill and speed. The sailor left first. He paid for his purchase and made his way through the heavy, brass revolving doors, turning right on Wellington Street. The other followed a minute later, making his way to the pedestrian crossing in front of the hotel. He hunched inside his raincoat, pulling his fedora down to give some protection from the heavy rain, which, driven by a gusting wind, made it impossible to see more than a few feet in any direction. He was alone at the crossing. As the light changed to 'walk' he stepped off the curb in front of an airport bus parked before the hotel. He was hit with such force by the low-slung sports car, that his body was lifted ten feet in the air before coming to rest in the middle of the road. The driver of the car which hit him applied the brakes so hard that his car slewed on the wet pavement and smashed broadside into a metal lamp-standard, snapping it off at the base.

The sailor hearing the screech of brakes and the impact, quickly retraced his steps, joining the quickly growing crowd of onlookers. Reaching into his jacket pocket, he pressed to the front of the crowd, to establish the identity of the victim and that he was still alive and conscious. He slipped his hand into the injured man's. Their eyes met. The sailor nodded and Thomas Volker removed his hand from the sailor's grasp and brushed it across his mouth. As a police cruiser materialized as if from nowhere, the sailor slipped away, and walked to the CNCP cable office on Metcalfe Street, where he sent a short cable to Euromitlex Corporation in Copenhagen. He was assured that, at the full rate, the cable would reach its destination within the hour. The Centre in Moscow would have it within three hours. The message read:

RS/D COPENHAGEN 24z 1452

PRESIDENT
EUROMITLEX CORP.

LIQUIDATION SOME INTERESTS PROVED NECESSARY. HAVE
ENCOUNTERED UNEXPECTED SET BACK. CAPITAL RESOURCES
REDUCED BY FIFTY PERCENT. ALTERNATIVES ARE ONE WITHDRAW
FROM MARKET TWO PROCEED WITH EXISTING RESOURCES THREE
SEND CAPITAL INJECTION. PLEASE INSTRUCT.

HARRY FOSTER
EMBASSY APARTMENT HOTEL
OTTAWA 70

ELEVEN

INTERNAL MEMORANDUM

SECURITY
CLASSIFICATION:
Most Secret
DISTRIBUTION:
Dept 'V' — Special
URGENT

TO: Director I.V. Zagorin
FROM: Krivolapov (Dept V)
SUBJECT: Operation Orestes

Operation support agent (V127) reports he has taken
'executive action' against Agent V90 for unknown reasons.
Given the information received from London earlier today, it
is imperative that Operation Orestes be successfully
completed. Agent V127 does not have the experience to be
entrusted with sole responsibility for the mission. Nor is
there time to brief a replacement.
As 'control' for Operation Orestes I therefore request
authority to assume assignment personally and proceed to
Canada immediately. My deputy, Boris Sorokin, can assume
control and responsibility for Department 'V' during my
absence.

* * * * * * * * * * * * * * * * * * *

  Heide's continued absence required some plausible explanation
to her circle of friends and, more particularly to Marc Grandpre. With
Brad's agreement she put it about that she had been experiencing
certain gynaecological problems requiring rest and eventual surgery.
The subterfuge was supported by the Privy Council Office granting her
sick leave upon the recommendation of a friendly doctor. Apart from
being an effective way of satisfying the curiosity of casual acquaintances, it also served to cool Marc Grandpre's ardour.
  Her interrogation continued at the country house with Brad
attempting to concentrate on the period when she had first been
activated and the development of her relationship with Armand
Latour. Heide showed little enthusiasm for recounting this period in
her life. She could remember it well enough but she did not want it on
the record. Brad and McCain had to push to get what they wanted.

The breakdown of her marriage to Latour still bothered her. She delayed dealing with it by going into considerable detail about her entry into the Civil Service. She recounted the interview that led to her job in External Affairs, some years after she had first come to Ottawa to work in the Department of Labour.

* *

A young woman with a professionally pleasant manner opened a door at the end of the nondescript, stuffy room in which Heide had been waiting.

"The Board is ready to see you now Mrs. Hlinka."

Heide followed her into an equally nondescript room. The only furniture was a rectanglar table surrounded by an assortment of chairs. A green cloth had been spread over the table. On top of it was a water jug and six glasses, two ashtrays and an array of file folders, documents, scratch-pads and pencils. She was familiar with the yellow, government issue pencils. On each of them was embossed the slogan, 'Misuse is abuse'. The injunction was a source of considerable hilarity among younger civil servants who could not resist its double entendre. It was, however, still treated with deadly seriousness by the older generation of Ottawa bureaucrats who remembered tales of a former prime minister, Mackenzie King, going through his staff's garbage bins to retrieve pencil stubs with which he scrawled his illegible instructions on the margins of official memoranda.

It was ten years since she had come to Canada, thirteen years since she had taken the identity of Heide Prager and fifteen years since she had first entered the training school near Moscow. It had been a long time. The success or failure of her mission depended on the judgement of the six men and one woman who sat around the green baize covered table. The tall, fair-haired man at the head of the table spoke first.

"My name is Sommers, Arnold Sommers. I am acting as chairman of this board. On my left is Mr. Harris of the Civil Service Commission. Beside him is Mr. Barrett and on his left is Mr. Denault. On my right is Mr. Pritchard and beside him is Mr. de Poitiers. Miss Ainsley is the secretary of the board. I apologize for the room. The air conditioning doesn't work very well, and, as you can see, it is an inside room. It is not helped by smoking. I should add, however, that if you wish to smoke please do so."

Heide was surprised at the relative youthfulness of the Board. Sommers was the oldest but she guessed even he was only in his early forties. Most of them appeared to be in their thirties and the girl could not have been more than twenty-five. Sommers looked up from the papers before him.

"I see you were born in Berlin in 1929, Mrs Hlinka. Your first name is Heide and your maiden name was Prager. Have you a middle name? You didn't provide one on your application form."

Heide found herself annoyed with Viktor Aleksandrovich. He had mentioned oral examinations but she had imagined they would be similar to those she had experienced at the University of Munich; on questions of substance.

"Yes. I was christened with a second name: Hoettle, after a grandparent. It is not a name I like and I do not use it." Heide smiled as she looked around her.

"Quite. None of us is consulted in such matters. I see that, very unfortunately, your husband died shortly after you came to Canada. You must have found that a great shock and difficult to make ends meet since you were still at university. Incidentally, I approve of your choice. It happens also to be my alma mater."

Heide inclined her head slightly but said nothing. Sommers' style was disarming but, for all the syrup, he was no fool. She would have to watch herself.

"Let me see. Where was I? Oh, yes. I was remarking upon the untimely death of your husband. I see you continued with your studies. That must have taken determination and money."

"Yes. It took both. I would probably have ended up with some heavy debts except that Jan's mother also died around that time. She left some money to which I fell heir and I was able to finish my studies debt free. I also worked in the summers and I had a part time job in the law school library during the winters. I even made a little extra money through my hobby; photography."

Heide noticed that Pritchard looked attentive at the mention of photography.

"I think the Board would like to hear in your own words a brief resumé of what you have done, say, starting with your studies at the University of Munich."

Heide was thankful that they had started with Munich. She did not have to narrate a fictitious cover story, but simply tell of her experiences. Only the story of her first meeting with Jan was invented. She made her account concise leaving out no important detail of the information the board already had before them in writing.

"Thank you Mrs. Hlinka. You've certainly had some interesting experiences since coming to Canada. Perhaps you could tell us why you applied to enter the foreign service?"

"For several reasons, Mr. Chairman. I believe Canada has an important part to play in the field of international relations and I would like to be a participant rather than just a spectator. I have had an opportunity to take part in ILO meetings for the Department of Labour and I found that I like to travel and to be able to use the languages I have acquired. Finally, since my husband died I have learned to look after myself. I feel I want a career which will satisfy me and enable me to earn a good living. The foreign service seems to offer all of these."

"Eloquently put Mrs. Hlinka. The foreign service does indeed offer challenging careers for men and women. I only wish that more women with your qualifications would apply."

Sommers smoothed his blonde hair and straightened his old school tie. What a bloody hypocrite, thought Heide. He probably thinks women are baby factories and loathes sharing his profession with them. She smiled and waited. Sommers cleared his throat.

"I think some of the other members of the board may have questions. John? Yes, you lead off."

He turned towards Barrett.

"Mrs Hlinka. Given your age obviously you were too young to be involved in the Nazi movement. I assume, however, you were a Hitlermädschen. What were your feelings about the Nazis?"

Heide could feel a tenseness in the board members. Barrett must be the intelligence and security member. She would have to be careful of him.

"Yes. I was a member of the Hitlermädschen until we were bombed out of Cologne. As you know, Mr. Barrett, all school children of a certain age were required to join. As to what I thought of the Nazis; I did not like them. I was not very interested in things political at that age. After we were evacuated to Bavària I found the pressures to participate in such activities lessened. Village life is less easily regimented and the war obviously was drawing to an end. I was not particularly affected by the Nazis in Tützing.

"What about your parents? Was your father not a member of the Nazi party?"

"No. He worked in a laboratory as a chemist. He was not the type to be welcomed by the Nazis even if he had wanted to be one of them, which he did not. After we were bombed out he was badly crippled in his left leg. He couldn't march to any tune let alone one played by some Nazi fiddler."

She resisted the urge to light a cigarette. She hoped she hadn't overplayed it. Barrett seemed satisfied. He indicated to the chairman that he had no further questions.

Heide was quite unprepared for the question put to her by Denault.

"Madame Hlinka. Do you believe in God?"

The Jesuitical bastard. For a moment she said nothing, controlling her temper. She caught a quick exchange of looks between Harris, the Civil Service representative, and Sommers. Sommers cleared his throat.

"An interesting intellectual question Mrs. Hlinka. But it is not one that you need answer, unless you particularly wish to do so. I am sure M. Denault will agree with my ruling."

"Thank you Mr. Chairman. I will refrain from attempting a serious reply. I was about to suggest that even among Roman Catholics there are different perceptions of the word 'God'. I was going to ask M. Denault to give us his perception and then I might be able to say if I believe in it. "

She obviously had made an enemy. The other members of the board seemed to enjoy Denault's discomfiture.

In the end she was questioned by all members of the board except the secretary, who seemed too busy taking notes. The interview had taken far longer than she expected; an hour and forty minutes. The last question was put by de Poitiers.

"Mrs Hlinka, before you go. I notice you have indicated on your application form that you speak, read and write German, English and French. From the way in which answered some of my earlier questions in French I acknowledge your fluency in that language. The same is true of English and I assume that your mother tongue is beyond question. You do not mention other languages. Have you a working knowledge of other languages?"

She had to lie to conceal her knowledge of Swedishand her real mother tongue.

"No. I have no real knowledge of other languages although I have a desire to learn some Slav tongue. One of my classmates in my undergraduate years at the University of Munich spoke Russian and I tried to learn it from him I was only mildly successful. His German was too good and I found it a difficult language. Perhaps if I am successful in passing these examinations I might get the chance to learn it. "

"An interesting thought Mrs. Hlinka. Thank you for answering our questions so fully and so patiently. It will be some time before the results are published. There have been an unusually large number of candidates this year who have to be interviewed right across the country. It is a time-consuming business. Goodbye. "

The post mortem following Heide's departure took a good deal longer than normally was the case.

"She was the last today, am I right Miss Ainsley? Good. We can afford to spend some time discussing her. She certainly is a likely candidate. Most attractive, with a strong personality and obvious intelligence. I rate her highly. What about other members of the board? What do you think, John?"

"There can be no doubt she's among the best we've seen so far. I cannot fault her on the replies she gave. Certainly there is nothing in the record to contradict her profession of dislike for the Nazis. Perhaps her father was a bit more active than she admitted but that would be natural — a protective daughter. I thought she handled Michel's dirty ball with skill and dignity. I too would give her a high rating. "

Barrett grinned at Denault beside him. Denault loosened his tie and smiled at the others.

"Oh, all right. Perhaps my question was a bit unorthodox. We are after all dealing with a former enemy alien. I thought it might help to reveal what she does believe in. I don't disagree with your ruling, Arnold, and I'm sure that Bert Harris will find some regulation which says that such a question can't be asked at Civil Service interviews. It's just that I distrust very beautiful women — especially clever ones. I have to agree though that she is one of the best we've seen. There was just something a bit too — a bit too slick about her for my liking. Certainly she has style and intelligence. Her French is excellent — better than mine. She obviously has an ear for languages. I agree she is a good prospect. I just hope she doesn't end up working for me. Or worse, that I don't end up working for her!"

Denault was the only one who expressed any doubts. He did not push them any farther and the discussion ended with general agreement that she ranked among the top six candidates they had seen. Their view was expressed in numerical terms and duly recorded.

Heide heard nothing for several weeks. Being part of it, she knew how slowly the bureaucracy worked. A chance meeting with de Poitiers at a cocktail party encouraged her. He became sufficiently drunk as the evening wore on to seek to impress her with his charms and the fact that his wife and the children were away, staying with his in-laws. Happily his efforts to have her join him for dinner came to naught when he was led away in an alcoholic stupor by some kind friend. She was thankful. The smell of stale garlic, Canadian whiskey and decaying teeth she could not have supported. She had found out from him, however, that although the eligible list had not been finally approved her name would be on it.

When the results did come out she ranked fourth and was offered an immediate appointment. She accepted, and after complicated negotiations between the Department of Labour and the Department of External Affairs she was transferred and reclassified as a Foreign Service Officer, Grade I (Probationary). It was explained that confirmation of her appointment depended, among other things, on a satisfactory security clearance, which, because she had lived in Germany, would take longer than usual to complete.

As a trainee in External Affairs, she worked in a series of divisions in sequence. The fourth and last division to which she was assigned was headed by Armand de Salliers Latour. She had heard that he had an eye for the women and she had formed an impression of him which turned out to be quite wrong. She expected a good-looking, flamboyant 'debrouilleur', who spoke before thinking. He was good-looking. He stood over six foot one, and, although a big man, carried his weight well. He reminded her of Anatoli Ivanovich, particularly in the way he smiled. Quite unlike her preconception of him, he spoke little and only after reflection. One felt that what he did say was worth while. He was completely at home in French and English. Something about the glow of his skin, which, even in the midst of winter seemed tanned, suggested Indian blood, as did his coal-black eyes. There was about him a sense of tremendous, suppressed energy.

Heide would have judged him younger than the forty years ascribed to him in the 'stud book', containing the biographies of all foreign service officers. He was seven years Galena's senior and nine years older than Heide. At first she saw little of him. He assigned her to work in a section dealing with political affairs in south-east Europe, and more particularly Greece, Yugoslavia and Turkey. Since her security clearance was still pending she was excluded from much of the work of the division. She had been given a temporary clearance that allowed her to handle 'Restricted' and 'Confidential' documents. But they tended to be routine and everything from 'Secret' up was denied to her. She often saw the distinctive red folders on other desks, but resisted the temptation to pry. To be caught doing so would be to jeopardize her position. In time, if all went well, she would have legitimate access to all such documents.

Almost two months after Heide went to work for Armand Latour, Dave Holloway picked up the grey coloured inter-office telephone and dialled the number for the Chief of Personnel.

"Oh, Mary. It's Dave Holloway. Is he there? Good. May I speak to him please?"

"James — David here. We've received the last of the reports from the RCMP on the current batch of FSO trainees. You remember there were three still outstanding because of the overseas inquiries that had to be completed? They're in now. Not all favourable, I'm afraid. What? No, the girl and Cullen are O.K. The problem is with McAllister. Evidently he concealed some information in filling in his application form. One might forgive him that, except it involved a conviction in the United States for smuggling narcotics."

"Oh, shit, Dave. Why do people try to get away with that kind of thing? What was the conviction? Serious enough to refuse to confirm him? He's done extremely well during probation. Indeed, he appears to be brilliant."

"Well, the sentence was a light one since it was a first offence and he was only an accessory. However, it was for running hard stuff, heroin, for the purpose of trafficking. The really difficult part is that the FBI have reasonable grounds for believing that he was recruited by Castro's intelligence organization to act as a courier for them. They can't prove it, but given the reliability of their source they're pretty sure McAllister was trapped, probably for smuggling into Cuba, and agreed to work for them to keep himself out of prison. Given what we know of Cuban jails I can't say I blame him."

"Where does that leave us? Can we face him with this?"

"No. I'm sure the Americans won't allow us to use their information about his having being recruited by the Cubans. If you and the Under-Secretary decide not to accept him you'll have to do it on the grounds of his falsification of the Personal History Form. He lied and he knows it. He may be brilliant but he was pretty dumb to think we wouldn't find out. My guess is that if he's told that his probationary period will not be extended and that he cannot be made permanent, he will simply accept it. If he demands a reason you can confront him with the drug smuggling conviction and his failure to mention it to us."

"Yeah, I suppose so. But what a waste of time and potential talent. That means we have to start with the next one on the eligible list, Lucy White. I hope to God we have a clearance on her. We should, since she seems to have gone nowhere and done nothing."

"Yup. We had a clearance on her a couple of months ago."

"I always seems to be the purveyor of bad news. Jesus, I'll never know why I allowed myself to be conned into doing this damn personnel job. Lot of square pegs in round holes. So long."

In the early spring, when word of Heide's security clearance filtered down to her division Armand Latour was away on a trip to Europe. His deputy did nothing to inform her of the clearance or to upgrade her work assignment. He may not even have opened the envelope that contained the information since it was addressed to Latour personally.

In the hallways of the East Block, Heide heard that Cullen's clearance had come through. She also heard that McAllister's probation had been terminated. She had worked in Historical Division with McAllister during her first weeks in the department and knew him as a bright and capable young man. They had joked together about the foibles and eccentricities of the elderly spinster who supervised their initiation into the departmental archives, chuckling over the measures she took to ensure that no forty-year old document from the First World War, marked 'secret', should be seen by their unauthorized eyes. Heide guessed that McAllister had failed to clear the security screening process and she knew that she was the only one of last summer's recruits that still had not been told one way or the other. She feared the worst and tried to track down McAllister to find out how they had handled him. Perhaps she could find a weakness in their approach that would enable her to slip through the net. But McAllister had already left Ottawa for parts unknown. There was nothing she could do but wait.

It was beginning to seem to Galena Nadya Gribanov alias Heide Hoettle Hlinka (nee Prager), that her entire life would be spent as a spy-in-waiting. She had been eleven years in Canada and all she had been able to feed back to the Centre through Lavrov were a few bits and pieces of gossip picked up through Marie-Claire Houle who had also come to Ottawa and was on the personal staff of a Cabinet Minister. She met the minister at a couple of Marie-Claire's parties and learned that when he drank too much his tongue loosened and he talked about his more prominent cabinet colleagues. To date all she had heard was boastful, small talk designed for self-aggrandizement but, as she told Lavrov, a trained mistress could no doubt get a lot more out of him. That and a few similar snippets, was all she had to show for her time in the capital.

Suddenly the picture changed dramatically. The day after Armand Latour returned from Europe he called her into his office and told her she had been cleared to Top Secret. He assigned her new duties.

The new work was more interesting from the standpoint of her two quite different careers. Among other things it involved her in the preparation of memoranda for cabinet on questions having to do with Western Europe.

During her first period of access to sensitive material she chose three areas upon which to concentrate. Since coming to Ottawa, and more so since moving to External Affairs, she had been surprised at the extent of the rivalries she had encountered. They existed not only between Canada and its allies, but between different government departments. Now she discovered how deeply these rivalries could run even within a department. Different divisions within External Affairs often held opposing views, which divisional officers defended fiercely in an effort to influence the shape of decisions. There were also strong rivalries between individual officers, not only among the junior and middle ranks but at the very top. Often these semed to have more to do with personalities than substance. There was in addition an unspoken, but no less sharp, rivalry between senior bureaucrats and Ministers and their staffs.

She selected examples of how the rivalries affected the development of policies, and committed them to memory to relay to Viktor Aleksandrovich. No doubt a knowledge of such differences and her assessment of the principal actors would be helpful to the Centre in establishing targets.

At first most of the material she came across was not worth attempting to copy. However, on the Top Secret docket of one of the working files she found gold in a series of telegrams about de Gaulle and his potential for disrupting NATO. She decided to photograph and reduce it to microdots for Lavrov. She wished she had been given one of the disguised miniature cameras Krylov had shown her. Instead she would have to use her regular equipment, which would be dangerous.

The opportunity she was looking for soon presented itself. It was just after 7.30 on a Friday evening when she and Armand Latour were still working in the office. The Geneva Four Power meeting of the foreign ministers of France, Britain, the United States and Russia was trying to find a solution to the crisis raging over Berlin. The Cabinet had decided to issue new instructions to Canadian representatives in Europe who had all been given watching briefs. Latour was drafting the telegrams and was using Heide to do a lot of the legwork and the research. They were nearly finished, when Latour's telephone rang. Heide was revising a page of the telegram at the secretary's desk outside his office and overheard the conversation.

"Latour speaking . . . .Yes sir . . . .Well, we're almost finished now . . . .No. We haven't talked to them. Now? Very well, but it will delay things. Noon, tomorrow? Will do. Goodnight sir."

Latour replaced the telephone and came to the door of his office.

"Are you free to work overtime tomorrow?" he asked the secretary.

"Love to," she said sarcastically.

"Good. How about you Heide?"

"Well," she thought fast, "I was planning to take my camera and get some shots of the tulip beds before they fade. But I guess I can bring it with me and do that after we finish — if you will let me out before the sun sets."

Latour smiled.

"If you're in by nine, you'll be out by noon, I promise. I have to rush off now and talk to some of the people at National Defence. Could you lock up for me?" He waved towards the files on his desk.

"Stick the files in your cabinet, Heide."

With that he shut the heavy steel door of the security shell which enclosed his filing cabinet and twirled the combination lock, grabbed his coat and left. Heide and Jeanne cleared off the desk and carried the files into Heide's office. They placed them in the top drawer of her cabinet next to the file on de Gaulle. They did the same with the files that lay on Heide's desk and repeated the locking procedure that Armand had gone through a few minutes before.

"Let's go," said Heide breezily and the two women walked together into the spring twilight.

Next morning, Heide signed into the building at 8.32. She had been up and ready to go at 7, but restrained herself knowing that when Armand arrived he would sign the same sheet beneath her signature. If she were there too early, his suspicions might be aroused. As it was she wrote the '3' so sloppily that it could easily be read as a '5'. It was not crucial that Armand not know that she was there half an hour early. But if she could readily conceal it, so much the better. She went immediately to her own office, entering through the secretary's room which acted as a reception area and let the outside door lock behind her. The sound of a key would give her a moment's warning if Armand or Jeanne arrived too soon. It was 8:39 am. She went quickly to her cabinet, opened it and removed the files from the previous night, together with the de Gaulle file. She took the camera from her purse. She had pre-set its focus and exposure time. With the de Gaulle file spread on the table by the window where the light was good, she quickly snapped the ten pages of the three documents she wanted. It was 8:44 am. She selected the Top Secret docket of the Berlin file which she had removed from Armand's desk the night before. She knew it contained the instructions to Ambassadors which she had seen, and a series of subsequent reports, which she had not seen. The most recent documents were on top. She took the folder to the window and quickly snapped everything down to and including the copy of the instructions.

It was 8.47 am. She went through to the secretary's office, checked that there was water in the electric kettle and plugged it into a socket. She returned to her own office, separated her Berlin files from Armand's and took the latter, neatly stacked, to his desk.

It was 8.51 am. She removed the roll of film from the camera and put it in the make-up pouch of her purse. She put a fresh roll of film in the camera and hung it and her purse from the same hook on the brown wooden coat-tree in the outer office next to her light spring coat.

It was 8.54 am. She unlocked the outer door, unplugged the kettle and mixed a half cup of instant coffee. It was 8.56 am. She perched herself on the table which held the pigeon holes for the distribution of mail within the division. She blew into the cup to cool the coffee.

It was 8.57 am. Armand entered.

"Ah, good, the coffee's ready."

He mixed himself a cup and did not notice that the water was too hot for Heide to have consumed half a cup without scalding her mouth.

"How did things go at DND last night?"

"Badly," he replied. "You know those National Defence types. They wanted our ambassadors to add information on Soviet build-ups to their reports. How the hell they expect our people to get that type of information when they're working their asses off trying to keep abreast of closed-door political talks is beyond me. I told them to use the military attaches and the commanders of our NATO forces to get the technical dope and then pass it to us for analysis. I don't think I made any friends. Anyway we have to amend the instructions to make it look as though we're complying with the request. If you want to finish the section on Commonwealth co-operation I'll do the new part. Put something in about military attaches taking special responsibility for consultation with their counterparts."

Jeanne came in as Armand finished speaking. She apologised for being late and they all set to work. By 11.15 they were finished. Armand went off with the text of the telegram to clear it with his superiors. Jeanne said she was going back to bed to catch up on the sleep she had missed the night before. Heide slung her camera over her shoulder, and walked jauntily down to the canal and along its banks to the tulip beds at Dow's lake. She spent the late afternoon in her darkroom developing the two, somewhat different rolls of film. From the shots of flowers she chose the most aesthetically pleasing and made a print of it to add to the collection on her office wall, suitably drawing Jeanne's or Armand's attention to it.

The other photographs she reduced to microdots and incorporated into a letter to Maria. The letter itself was purely personal, but it began with a phrase about the weather which was a signal to Maria to turn it over to Lavrov. At dusk she walked along Rideau street and mailed the letter at a post box. It was her first theft of documents and the first time she had used microdots for communication with the Centre. She was on edge for the next fortnight until Maria's reply arrived. In the first sentence Maria wrote that Heide's letter had been received on the nineteenth. The second sentence complained that they had been worried because it had been almost ten weeks since they had last heard from her. Heide substracted the second number from the first and knew that all nine microdots had been received by Lavrov. She rested easy.

By the nature of their work, Heide and Armand saw a great deal of each other. The secretary's office was a common passageway for entrance to each of their offices and was also the source of coffee. The daily routine involved more or less constant consultation between the head of the division and his officers. The game of diplomacy is a game of words. Documents are put together with great care and are taken apart with equal care. Even when they say nothing, how they say nothing can be of great significance. When she went into his office with a draft memorandum she had prepared he would often tell her to pull a chair over and they would sit together huddled around one corner of the desk discussing every word, clause, sentence and paragraph. Each time they did so she became more conscious of the animal attraction of the man. She was sure the growing closeness was shared by him, although she guessed he also felt that office romances were too complex to be risked.

She was, therefore, more than a little surprised when, with the July 1st holiday in prospect, he suggested that they might spend it together. They were walking up to Parliament Hill together after a luncheon at which they had sat across from each other. They had each concentrated their conversation on the people at either side of them. Whenever their eyes had met, however, they had held for a moment before passing on. As they approached the East Block, Armand said,

"What are you doing for the weekend, Heide?"

"Nothing planned. My car is in the garage. Some part they had to order. I thought I would take in the festivities on the Hill. Why?"

"I thought you might want to see the most beautiful city in North America — my city, Quebec. I'm leaving some time Friday morning and motoring to be there for dinner. I have a cottage at Lac Beauport. Perhaps you would like to meet my parents. They have a house in the Saint Foy district."

He stopped talking and smiled in the manner that reminded her of

Anatoli Ivanovich. She felt her stomach muscles tighten. Why not? There was nothing in the timing that was against it.

"Armand, what a nice surprise. Yes. I should love to see your beautiful city and to meet your parents. I'm afraid I can't reciprocate unless we take a weekend in Berlin."

Armand didn't waste any time after they left Ottawa. The highway to Montreal was crowded with week-end traffic, but once they hit the Montreal-Quebec highway the BMW ate up the miles despite the twists and turns of the road. They did not encounter a single police patrol car the whole way. Dusk was settling over the city when they hit the outskirts. It was her second time in Quebec City. The first had been when she arrived in Canada with Jan Hlinka more than a decade before. They had seen nothing of the city on that occasion. As Displaced Persons they were taken straight from the ship to a waiting train, shunted onto a siding and then transported to Montreal.

The street lights were coming on as they threaded their way through the traffic to the Grand Allee. Although she had seen photographs of Quebec, she was unprepared for the European flavour of the city and the impression of compactness it created; the narrow, winding streets, the low gabled houses, the wrought iron fences and turreted fantasy which was the Chateau Frontenac.

"Oh, Armand, you were right. It is a beautiful city."

She had to check herself from exclaiming that Upper Town looked like a miniature Kremlin.

He swung the car under the arch of the Chateau Frontenac and greeted the red-coated doorman.

"Bonsoir, Victor. We are thirsty. Can I leave it with you for a while?" He slipped a dollar bill into the pocket of the red coat.

"Mais oui, Monsieur Latour. Il y a place dans le cour, ici."

After Armand had ordered their drinks he telephoned to reserve a table at one of his favourite restaurants.

"You will see. It doesn't look like much on the outside but the cooking is superb. Since it only has fourteen tables one must reserve. The owner is an old friend. He will keep a table for us."

Armand almost seemed to acquire a different personality in Quebec. The quiet deliberation which marked his official style in Ottawa, slipped from him. He was carefree, almost boisterous; a child let out from school. He was proud of being québecois and occasionally let slip some nationalist sentiments that surprised Heide. Although vaguely familiar with the radical separatist philosophy of many Quebecers, those French-Canadians who felt stronger spiritual ties with France than Canada and wished to establish an independent Quebec, Heide had never before experienced first-hand the fierceness with which these men and women believed in their cause. The only sour note, in fact, was when they were interrupted by a raven-haired girl with sharp features. Armand introduced her as Charlotte

Boisvert, an old 'friend'. Charlotte's response was a muttered comment about Armand's bringing 'Les Anglais' to Quebec. He quickly silenced her by a reference to Heide's German heritage. When Charlotte left, they quickly finished their drinks and walked out of the hotel onto the boardwalk, high above the old town.

The night was warm and clear. The stars seemed almost to touch the turrets of the hotel. Below, the lights of Lower Town outlined its narrow length along the river bank. The noises of loading and unloading ships in the harbour rose in the still air. They could even hear the throb of the engines of the ferry pulling away from Levis on the opposite shore, festooned with lights reflected on the blackness of the St. Lawrence. Directly below, the ancient elevator connecting Lower and Upper town moved silently on its greased tracks. They stood for some time without talking. The tension of a few moments before had vanished.

"I don't know about you but I am famished. If you don't mind the walk, its only about five minutes from here. We can leave the car with Victor. We would never find a parking place near the restaurant at this hour."

The food was indeed superb. She did not stint herself; quenelles de brochet Lyonnaise, quail under embers and a soufllé au chocolat, ending with a sharp goat's cheese. The effect, however, was light and satisfying. The wines which Armand chose showed his knowledge of what the cellars held and his discrimination.

They must have been physically transported otherwise she would not be lying in the sun-filled bedroom of this small chalet overlooking lac Beauport, with delicious smells of brewing coffee and grilled bacon, wafting up from below. She had no clear recollection of anything but wave upon wave of deep satisfaction. Armand did indeed possess unseen pools of energy, which, even at the height of her pleasure, she sensed had not been entirely tapped. He was the first man to completely satisfy her physical needs while at the same time reaching the hidden well-springs of her inner self.

Armand appeared in the doorway of the bedroom stark naked but for the tray he was carrying, on which was heaped toast, bacon, jam a large pot of coffee and two glasses of freshly squeezed orange juice. The sunlight played on the red-brown skin and the jet black hair of his head and body. He was an impressive man.

"Good morning, my little one. Refreshment after an active evening. What a beautiful day. Where better to enjoy it than here, eh?" He set the tray on the bed and sat beside her. They ate hungrily.

"Armand that was a beautiful dinner. Your choice of wines was so good that I have no recollection of getting here."

"I hope you remember something of the rest of the evening?"

"Oh yes, my love, I remember it well." At the memory of their lovemaking, she sensuously stretched her body beneath the sheet. Her leg pushed against the tray.

"Move it Armand before something gets spilled."

He did and with the bed cleared they returned to where sleep had intervened the night before.

Lunch with Armand's parents was a subdued affair. Armand's mother responded to their effervescent mood with reserve. His father on the other hand went out of his way to make her feel welcome. Madame Latour, although shorter than Heide, had a commanding presence, created in part by her steady grey eyes and strong, almost masculine face. In appearance Armand was very like his father, although taller. They shared the same smile, black eyes and red-brown skin. They also had the same sense of humour. Conversation was entirely in French.

"You must come and see us again, my dear. We shall always be glad to see you, eh Pauline?"

Madame Latour smiled but did not reply. Instead she said,

"Armand, drive with care. You know I am frightened of that fast car you bought in Ontario. Oh, I wish that you had found something to do in Quebec city. Then we might see you more often and not just on some weekend expedition." Madame Latour managed to give the last word a special meaning. The tone of disapproval was not lost on Heide, but she did not care.

Two months later she emerged from the doctor's office, her suspicions confirmed. She was pregnant. Armand was on a trip to the United States and it was the end of the week before they met for dinner in his apartment. It was only after they were in bed that she was able to tell him. She added that she was willing to have an abortion. His reaction was immediate.

"Get rid of it? What blasphemy. I won't hear of it. It is ours — yours and mine. This merely brings me to ask what I have not had the courage to ask before. Will you marry me?"

Heide remembered little of the rest of the night, which was love, passion, tears, joy, fear and a tremendous feeling of security; the kind of security she had only before experienced as a child in her father's arms.

They were married in a small Catholic church on the Ile d'Orleans. Armand's parents had not been told that she was already pregnant, although Heide had a feeling that her mother-in-law suspected. Madame Latour was not openly hostile, but she made it plain that for her, Heide was a foreigner.

"Don't worry. Mothers are like that. You will just have to accept it. I wager her attitude will change after her first grandchild appears, and especially if it's a boy. You'll see. In the meantime it is better to let her pretend that she doesn't know that you are pregnant. When the time comes she won't want to do the arithmetic.'

Their marriage caused fluttering in the dovecotes of the Personnel Division of the Department of External Affairs. While the marriage between Foreign Service Officers was not unique, it was unusual. There had been a good deal of havering about whether she should be asked to resign. Eventually it had been agreed that she could remain a Foreign Service Officer, largely on the grounds that her work had been outstanding. Indeed, she had been slated for promotion before they announced their marriage plans. To her satisfaction, when it was decided to continue her employment, it also was decided to give her the promotion.

Heide suspected that Armand had done some arm twisting. She was glad, not only because she preferred to be able to continue with the work which she liked, but because she knew she would eventually have to face Viktor Aleksandrovich. His displeasure would know no bounds if she had excluded herself from direct access to this aspect of Canadian government operations. As it was she was apprehensive about his reaction to her marriage and pregnancy. She had no regrets but memories of what had happened to Frank Delacourt made her fear for Armand's safety if her masters took serious exception to her new husband.

Despite the dire predictions of the obstetrician that due to some apparent hormonal imbalance she might have trouble with the birth, the baby, a boy, was born without difficulty, on time. Heide thought him by far the most beautiful human being she had ever seen. He had Anatoli's smile and grey eyes, Armand's skin and physical strength. Although not quite so ecstatic, Armand was proud and pleased. Heide had great difficulty suppressing her emotions when they discussed the choice of a name for the baby. He wanted André or Marcel, names with a connection in his family. She insisted on Paul, without divulging her reasons. In the end they compromised and the child was christened Paul André.

As Armand predicted his mother was almost warm in her conversations with Heide on the telephone.

"Are you sure, my dear, that he is getting the right food? I don't set much store by all these new fads. You should nurse him for as long as you can. I did with Armand. Beginnings are so important. You must take care of yourself, too."

Heide intended taking care of herself, and had no intention of staying home nursing the child for nine months or more. It was not that she lacked a mothering instinct, only that she knew herself, and the work she had undertaken, well enough to know that she and Armand and Paul would all be better off if she returned to the Department and picked up her two careers. Her marriage severely limited her ability to feed material to the Centre though she was constantly alert for information on personalities to be given to Viktor Aleksandrovich when next they met.

For four months after Paul's birth she was off work. She used the time to prepare for the future. Armand had agreed that they should abandon apartment living in favour of a house. They managed to purchase one at a bargain price in mid-February when the real estate market was at its weakest for the year. The house was unoccupied and while Heide was still in hospital, Armand took a few days leave and moved them in. A large old sandstone structure not far from the Russian embassy in Sandy Hill, it gave them lots of room.

After they purchased it, Heide supervised the extensive redecorating that was needed to put it in shape. She claimed an attic room and bathroom on the third floor for her own study and darkroom. Two rooms on one side of the second storey landing were set aside for the baby and a nurse they would have to hire. On the other side of the landing was a large master bedroom and an adjoining sitting room, dressing room and bathroom. The smallest of the main floor rooms was set aside as a study for Armand. When she looked at the massiveness of the house and considered how well they filled it, she wondered what they would ever do if they had another child.

It took her a few weeks after getting home from hospital to adjust to the new surroundings. Once she did, however, she set to work hunting for a suitable nurse for Paul. The first two attempts were disastrous. The Jamaican girl lasted only a week. The second was a recently-widowed middle-aged woman. Although gentle with the child she tended to be so wrapped up in her own misfortunes that Heide feared to leave the child with her lest absent-minded neglect lead to disaster. The third attempt was successful. Janet Brown was a recently arrived Scottish immigrant. She was shy and overweight, had an almost unintelligible accent and was a natural mother. When Heide showed her the baby at the interview, she said:

"Aw the bonnie wee thin', can a hawd him Missus Latoor?"

Without waiting for an answer she lifted Paul from his crib and nestled him in her arms. The baby cooed, and Janet was hired.

With the domestic arrangements in place and working smoothly, Heide informed the Department that she was ready to return. Before her maternity leave she had stayed in Armand's division but the personnel people thought it best to reassign her now to avoid the difficulties that could arise from a husband and wife team being too closely associated professionally. She was assigned to the office of the Legal Advisor. The work was interesting and she was not unhappy at the prospect of polishing up her never-practiced law. It even promised to yield good returns for her masters at the Centre for, among her duties, was the monitoring of the cases of Canadian officials abroad who got into scrapes with the law. It was precisely the type of information the Centre could use in recruiting drives.

Before the job yielded much, however, yet another change occurred in their lives. Armand was asked if he would accept a posting to Bonn. It was an important step in his career. He would be counsellor at the Embassy, next to the Ambassador in rank. It meant a promotion for him but there was a difficulty over Heide. Departmental policy was opposed in principle to sending natives of foreign countries back to their homelands as diplomatic representatives of Canada. As is the way with these postings, however, Armand's move was part of a mass shifting of officers. If one dropped out it meant planned moves of a dozen or more other officers would be affected. In the end he was able to pressure those responsible into agreeing to Heide being posted to the same embassy to take over responsibility for cultural and information programmes, provided the Ambassador agreed. A telegram was sent, and the Ambassador, who had met Heide and had an eye for pretty women, did not hesitate.

Janet, to Heide's great delight, agreed to go with them and in September they rented their house and put their belongings in storage. After a short holiday in Quebec during which they stayed at the cottage on Lac Beauport where Armand's mother visited her son and grandson and tolerated her daughter-in-law, they flew together to the only European capital that was the match of Ottawa for dullness.

* *

The American Secret Service advance party arrived in Ottawa in strength. A whole plane load. They were thorough and very professional and, for the most part, diplomatic in the way did their job. They did a detailed survey of Government House, where the President and some of his party would stay. They went over every inch of the routes between the airport and Government House and Government House and Parliament Hill, where the President was to address a joint session of the Senate and the House of Commons.

Nobody in the advance party was able to offer an explanation of why the KGB might want to assassinate the President. As one Secret Service agent   put it:

"Makes no sense to us. But we can't afford to laugh it off or take any chances. I've seen some screwy attempts on Presidents in the last twenty years. Our job is to protect the man and that's what we're going to do."

As the date fixed for the visit approached the pace of preparations quickened perceptibly. Lists of all the guests to the State dinner and the luncheon to be given the next day by the Speaker of the House of Commons, as well as every single waiter, waitress, cook, gardener, bottlewasher and member of the Governor General's household were run through the RCMP and American computers. The Secret Service set up a control centre at the U.S. Ambassador's residence, where some of the Presidential party, including the Secretary of State and the Secretary of Defence would be staying. Residual members of the party were to be accommodated at 7 Rideau Gate, at the entrance to Rideau Hall. The Canadian government crisis centre, which had been established to handle such situations, was activated and linked directly to the U.S. Secret Service control centre.

In the meantime, the search for the man with the missing finger was about to end. The Canada-wide alert which had gone out turned up a surprising number of sightings, but none that stood up under investigation. The Mongolian looking man sighted in a government building was a typical example. He appeared to answer the description of Okulov until it was established that he was an eskimo who had lost his finger while seal hunting as a young man.

The injured man was taken from in front of the Chateau Laurier Hotel on Wellington Street and rushed in an ambulance to the Ottawa General Hospital, a few blocks away, where he was admitted to the emergency ward.

Ten minutes after his arrival an intern appeared from the operating room to speak to the policeman who had accompanied the ambulance.

"He's dead. We won't know precisely why until there's been an autopsy. There doesn't seem to have been enough damage to have killed him. He has a broken collar bone and arm and severe lacerations. Seems to have a finger missing on the left hand. Not from the accident. Must have been amputated years ago. There may have been internal damage, though there's no sign of haemorrhageing. Here are his clothes and effects, which may help to identify him."

The policeman methodically sifted through the effects. He was puzzled to find a Canadian passport in the name of Thomas Rolf Volker. A Manitoba driver's license in the name of Adolph Semper and a card with a social insurance number in the same name. The wallet of the injured man contained an open airline ticket from Montreal to Amsterdam in the name of Volker and an Avis car rental contract in the name of Semper. In the raincoat pocket he found a map of the Ottawa-Hull area. There appeared to be no marks of identification on his clothing; no laundry marks, no manufacturing label, nothing.

Later, the policeman was never sure whether it was the lack of markings or the two names on the documents that first aroused his suspicions. He called the intern and asked to see the body. There could be no mistake about the missing finger on the left hand. It was then he remembered the APB he had seen at the police station a few days earlier. He gathered up the man's belongings.

"Look, there's something not right about this man. I'm going to the station and I will take the man's effects with me to help us establish his identity. I'll sign for them at the front desk. In the meantime don't let anyone near the body — not even the coroner. The inquest can wait."

At Ottawa police headquarters when the duty sergeant heard the story and studied the man's belongings he immediately called his contact at the RCMP Security Service. By the time Brad was brought into the picture when he returned from the country house that evening, Okulov had been positively identified.

J.B. received the news with an audible sigh of relief.

"Too bad we couldn't have talked to him. We still don't know his target. All we do know is that he is no longer able to achieve it — though he may have had a partner. By the way Brad, that young Ottawa police constable was on his toes. Let's make sure his chief knows about it and also tell our recruiting team to keep an eye on him."

The American Secret Service took the news of 'Missing Fingers' death in their stride. The death made no difference to their plans, which they pursued vigorously in the days remaining before the visit was to take place.

TWELVE

The man known as Krivolapov fingered the memorandum he had sent to his chief earlier that day. Scrawled across the bottom of the sheet was one word: 'Approved' and the initial 'Z'. He pressed a button on the side of his desk. A secretary entered almost immediately.

"You called, Comrade General?"

"Yes, Sonya. I want the following messages sent immediately." The secretary opened her notebook and waited.

"First message to be sent *en clair* in English through Euromitlex Corporation, Copenhagen."

He paused, looking at the open file on the desk before him.

"Address it to Harry Foster, Embassy Apartment Hotel, Ottawa, Canada. 'Vice President arriving to assist you and assume responsibility for conclusion business. Will contact on arrival.' Sign it, 'President, Euromitlex Corp.' Read that back please."

Krivalopov listened attentively.

"Good. Second message to be sent via East Berlin for delivery immediately by safe hand to Maria Prager. You will find the address on file K.10-40-70. Maria Prager is to be instructed to send her daughter Heide Latour the following telegram, the message to be phrased in German.

'Paul Thorvald husband of Hilde Richter the baker's daughter, Tützing, will be in Ottawa on business next ten days. He represents Berlin chemical firm. Have given him your address and telephone number. Love, Maria'

"Read that back please."

"One correction. After 'husband of' and before the word 'Hilde', insert 'your school friend'."

"Thank you, Sonya. See that those get off at once. You are familiar with the routing of messages to Euromitlex? Good."

* * * * * * * * * * * * * * * * * * * *

At the country house, Heide's story continued to unfold. They had reached the period when she had had her most frequent contacts with her handler, following their posting to Bonn. It had been a happy time when she had been in love with Armand Latour. The reluctance that had marked the interrogation of her first contact with Armand had vanished. Now each memory seemed to rekindle the old warmth of their relationship.

Heide and Armand inherited a house in Bad Godesberg in a British built enclave which the Canadian government had acquired through an arrangement made when Britain was still an Occupying Power. Apart from being relatively modern and well maintained it fitted their needs. Heide liked it because it was light and airy, sitting on a hillside in what had been orchards of apple, plum, pear, cherry and apricot trees. Some of these had been retained in the garden at the back of the house. It was an ideal place for Paul and Janet Brown found companionship among the British community surrounding them. The house was large enough to allow Heide a dark-room for the paraphenalia of her hobby.

Running a fair sized household and entertaining, while at the same time carrying out her duties as an officer of the embassy, presented problems she had not experienced before. Happily, Armand's years as a bachelor at different posts abroad made it posible for him to help with the niceties of entertaining. In addition they inherited a first class staff, who took care of the day to day running of the house. Her fluency in German created an instant rapport with them, something her predecessor had not achieved in the four years she had been in the house.

Shortly after their arrival one of the foreign service officers responsible for political reporting contracted a form of emphysema. The doctors recommended his transfer to a less humid climate. The Ambassador filled the gap in the embassy's resources by asking Heide to take on his duties as well as on the cultural and information side of the embassy's work. At once her contacts in the German Foreign Office, and with British, American and French officials increased greatly. In particular she came to know officials of these countries dealing with intelligence and security matters. She felt sure her new duties would be of interest to Viktor Aleksandrovich.

Maria had responded to the news of her marriage, and subsequently the birth of Paul, with what appeared to be genuine enthusiasm. Her letters to Heide had been filled with warmth and interest. Heide had been strangely touched and reassured. Although Armand had offered to pay for her parents to come to Canada for the wedding, Anton's ill health had prevented it. By the time Anton had recovered enough to make the trip their posting to Bonn had been decided and it made more sense for Heide and Paul to visit Berlin. A few weeks after their arrival in Bonn, Heide took some of her annual leave and flew to Berlin with Paul. Armand followed a few days later, using the occasion to make his first official visit to the Canadian Military Mission in Berlin. Maria in one of her letters confirming the arrangements mentioned that some of her friends were looking forward to seeing her. Heide was not sure that she looked forward to her next meeting with Lavrov.

The trip from Wahnerheide airport to Templehof was surprisingly quick. The officer in charge of the military mission, a young foreign service officer, met her with the official car, flying an outsize red ensign.

"Welcome to Berlin, Mrs. Latour. You have brought summer weather. We've had nothing but rain for the past three weeks."

Hugh Yarrow smiled as he offered to help her with the luggage and with Paul.

"Thank you. Perhaps you could hold the baby. I think my passport is in the attache case. I didn't have room in my purse."

Anton and Maria's house was in the Charlottenburg area, on a street which appeared to have escaped any heavy damage. It was a two storey, brownstone, with large bow windows on the front and back. It was not beautiful but it was comfortable. Maria greeted her with warmth, and she and Paul became friends at once.

"Oh, Heide. Such a beautiful baby. Those eyes and his skin. You must be proud of him. He is bigger than I expected."

She took Paul in her arms.

"Anton? Yes, he is here, but he has not been well again. He is in bed upstairs."

Heide was shocked at Anton's appearance. He had lost a great deal of weight. His skin had an unhealthy, yellowish pallor. He appeared shrunken and old. His eyes had a feverish glaze. However, he still had his wits about him. He gave her precise and detailed instructions for her next rendezvous with Lavrov.

"With a diplomatic passport you will have no difficulty getting into East Berlin. No need for you to use the S Bahn route. You can cross at Checkpoint Charley as and when you wish. The people at the Canadian Military Mission will know the ropes — they go across quite frequently. There are lots of valid reasons for you to visit East Berlin — shopping, sightseeing and entertainment. The latter is the most plausible and the most convenient from the standpoint of arranging a meeting with your handler. 'Sauber Flotte' is on at the comic opera this week. Get tickets for the Thursday night performance and arrange to go on your own. You will be contacted."

The effort had exhausted Anton. He lay back on his pillows, his breathing heavy.

"Good luck." Anton opened his eyes, and then appeared to go to sleep.

At first Hugh Yarrow was reluctant to let Heide attend the opera on her own. However, when she pointed out to him that she had been born in Berlin, that German was her mother tongue and that she had the protection of her official position, he relented. She suspected that his agreement in part was based on the fact that he had been to Sauber Flotte at least twice in the past year. He offered the official car with a British driver to get her there and back.

The crossing was simple. The British army driver showed his

identification. As instructed, she showed her open passport through the window of the car, turning the pages for the benefit of the rather bored looking Volkspolizei. The procedure avoided having the passport stamped by the East German authorities, which might be construed as tacit recognition of a regime with which Canada refused to have relations.

The car left her at the door of the comic opera and the driver arranged to pick her up at the same door when the performance ended. To Heide's surprise the foyer and the upper halls were jammed with people. The air was thick with the smoke of cheap cigarettes, sweat and what smelled like kitchen soap. As she made her way to her seat, she felt a hand on her sleeve. Lavrov motioned her to follow him. He led her to the office of the manager on the floor above. He admitted them with a key, crossed the office and opened another door which led to a large well lit room.

"Greetings Galena Nadya. We will not be interrupted here. Be seated. Would you like a vodka?"

He motioned towards a small bar set up in the corner. At the door he pulled a handle on an electric switch box.

"There. We are electronically protected as well. We can talk freely. We have much ground to cover before the opera ends. Your seat will be filled by a woman who bears some resemblance to you."

Galena helped herself to a glass of vodka.

"It is a long time since I have had real vodka." She savoured the fiery liquid.

Helping himself to a drink from the same bottle, Viktor Aleksandrovich raised his glass.

"To you Madame Latour."

Galena braced herself.

"Well, Galena Nadya. You decided to get married without the permission of the Centre. They were very displeased. It could have meant the end of your mission. Through good fortune it has worked out that you will remain in the employ of the Canadian governement. It could have been otherwise. You acted impulsively. Something someone in your position cannot do."

Galena said nothing. She poured herself another drink. She sat down and faced Lavrov.

"There is little I can say. I fell in love."

"Fall in love if you must. You don't have to marry everyone with whom you go to bed. That was a stupidity. There is no point in driving the troika further, as we Russians say. What is done is done. We have checked Latour and happily he is exactly what he appears to be. However, he presents problems for your mission. It will make things more complicated but not impossible. Your appointment to Bonn, however, does open up new opportunities. Before we get to that though, there are questions I have for you."

Viktor Aleksandrovich lit a cigarette and got up and switched on the Uher tape recorder on the table between them. The debriefing took the better part of an hour as he worked his way through a list of questions.

"Good. Some of what you have related is new. Other comments confirm what we already know. There seem to be no important contradictions. Your evaluation of various personalities will be of interest to those dealing with talent spotting and recruiting.

"We have about an hour before you must go. First your new tasks. We would like you to continue to gather information about the embassy staff and their families, and contacts you have with the staff of other missions in Bonn. We want anything you can obtain about the weaknesses and habits of the Canadian and locally employed staff, from the Ambassador to the most junior. We are especially interested in the stenographers, the cypher staff, the security guards, the staff handling the archives and the couriers. We would like any information you can obtain about the schedules of the couriers, the locations of telephones in the office and particularly in the cypher rooms and other restricted areas. We would like to have the duty roster of the security guards, with emphasis on the quiet hours and holidays and week-ends. We can discuss this kind of information when we next meet."

Lavrov rose and went to the bar where he switched on a small hot-plate for making coffee.

"You also can start photographing documents on a very selective basis. We want you to take no risks. Certain categories you can overlook completely. For example, we have no need of NATO documents. These we get at will from other sources. Similarly there is no need to bother about documents about Canadian forces in Germany as most of these relate to questions of housing agreements and the NATO Status of Forces Agreement. They are of little value. We are interested in matters dealing with East-West trade, German reunification, political relations between the Federal Republic and Canada and any documentation relating to the views of the British, the Americans and the French on these and other matters. You will have to exercise judgement and to be highly selective. You are to take absolutely no risks."

He got up and poured them both a cup of coffee.

"As I remember, Galena Nadya, you like it black. As to methods of communication. Here is a lighter to replace the one you are now using. As you will see it is of a different style and perhaps a bit bigger. At one end is a lighter. At the other end is a miniature camera. To operate it you hold it, lighter end up, with your elbow placed on the table. The distance from your hand to the table and the documents you wish to photograph will give you the correct focus. The film cartridge is sealed, giving you sixty exposures. You only require a strong light from an ordinary desk lamp. When you have exposed all the film you will buy a new lighter at the tabac on the bahnhofstrasse in Bad Godesberg, at the point where it intersects with the Koblenzerstrasse. You will ask for a new lighter, saying that you prefer the same colour, red. If the response is that the only colour they have in stock is blue, you will accept it, giving him your old lighter to throw away. He will ask you for four marks fifty, which you will pay with a fifty mark note. You will maintain this procedure for the present. The colours for succeeding occasions will be, yellow, white, green and black. Should the reply be that they are out of the brand of lighter you are seeking, this will indicate that he cannot receive your exposed film, perceiving some danger in so doing. He will indicate when he expects a new shipment, after which date you may approach him again."

A buzzing sound, accompanied by a flashing red light above the door, interrupted them.

"There. The opera is ending. We will wait five minutes, after which you must rejoin the crowd and return to West Berlin. One final reminder; do not take any risks. Your long-term potential is far more valuable to us than any short-term advantage which can be gained from obtaining any particular piece of documentation. Your oral reports are at least as important at this stage. Goodbye, Galena Nadya."

Armand joined her in Berlin at the end of the week, and the three of them went to Kempinski's hotel. They had planned to leave Paul with Maria for the remainder of their stay but Anton's condition worsened, making this impossible. Armand was able to meet Anton briefly, but it was evident that they did not like one another. With Maria, on the other hand, there was an immediate rapport despite the language barrier. It was not an easy time for any of them and Heide was relieved when they flew back to Wahnerheide. Two months later Anton died and Heide flew back to Berlin to be with Maria. Armand had wanted to accompany her, but since he was acting as Chargé d'Affaires in the absence of the Ambassador, this proved impossible. Heide had no feelings about Anton's death, but she was glad to be there for Maria's sake. She was able to help with the funeral arrangements and be with Maria as she sorted through Anton's personal effects and rearranged the house.

Heide's next meeting with Lavrov did not take place for several months. She received a letter from Maria suggesting that Heide come to Berlin since there were a number of matters concerning the settlement of Anton's estate on which she needed advice. As soon as she was able to arrange it, she flew to Berlin and stayed with Maria. As before she arranged to get tickets to the Comic Opera in East Berlin, where she met Lavrov in the manager's office on the third floor.

"Greetings, Galena Nadya. I felt we should meet. You will be sad to learn the first two rolls of film you sent were completely useless. No, no, not your fault. It appears the seals were imperfect and the fluid in which the cameras were concealed destroyed the film. Since the liquid was gasoline, perhaps it is not surprising. A pity. However, in our trade one must expect failures along with successes."

"But Viktor Aleksandrovich, I cannot posibly remember the contents of the documents I photographed. I can't even remember which documents were on those rolls of film." She was upset.

"We do not expect you to remember. Forget it. We have other business to attend to."

They spent the remaining time with the Uher tape recorder between them. They paused only to replace the tapes. Lavrov was particularly interested in the Ambassador's wife. Heide reported the common gossip, that she was having an affair with the Ambassador's chauffeur, a muscular, blond rejoicing in the name of Sigismund.

"Perhaps we can exploit the situation."

"I doubt it. The Ambassador has been told that he is to be moved to Latin America. His wife is Chilean, and the rumour is that the Department of External Affairs feel that in Santiago, where she has a large family, the opportunities for carrying on her amorous escapades, of which the chauffeur is but the latest, will be sharply reduced. The Ambassador is furious since, quite rightly, he regards the posting as a demotion. Moreover, he is not happy about his proposed replacement, a French-Canadian, who has been Ambassador in Rome for several years. Armand tells me he is a distant cousin. Apparently he is less than enthusiastic about being moved from the delights of Rome to the small-town atmosphere of Bonn, amid what he obviously regards as a barbarous society."

"Hmm. Interesting. If the Department of External Affairs has its way, and I suspect they will, this probably means Armand will be moved since it would be unusual for two very senior French Canadians to remain at the same post."

"Possibly you are right. Certainly Armand has no love for his cousin and would not be happy to have to serve under him."

"Have you any idea where you and Armand might be sent?"

"No. I haven't. But given the relatively short time we have been in Germany we would be more likely to be cross-posted than to be brought back to Ottawa. I have no idea where we might be sent. Nor does Armand."

She also told Lavrov more about the routine of the Embassy, and was able to give him an accurate description of the cypher machines; their location, power source, proximity to telephones, maintenance schedules and an estimate of the volume of traffic in and out.

Lavrov asked her to supplement her oral report with sketches. He also showed some interest in her report that one of the security guards had been had up on the mat for having been found drunk, one evening, while on duty. He had been let off with a reprimand. The Ambassador had decided not to report the matter to Ottawa since this probably would result in his recall. Armand had said he did not agree with the Ambasador's decision as it was his belief that no amount of warning would cure the problem. Lavrov took careful note of his name and everything that Galena could tell him about the man.

When the warning light went on and the buzzer sounded, they parted company.

"Goodbye, Galena Nadya. Remember do nothing to place yourself in jeopardy. Your next assignment may be important to us."

After endless farewell parties given by other Ambassadors, the German Foreign Office and friends, the Ambassador and his amorous wife left. The farewell scene at the airport amused those in the know, since it involved permission to drive the Ambassador's Cadillac onto the tarmac, with Sigismund at the wheel. One of Armand's first acts as Chargé d'Affaires was to fire Sigismund. He disliked his cousin, but he was not prepared to have him saddled with a driver whom half of Bonn knew had cuckolded his predecessor.

The reluctance of the Ambassador-designate, Jacques Basdevant and his wife, to leave Rome meant that Armand had a lengthy period as Chargé d'Affaires. Heide found this period particularly trying as it happened to coincide with the advent of numerous visitors, most of whom had to be entertained in one way or another. The wives of these visitors took it for granted that since Heide spoke German she should act as their translator-cum-ladies-maid on their shopping and sight-seeing forays. For the first time in years she was homesick. She longed for the sights and sounds of her homeland. The Department finally dislodged the Basdevants by the simple expedient of putting their successors on an aircraft for Rome via Paris and giving them forty-eight hours to be out of the country. Even at that, the Basdevants delayed their arrival in Bonn by another two weeks on the grounds that they needed a fortnight on the French Riviera, 'to recuperate from the tiring round of farewell parties'.

The Basdevants tended on almost every occasion, and volubly, to compare Bonn unfavourably with Rome. They made few friends. Neither Heide nor Armand were sorry when they received word that they were to be cross-posted to the Canadian Delegation to the United Nations in New York. Armand was to be deputy-head of the delegation, a promotion, and Heide was assigned to look after the work of the specialized agencies.

Despite Basdevant's dislike of Armand he tried to oppose the transfer but failed. Head Office was still annoyed at his procrastination in leaving Rome and curtly dismissed his entreaties about Armand.

In the hectic month before their departure Heide managed one more trip to Berlin. In arranging dates with Maria she had mentioned that she would like to take in one last performance at the comic opera in East Berlin. Lavrov was waiting for her in the manager's office.

"Well, Galena Nadya. Maria tells me you have interesting news. The situation in New York is very different than it is in Bonn. For one thing the FBI and the CIA are much more active than the Gehlen organization and the BfV. Their coverage of the United Nations is excellent."

He paused to offer Galena a cigarette. He lit one for himself. They were both silent, savouring the pleasure of Russian tobacco.

"I can no longer be your contact. Instead, it will be Terence Sean Flaherty. You may recognize him. You were both in training camp at the same time. He has been a member of the United Nations secretariat for the past twelve years. He has steadily risen and now holds the post of Director-General of Information. Your contacts with him both socially and professionally, should cause you no problems. You could pass documentation to him but the Centre sees little point in your taking the risk since they are getting what they require from other sources. For example, most of the cypher traffic between the Canadian Delegation and Ottawa is already being intercepted at the Ottawa end from the Rezidentura. Most of the traffic is only of ephemeral interest; how the delegation will vote on various issues and reports of negotiations with other delegations."

"What then do I do, comrade?"

"For the most part we would be interested in knowing more about the daily routine of the delegation. Who deals with what. Assessments of the officers and their wives. We would be particularly interested in assessments of ministers and members of parliament who are attached to the delegation during sessions of the General Assembly. We also would like to have any information you can gather concerning matters discussed at regular meetings of the delegation, which usually take place every morning. None of this requires documentation and we do not envisage your having to use your camera. Should there be some document which you think important to photograph, arrangments can be made to pass it to us through Flaherty. In due course the Centre would like you to establish regular contacts with Flaherty, which, given what you have told me about your responsibilities, should be entirely natural."

Lavrov got up and poured coffee for them both.

"The Centre was pleased with the material in your last batch of films. It all came out well. Some of the documents, especially those dealing with the meeting in Vienna of Canadian Heads of Mission in Europe, were very valuable. The Centre also asked me to congratulate you on the telegrams from the Canadian Embassy in Paris, dealing with French views on the European Community and defence. The disinformation people think they can use it to advantage."

Lavrov got up and walked to and fro.

"There is one other matter about which the Centre asked me to inform you. As you know the Centre was displeased about your marriage. As I mentioned earlier our investigation of Latour shows that he is exactly what he seems to be. However, as a precaution, we have kept him under surveillance."

Galena got to her feet angrily.

"Sit down Galena Nadya. It is a precaution we felt obliged to take. After all we have a big investment in you. Nothing in our investigation suggests he is a threat to us or to the success of your mission. He appears to have a number of relationships with persons active on the ultra-nationalist fringe in Quebec. We see nothing disadvantageous in this. Indeed, we may be able to exploit it. However, we have noted some extra-marital activity, which, no doubt will not please you and could lead to difficulties for your mission."

Galena, her eyes blazing, her face white, stamped her foot.

"You lie Viktor Aleksandrovich. It is a filthy lie. He wouldn't."

She lit a cigarette and quickly butted it.

"I am sorry Galena Nadya. It is no lie. There is proof if you need it."

He handed her an envelope from which she reluctantly extracted half a dozen photographs. Taken with a wide-angle lens from a short distance they left no doubt of Armand's identity or of the fact that his partner in bed was a well built, dark-haired woman, probably several years younger than Galena.

"Those were taken in an hotel in Dusseldorf, three months ago."

She threw the photographs on the ground in disgust.

"I'll teach the son of a bitch."

"You will do nothing, Galena Nadya. To face Armand with your knowledge will indicate to him that you, or someone, has had him under surveillance. I do not want you to do anything. We felt that you had to know about his womanizing, and that it was better to learn from us than to stumble upon it. Had that happened, you might have reacted in a manner which could affect your mission."

Galena got up and poured herself a large glasss of vodka, which she tossed down.

"The dirty son of a pig."

She thought of Madame Latour and her prim opposition to their marriage. Perhaps the old sow had been trying to warn her? She picked up her purse as the buzzer and the flashing red light signalled the end of the performance. She made her way to the door without a word.

* * * * * * * * * * * * * * * * * * * *

FROM: Special Analysis Group (Merrivale)
TO: Director-General
SUBJECT: Opal

As you have requested we have examined the pros and cons of telling Opal now of the death of the man with the missing finger. The American Secret Service are opposed, on the grounds that nothing should be done, which might complicate their principal task, the protection of the President. On the other hand, they do not see how her knowledge of Missing Finger's death can have any effect on the visit, as she is under our control.

On balance, given the importance of de-briefing Opal as quickly and thoroughly as possible, S.A.G. believes that there is no obvious and compelling reason to keep the information from her. It could be that her knowledge of his death will assist us by increasing the scope of her co-operation.

We continue to believe that it is important to conduct Level II searches of her house. Unfortunately, so far we have been unable to arrange for the house to remain unoccupied for more than a few hours at a time. We have managed brief surreptitious entries on two occasions. One in a locked room in the basement, and the other in the attic, which were given only cursory treatment during the original Level II search. Neither the basement nor the attic appeared to contain anything suspicious. The locked basement cupboard is for wine. The only slightly suspicious item found was a plastic covered metal clothes line strung the length of the attic. Although obviously used for hanging clothes, it measured exactly 926 centimetres, ideal for certain types of short wave transmissions.

As you are aware, we intercepted a telegram from Maria Prager in Berlin, addressed to Opal. The message, which is in German, has been subjected to the most detailed examination by the crypto-analytical experts, who have been unable to read anything sinister into the text. There would seem to be no point in witholding the message further, but we suggest that her interrogators, when giving her the message, watch closely for any unusual reactions on her part.

THIRTEEN

By the time Brad picked Heide up for the drive to the country house, it had begun to rain. They spoke little during the journey. The rain became heavy and was accompanied by thunder.

At the country house and before they started the tape recorders, Brad decided to tell her about the death of MissingFinger and to give her Maria's message. J.B. had given his agreement the night before.

"It's okay to go ahead Brad. Sorry not to have been able to give you the green light earlier, but given the PM's jumpiness I thought I had better clear it with him. He has no objection."

Brad handed Heide a steaming mug of coffee.

"Before we begin I have a couple of matters I would like to discuss. Let's sit in the other room."

When Brad told her about the death of the 'V for Victor' agent she hardly reacted at all. She shrugged and lit another cigarette. Brad handed her Maria's telegram.

"We intercepted this. Sorry we had to delay it a day or so."

Heide opened the envelope and read the message carefully. The name Paul Thorvald leapt from the text. The significance stunned her. He was alive. Alive, alive. She wanted to shout with joy. Only the discipline which years of training had instilled in her suppressed the wild emotion. She was a consumate actress. Brad was unable to detect any unusual reaction. She re-read the message carefully and handed it back to Brad.

"I guess Maria was trying to be kind to Hilde's husband. I didn't know she was married. Hardly a convenient time for his visit. What will I do if he contacts me?"

Brad shrugged.

"The timing's inconvenient, I agree. If he calls, you'll have to play it by ear. Maybe his visit will be postponed."

Heide made no reply. Her mind was racing, exploring all the meanings of the information contained in the message. He was alive. She would have to act quickly. But she would have to keep a tight rein on herself — on the tremendous impatience she felt. She must do or say nothing to arouse suspicion.

Brad handed her back the telegram.

"Here, you can keep it."

"I don't need to."

Heide tore the message into small pieces and put them in the ashtray. Only the care she took in tearing up the message suggested to Brad that perhaps the telegram was more important than she had let on. He cast the thought aside. With the President arriving in two days every availabe man was being switched to security duty. He was determined to reach the end of Heide's account of her life before the end of the day. If they could accomplish that, they could start into the cross-examination after the visit. With luck, they might even be able to start using her as a double agent.

To Brad's surprise, the interrogation about the period following the transfer of the Latour's from Bonn to New York and the break-up of their marriage went quickly. He was surprised since some of the memories were painful, and on previous occasions when she was recalling periods she did not like the going had been slow. On this occasion her memory of past events came evenly and without hesitation. By lunch they were almost into the period when her relationship with Marc Grandpre had begun to develop.

* * * * * * * * * * * * * * * * * * * *

Although Heide had prepared herself well for living in the United States, she had found the first impact far more unsettling than she had anticipated. The sheer size and the wealth of New York City; the vibrancy, the diversity and the rawness of it shocked her. The Latour s inherited a large, well appointed apartment on the top floor of a new building overlooking the East River, within walking distance of the United Nations buildings. Happily the greater part of the rent was met out of departmental funds since the cost was astronomical. There was more than enough room for the three of them, together with Janet Brown and a maid and a cook, who lived in. Heide was able to convert a utility room into a darkroom. There was even a large guest room, which with a bathroom and a dressing room, provided a self contained suite.

Heide liked the Head of Delegation and his wife. He was a professional public servant, who had served both the Liberals and the Conservatives as a deputy-minister in various portfolios. He had the confidence of the bureaucrats and he was on first name terms with many members of the Cabinet and with many former Cabinet Ministers, now in the official opposition.

He worked hard, and, in the two years he had been in New York, established a reputation with the Secretary-General and the United Nations secretariat. Unlike some of his predecessors he had no greater ambitions. No aspirations to public office, a fact which was obvious to those working with him and added to their respect for him. His wife, an English speaking Montrealer, who spoke excellent French, was universally liked. She worked very hard at that side of diplomatic life, which so often is ridiculed, but which is inescapable and demanding. She entertained with discrimination and skill. She had a flair for dealing with people. The wife of the most junior clerk was treated in exactly the same way as the wife of a Cabinet Minister. She also happened to be intelligent. Heide felt that she could have had a rewarding career of her own if she had so chosen.

Heide's first meeting with Terence Sean Flaherty occurred ten days after their arrival in New York. They were at a dinner party given by the French representative to the United Nations. She was astonished how completely her former classmate had assumed the identity of Flaherty. Not only had he perfected the speech of an Irishman born in Cork and educated in Dublin, but he had acquired the appropriate mannerisms. He also managed to give an impression of feyness, which one associated with the Irish. Heide could detect nothing about him which was Slav.

"Ah, Mrs. Latour. And what a pleasure it is to meet you. It'll be Bonn you are coming from, now? Like a village it is, I'm told. You'll find that New York is nothing but a collection of villages and the languages they speak are incomprehensible.

"I understand, Mrs Latour that you share your husband's profession? I expect you have certain areas of work for which you will be responsible?"

"Yes. I have been made responsible for the work of the specialized agencies; mainly Committee 4. And what do you do in the secretariat? "

"Well, now, I am in the information business, as they say. Telling the world what the U.N. does. In America, where there are almost as many journalists as there are Irishmen, the task is never ending."

They had been joined by the wife of a member of the French delegation. Born in Cairo, she looked and sounded as if she had stepped from the pages of one of Lawrence Durrell's books.

"Ah, Natasha me love. You have already met one another? I was just telling Mrs. Latour about my work."

"Terence. Why do you always have to talk about such boring subjects? Have you seen the new Serengi exhibition on 53rd? Delicious colours and dripping with sex. The piece de resistance is entitled 'Ivoire'. Some see a resemblance to the Secretary General's mistress. I don't, although I've never seen her in the nude."

Heide disengaged herself but not before Flaherty had suggested they eat lunch together after she had settled in to her new work. At dinner Heide found herself beside the husband of Natasha. Tall, rather supercillious, he spent some time telling her that among the upper middle class in France it was customary for mothers to initiate their sons into the delights of sexual intercourse. He assured her that his first sexual experience had been with his mother.

"After all, Madame, who could be more loving and understanding than a mother?"

Heide tried to conceal her disgust. She regarded his story as a good illustration of Western decadence. On other subjects, however, he was witty and entertaining. She might even have been prepared to like him had it not been that she believed his story about having sexual intercourse with his mother.

Ever since her last meeting with Lavrov in East Berlin Heide had allowed a certain coolness to govern her relations with Armand. The effect had been to increase his attentiveness. Indeed, he had become almost uxorious. At first she found his renewed interest merely amusing, but her amusement turned to irritation when she discovered herself responding to his love-making with passion. During this period Heide drew closer to Paul. He had grown into a sturdy, handsome, highly intelligent child. She knew that she loved him more than anything else in the world. She could see in him a clear resemblance to Anatoli Ivanovich.

Summer weather and the absence of any crises in world affairs provided the Latours with a period of inactivity, during which they took three weeks leave at Armand's cottage at Lac Beauport.

Back in his home environment, Heide noted how his old nationalism was taking a more separatist tone. After she returned to New York she made a point of seeking out Terence Flaherty at the bar in the U.N. building.

"Well, now. The summer is all but gone and I haven't had a chance to see you. How about lunch next Tuesday?"

The following Sunday they had a late breakfast after which Armand settled down to read the week-end edition of the New York Times.

"Well, that shows you can't trust anyone."

Heide, immersed in the Book Review section, only half heard.

"Imagine Terence Flaherty being a spy."

Armand's words struck like a thunderclap. She felt sudden panic and struggled to keep her composure.

"What on earth are you talking about? Terence Flaherty a spy. What utter nonsense. Who says he is?"

"The U.S. government. Here, see for yourself."

Armand handed her the newspaper. She read it quickly.

"The FBI, acting on a warrant issued by a Judge of the U.S. District Court, arrested Terence Sean Flaherty, a Director-General of Information in the United Nations Secretariat, early this morning. He is charged with possession of a false passport, illegal entry to the United States and various acts of espionage while a member of the international body.

"The arrest was carried out in the early hours of the morning in Mr. Flaherty's apartment in Brooklyn, to avoid the complications which might have been caused had an attempt been made to arrest him in the United Nations building.

"The FBI would not comment on the case other than to say that a preliminary hearing would take place tomorrow, at which time a decision would be taken on whether bail would be granted. The U.S. Attorney General was recommending that bail not be granted. The FBI spokesman suggested that any further questions should be addressed to the office of the U.S. Federal Prosecutor.

"Reliable sources in Washington suggested that Mr. Flaherty had been under investigation for several months, following a tip-off from a high level Soviet defector. These sources would not speculate on exactly how investigators had discovered Mr. Flaherty's false identity."

Heide handed back the newspaper to Armand.

"Extraordinary. I find it difficult to believe. He seemed such a nice person. I rather liked him. Heavens, I just remembered. He asked me to have lunch with him next week. I can't imagine what he could have expected to get out of someone like me. The Specialized Agencies aren't exactly the kind of stuff to interest a spy."

Armand had continued with his reading. He stopped, realizing that she was waiting for a response.

"Yes, too bad. I quite liked him, too. Not my idea of a spy. Speaking of the Specialized Agencies, aren't you slated to attend some seminar the U.N. has organized in San Francisco, soon? The Ambassador spoke to me about it, and asked if your absence for a few days would be difficult. I told him I begrudged any time we had apart, but I thought that you wanted to go."

Heide answered absent-mindedly, "Yes, he spoke to me about going."

Her mind was racing over the implications of Flaherty's arrest. Would her contacts with him cast any suspicion on her? She thought it unlikely. All her contacts with Flaherty had been within a normal framework. Happily their luncheon date had not yet taken place. She felt certain that Flaherty was far too professional to have left any trace of the true nature of their relationship. She also was certain that no matter what kind of pressure the FBI brought to bear on him he would reveal only that which could not be avoided. It was idle to speculate on how he had been discovered. It could well have been some defector or perhaps that was just to cover that his communications with the Centre had been compromised in some manner. If so she might be in danger. There was also a possibility if a defector had really identified Flaherty, he might also have identified her. Could it have been her youthful lover, Oleg? There was nothing to be gained from speculation. She would simply have to continue as if nothing had happened. As had been emphasized throughout her training, often waiting would prove to be the most difficult of her assignment. She decided to put the matter out of her mind.

Although the seminar lasted only a few days Heide welcomed the chance to see San Francisco. It was a delightful city, far beyond her expectations. It, like Quebec, had a European quality to it, which, coupled with its climate, made a most welcome change from New York City. She stayed at the Biltmore-Ambassador with its high-vaulted glass-domed rotunda, potted palms and turn of the century furnishings. Not only did the decor remind her of Moscow, but she discovered that the bar in the hotel carried an excellent brand of Russian vodka. She did not lack for evening entertainment. A number of the delegates and members of the secretariat had left their wives in New York. Particularly memorable was an evening in the company of a Peruvian and a number of other Latin-American delegates. The Peruvian, Ortez Jiminez, having spent his undergraduate years in San Francisco, knew the bay area well and suggested dinner at the Alta Mira Continental Hotel at Sausalito, a half-hour drive north of the city. The evening had a distinctly Mediterranean flavour, heightened by the fact that no English was spoken. For several hours on the broad terrace of the hotel they savoured the superb cuisine, the cellar's choicest wines and the view. Heide was relieved when her offer to share the cost of the evening was politely but firmly turned down; the figure had been astronomical.

When Heide discovered that the final day of the seminar was to be entirely given over to discussion of items of primary interest to the secretariat, she decided to return a day early. The first available direct flight to New York got her in at ten o'clock. At the airport she tried to telephone Armand but gave up after waiting ten minutes at a row of telephone booths, each of which had a queue in front of it. She reasoned that he might well be out since Paul and Janet Brown had flown to Quebec City to stay with Armand's parents. She hoped they were safe.

The taxi ride took almost an hour in a driving rain, which had created enormous pools of water under some of the overpasses. The doorman greeted her warmly. As she let herself into the apartment an unfamiliar smell hung in the air. She put down her suitcase and briefcase. She recognized the smell, Gitanes cigarettes. Certainly, Armand didn't smoke them.

Suddenly the photograph that Lavrov had shown her flashed before her eye. It had been over a year since that meeting and she had allowed its disquieting news to recede, persuading herself that everyone was allowed one error.

"God damn his filthy hide; he wouldn't dare, not here."

She moved quickly down the long, heavily carpeted corridor to their bedroom. She threw the door open and switched on the lights. A pair of dark brown, shapely legs with dark-red painted toenails were wrapped around Armand's thighs. The long, blue black hair of the woman lay over the pillows. Heide recognized her. Charlotte Boisvert, the bitch. Heide had heard that she had been in New York a few weeks earlier trying to drum up support among Third World delegations for an independent Quebec. Her own opinion of Charlotte was so low as a result of their encounter in Quebec City on her first outing with Armand, that she had not considered the possibility of her husband climbing into bed with the slut. She had been wrong.

Like two copulating flies, caught for eternity in amber, the couple on the bed remained transfixed. Suddenly the frozen figures came to life as they frantically tried to disengage themselves.

"You dirty bastard. In my bed. You rotten pig. Get the hell out of here and take that separatist whore with you."

Armand with his recent lust still very obvious stood up.

"Heide. I'm sorry. I didn't know you were coming back until tomorrow. I . . . ."

His words and the sight of him filled her with an uncontrollable rage. She scooped up the first thing that came to her hand, a large Eskimo carving, and flung it at him. The stone hit Armand on the temple and he went down like a polled ox. The woman fled screaming to the bathroom. Heide took one look at the slumped figure of her husband before slamming the door. She did not care whether he was alive or dead. She spent the night locked in the guest suite at the other end of the apartment.

It was several days before she agreed to talk to Armand. Eventually they reached agreement to separate and at least until they could work out separate quarters, to share the apartment. Happily the place was large enough that they were able to manage this with a minimum of contact between them. She was adamant that she should have custody of Paul. When he demurred, she threatened to sue for divorce and make their differences public. He changed his mind. Armand managed to spend an increasing amount of time in Canada and Heide was certain that Charlotte was the reason. She accused him of this and he did not deny it.

"Yes. I see Charlotte whenever I can. So what? Apart from her obvious attractions we happen to share the same policitcal views about our country; Quebec."

They nearly came to blows again, not so much because Armand obviously preferred Charlotte to Heide, which certainly irritated her, but because of his attitudes about Canada and Quebec. She regarded his espousal of a separate Quebec as beyond comprehension. Viewed from the perspective of her political upbringing, the differences between French-Canadians and English-Canadians were minimal while the similarities were so vast as to make them virtually indistinguishable.

Brad interrupted her story to ask if she ever considered Armand's split loyalties in the light of her own commitments to Canada and to Russia.

"Until you caught me, my only commitment was to Russia."

Brad decided not to pursue the matter, at least for the time being. He changed the subject.

"You mentioned that on one occasion you had a handler other than Lavrov. Molev, I think you said was his name. Tell us about your meeting with him. When did it take place and where?"

"Molev is his name. Fedor Nikolaivich. I think it was in September, while I was still in New York, not long after the FBI caught Flaherty. I felt I needed to see Lavrov. I wrote to Maria suggesting I might visit her. She replied in a couple of weeks saying that following Anton's death she felt the need for a holiday, away from West Berlin. She proposed we meet in Austria. I was able to get permission to take some of my annual leave. By this time Armand and I had separated and the Ambassador, who tended to take my side, readily agreed I might take some time off."

"I flew directly from New York to Zurich. From there I took the Arlberg Express to Innsbruck. We were to meet in a small village called Igls, in the mountains above Innsbruck. In normal circumstances, I might have enjoyed the trip. The railway runs through a series of beautiful valleys, between the Glarner Alpen to the south and the Lechertaler Alpen to the north. However, I wasn't in the mood for scenery. It was dark when I got to Innsbruck. I caught a post bus, one of those canary coloured things."

"Did you know then that Lavrov was sick?"

"I knew only what Maria had written in her letter. She was waiting for me at the hotel, and it was only then that I learned I would be meeting someone other than Lavrov. The meeting was to take place in a small chapel half way up the Patcherkoffel, above Igls. It was arranged for the next morning."

"What happened?"

"When we got up early next morning it had started to rain. By eight o'clock a storm broke. Strong winds and driving rain. By nine-thirty the worst of it had passed but it was still raining. Maria lent me some walking boots and her Lodenfrei cape. I took bread, sausage and some chocolate."

Heide stopped to light a cigarette.

"The path was well marked but it took me longer than I had expected. By the time I reached the chapel the rain had stopped and a thick fog had rolled up from the valley. It was almost an hour before Molev appeared. He was a surprise."

"In what way?"

"He was enormous. Quite the opposite of Viktor Aleksandrovich. He wore one of those shepherd's capes and black lederhosen and was smoking one of those long curved wooden pipes. He greeted me in the dialect. I didn't think he was my contact until he produced the other half of a torn music program which Maria had been instructed to give me."

"Did he deal with you differently than Lavrov?"

"No. He used a small tape recorder to take my oral report. I found him well informed about my reports and about my own affairs. For example, he knew that I had separated from Armand."

"Did he give you any new instructions? Anything specific?"

"No."

"Would you have preferred Molev to Lavrov as your principal handler?"

"I don't know. They are quite different. Perhaps it was his sheer size and obvious strength, but I found Molev frightening. Nothing he said or did, but rather his manner. He is not the kind of man I would ever want to cross. Nor would I want to be opposite him in a fight."

"Did you come right back from Austria?"

"No. I enjoyed seeing Maria again. After all, the Ambassador had given me leave, and I decided to take advantage of it. We spent five days in Igls. Moreover, I needed the rest."

Brad reflected that throughout the many days of interrogation this was the first time that Heide had admitted to any need. The more he saw of her the less he felt he knew what made her tick. She was tough, very tough. At the same time she obviously was a passionate woman and her love for her son, Paul, was unquestionable. Never once had she allowed her interrogators to dominate her. He had to admit, ruefully, that at times, it was she who had dominated them. Brad had a gut feeling that despite appearances, there was within her a hard core, quite untouched by the Western civilization into which she had fitted herself with such consumate skill and ease. He couldn't put his finger on it but he would bet anything that the chic exterior successfully hid deep feelings which only a Slav would understand.

He remembered the day at the country house when they had taken a break and had gone outside for a breath of fresh air. Suddenly they heard, then saw, two large flocks of Canada geese flying south, high above them.

"Boy what a beautiful sight."

Heide's reaction had been to say:

"I think it is one of the saddest sounds and sights in the world. They are creatures driven by instincts implanted in them at birth. They have no choice in life. They must fly where their destiny takes them."

Brad was honest enough to acknowledge to himself that he was strongly attracted to Heide. She had an animal magnetism it was impossible to ignore. He knew enough of the psychology of the relationships which sometimes develop between captor and captive, hostage and hostage-taker, interrogator and interrogatee, to appreciate there probably had been at least a partial transfer of his sympathies, helped no doubt by the fact that she was a woman, and a very beautiful woman.

George McCain, on the other hand, probably harboured no such feelings. His approach was straightforward. She was an enemy agent to be countered and, in this case, used. Her beauty left him unaffected. It would never have occured to McCain to find out what made her tick, except, insofar as it might assist his professional needs.

"Okay, Heide. Let's stop there. Let's have lunch. You must be hungry. I certainly am."

"Yes. I am hungry."

Brad thought to himself that she might be hungry, but she obviously wasn't the least bit tired. Indeed, he had never seen her look more radiant — more beautiful.

When they were alone McCain spoke to Brad.

"What's got into her? She sure as hell didn't waste much time this morning. Must have taken Geritol or something."

Brad answered slowly.

"Couldn't have been that damn telegram. She hardly reacted at all when I showed it to her. Seemed put out that this guy might try to get in touch with her. More likely due to some female change of rhythm."

"Good an explanation as any, Brad."

"Perhaps. Let's hope so."

After lunch they resumed. Heide picked up the story from the moment following her return to New York and her relationship with Marc Grandpre began. Brad had the impression she derived a certain pleasure in retelling the story of this part of her life.

When Grandpre was appointed the Canadian delegate to the fourth committee of the Assembly was still one of the youngest members of parliament to have served as a parliamentary secretary. Although his name was French in origin, he was born in Manitoba and spoke little French. His mother's name had been O'Malley. Heide learned during a business lunch of sandwiches and coffee, that he also had Dutch and Scandinavian roots. His Scandinavian ancestor, a sailor, appeared to have got mixed up with a Creole lady, whose charms caused him to abandon a wife and children. Eventually he married the Creole.

"To her my mother attributed her curly hair, dark skin and eyes, which I seem to have inherited." He ran his hand through his thick, black hair and grinned. He was not handsome but she found him attractive. He possessed enormous vitality and his ego was only matched by his ambition.

Towards the middle of the General Assembly session the Prime Minister joined the delegation. His speech was intended to reinforce a Canadian initiative in one of the areas of the United Nations work for which Heide had been assigned responsibility. She found herself very busy and, of necessity, working closely with Marc Grandpre on the speech, who rightly saw in the occasion an opportunity to impress the Prime Minister. The long working hours meant that she and Marc found themselves dining together, alone, with increasing frequency. Their attraction to one another was obvious and it was no surprise to either of them that they ended up in bed together; usually in his bed, in the comfortable mid-town hotel suite he occupied.

The evening following the Prime Minister's speech they had a special celebration. The speech was well received and given wide coverage in the Canadian news media. The Prime Minister was delighted and made his satisfaction known before leaving the Assembly to catch his airforce plane back to Ottawa. Marc was elated.

"Heide, my love. To you. Your help made it all possible. Although he didn't say it in so many words, the P.M. hinted that he would be considering me when he shuffles his Cabinet next month." Marc raised the glass of champagne he was holding.

"I am so glad Marc. It was a good speech and the Prime Minister delivered it well."

"And now to important matters. The menu. I am torn between beginning with snails or frog's legs and then having the Long Island duck with wild rice. The soufflé Grand Marnier was superb the last time we were here. What tempts you?"

The small restaurant in the Village was one of their favourites. It was run by an Englishman and his French wife who both cooked, although she tended to spend more time with their clientele. The decor was subdued but attractive. The food was expensive but exceptionally good. The wine list, even by New York standards, was unusual in the quality of the vineyards and the quality of the vintages. They returned to the hotel suite and happened to go up in the elevator with a couple of Marc's parliamentary colleagues. Neither of them said anything but it was clear what they thought.

When they were in the suite Marc raised the subject.

"I guess there isn't much point in trying to hide our relationship. Most of the people in the delegation must assume that we are living together. One of those guys knows my wife pretty well. But he also knows that Hermione and I broke up about a year ago. She has the children and she has a pretty handsome monthly allowance. I guess you and Armand have the same problem?"

"Yes. Pretty much." Heide shrugged.

"Un-zip me at the back. It has been — it is a lovely evening. Why spoil it with more talk?"

There was none of the passion in her sexual encounters with Marc that had been the hallmark of her relationship with Armand. It was, as she now recounted to Brad, not a question of his virility or stamina — that she could attest to — rather it was in her response. Marc Grandpre fulfilled a biological need in her, but she knew that after Armand's betrayal she would never let her emotions get the better of her in her love affairs. As with Major Krylov long years before, she would always hold part of herself in reserve. As she spoke, Brad wondered what success he might have in getting her to reverse that vow. He quickly abandoned the thought, at least for the moment, and brought her back to the topic of her growing relationship with Marc Grandpre.

After Parliament reconvened in Ottawa, she continued, she saw less of him. He came to meetings from time to time, but nearly always had to return the following day. At least this allowed them time together in the evenings. Marc called Heide from Ottawa during a period when he had been absent from New York for about ten days. She could tell from his voice that he was excited.

"Heide. I couldn't wait to tell you the good news. The Prime Minister will be announcing the changes in the Cabinet later this morning. He has asked me to join. I believe we are to be sworn in this afternoon. The only sad part is that it will mean that I won't be back in New York for a while. Perhaps I can get you posted to Ottawa. How would that be?"

"Oh, Marc. What good news. I am so glad for you. I wouldn't mind coming back to Ottawa. From what Armand tells me the Department of External Affairs has had the same thought recently. The Under-secretary spoke to him, when he was here for meetings of the Political Committee. It seems that he felt our interests and those of the department would be better served if we were able to work out our differences in Ottawa rather than in New York. I guess he's right. The other thing is that Paul's asthma seems to be aggravated by the air pollution here in New York, so the cleaner air back in Ottawa would relieve his difficulty breathing and ease my concern. It would be better if we were at home."

"All right, my darling. Leave it to me."

The next few weeks were difficult for Heide. The departure of many members of the delegation meant an expansion of her duties at the Assembly sessions and on the specialized agencies. Paul's condition did not improve. Their doctor could not establish a perfectly effective control for the asthmatic attacks and insisted on a series of tests. Aside from the worry which his illness caused, she also had to get him to and from the hospital. Armand was less than helpful. He was besotted with Charlotte and he spent an increasing number of extended weekends in Quebec City. Heide was content not to have him under foot all the time, but his colleagues on the delegation were not happy with his taking off early on Friday and only returning on late Monday. Even the Ambassador, who was a mild mannered man, was heard to murmur about the misfortune of having only half a deputy.

Shortly before Christmas, Marc telephoned from Ottawa to say that he was going to Washington for a meeting and could stop off the following Friday in New York on the way home if they could have dinner.

"I have some exciting news about you. No, I want to keep it until we can talk privately."

Since Armand would be away she suggested that he stay overnight in the flat. He agreed and within an hour she had arranged for Janet Brown to take Paul to visit friends on Long Island. They would have the flat to themselves.

She did not know whether it was their long absence from one another or simply that the chemistry was just right, but there was a new spark between them when they met. She liked the way he stood at the door with a bottle of champagne in his hand when she opened it and the way he held her when she let him in. He felt the same. Neither suggested that they postpone dinner until after they had gone to bed, it just happened. It was late before they felt sufficient strength to consider getting up, and then only to open the champagne which she had put into the refrigerator. While he prepared the glasses, she brought some water to the boil, added a bay leaf, a stock of celery and a cup of wine before tossing in a pound of fresh shrimps. Ninety seconds later the succulent pink flesh was ready to be eaten and the wine was bubbling from the stem of the clear glasses. He offered a toast.

"To us, my love. And more particularly to your new job in Ottawa."

Marc raised his glass.

"Uhm. That Veuve Cliquot is good. Bought it in a drug store in Washington. Why in hell can't we have that kind of system in Canada. Your new job? Ah yes. I think I have talked your undersecretary into lending you to the Privy Council Office for a while. He wasn't easy to persuade but we are old friends. We went to university together. The Secretary to the Cabinet was amenable, and why wouldn't he be with your qualifications? I hadn't realized how impressive they are until I saw them on a sheet of paper. Not only are you very beautiful but you are also very intelligent."

He put his glass down and kissed her shoulder. She responded with a new fervour, partly sparked by the thought of a job in the PCO — right at the heart of the Canadian government — which seemed the fruition of all her years of preparation. Her elation knew no bounds and Marc Grandpre, mistaking the cause, reaped the benefit.

It was well into the new year before news of Heide's transfer to Ottawa and secondment to the Privy Council Office became official. Disentanglement of her affairs from those of Armand proved to be more complex than expected. It was not so much the disposition of their personal belongings as the problems of re-establishing themselves in Ottawa. They agreed that they would each find their own quarters. This was not easy to do at a distance and it was made more difficult for Heide by Marc's suggestion that he give up his small bachelor flat and move in with her. She resisted the idea and in the end she prevailed. Her real reasons for rejecting the offer she kept to herself. The argument that dissuaded Marc was that since they were both still married there might be legal complications if they set up a menage together.

Eventually she decided to buy Armand's half of the house they still owned jointly in Sandy Hill. She liked the district and the house was sufficiently large that Janet and Paul could have an entire floor to themselves with an entrance at the rear. She felt that with a bit of money the house could be made very attractive. Marc helped her find a lawyer who completed the deal on her behalf while she was still in New York.

Before leaving New York, she wrote Maria a long letter telling her of everything which had transpired since she had last seen her. She was certain that it would reach Viktor Aleksandrovich. She had a brief post-card back from Maria thanking her for the letter and indicating that she would write, at greater length, later.

By the time they were finally installed the worst of the winter was over. Armand left New York almost a month before she did and since she was no longer working in the department of External Affairs she had not seen him. She heard through mutual friends that he had a small apartment in New Edinburgh and that his relationship with Charlotte was causing a lot of gossip in External Affairs, where her separatist activities were viewed with strong disfavour.

At first the nature of her work was so different that she had difficulty coping. It was particularly trying, when acting as Secretary to Cabinet Committees, to make sense out of discussions which often were so unstructured and interminable as to be virtually unintelligible. Happily she had as her mentor a man who had been doing the job for years under both the Liberals and the Conservatives.

"Don't let all their blather get you down. Half of them haven't read the documents and with the other half it wouldn't matter if they had. Get hold of your Chairman and make sure he is well briefed and does his homework. Work out some kind of game plan with him and get him to stick to it. There will always be a couple of ministers who have a stake in the outcome. Keep track of what they say. Keep your minutes of discussion short and your record of decisions even shorter. If you have any problem, take it to your Chairman. Get him to approve the minutes and any decisions. It's up to him to decide whether he wants to consult other members about wording and the kind of outcome he thinks desirable. For the rest, relax. The same rules apply to drawing up agendas and fixing dates and times for meetings. If the Chairman is happy you're home free."

After she got the hang of it, she liked the work. Her assignments were mostly in the field of social affairs, but from time to time she filled in on other committees when members of the secretariat were ill or on leave. One or two of these were in areas which she knew would be of interest to Viktor Aleksandrovich. Since there was no documentation which seemed to her of outstanding interest to the Centre she decided not to photograph material until she had a better grasp of the intricacies of the work.

Marc spent an increasing amount of time in her house in the evenings. She found his companionship amusing and interesting. She liked him although she knew she could never love him. She recognized, however, that he was in love with her. Their relationship was generally accepted by their friends and acquaintances. Certainly they were invited together to enough functions.

As Heide became familiar with her work in the Privy Council Office she felt more confident about photographing documents for the Centre. A majority of the documents she selected lay outside the sphere of interest of the Cabinet Committee of which she was Secretary. They derived mostly from other committees which from time to time impinged on her work. Their intrinsic value to the Centre was the indication they gave of the trend of Canadian government thinking. They were also interesting for the light they shed on the way in which the government machinery worked, or failed to work. Only rarely did she have access to material dealing with defence, national security, and foreign affairs. Occasionally, as when the social aspects of proposed new legislation on immigration were examined in her committee, she obtained access to documents she would not otherwise have seen. On one such occasion she photographed an entire document dealing with the government's priorities and future plans which ran to twenty pages: it obviously would be of interest to the Centre.

All of this documentation she reduced to micro-dots and despatched in the manner she had been instructed. This involved a good deal of work at night in her dark-room, but in time she found that she could complete the task in about half the time it had taken her at first. While Marc often slept in her house, he seldom arrived much before midnight. His Ministerial duties, particularly when the House of Commons was sitting, meant late hours. Only weekends seemed relatively free when he was in Ottawa. She found these arrangements gave her time to carry out her photography.

A year passed quickly for Heide. Her relationship with Marc Grandpre suited her although Marc increasingly raised the question of marriage, a step she was not prepared to contemplate even if their respective marital arrangements had made it possible. He argued that his wife was willing to have a divorce and he saw no reason why she should remain married to Armand.

"Get a divorce. Hell you wouldn't have difficulty finding grounds for it. I hear that he wants to leave External Affairs and move to

Quebec City. I gather there are serious doubts about his loyalty. Christ, that woman has him eating out of her hand."

Heide managed to elude his efforts to pin her down. She enjoyed his company and found his comments on his work, his Cabinet colleagues, officials and others interesting. She memorized as much as she thought would be valuable to Viktor Aleksandrovich when next she met him.

After nearly a year on the job, her big chance came. She was approached by the Deputy-Secretary to the Cabinet to take on a new job. The Secretary to the Cabinet Committee on Security and Intelligence had taken ill and there was an urgent need to find a replacement. It had been suggested by several ministers that she might take on the job of acting as Secretary until a permanent replacement could be found. It would mean more work since she would also have to continue as Secretary of the committee dealing with social affairs. As she knew they were very short-handed at the moment; two and three committees being serviced by the same person. And, of course, since the Prime Minister was the Chairman of the Cabinet Committee on Security and Intelligence, it did not meet as often as other committees. Moreover, its meetings could be scheduled in such as way as to avoid conflict with her other work, unless, of course, some urgent problem arose. He smiled.

"As you can imagine, that is unlikely to happen often. It is not the most active committee we have. I hope you can take it on Heide. I am sure the PM would appreciate it."

She hesitated only for as long as decency demanded. Weeks later she was approached by the Privy Council Office security officer to complete a new set of Personal History forms.

"A routine requirement Mrs. Latour. Your new job will require access to a good deal of sensitive material. The rules require an up-date to your Top Secret security clearance. When you have completed the forms bring them to my office. What? Yes, it is a bit urgent, since properly speaking we should have done this before you took on the job. I was away taking a French immersion course and some of the routine work piled up."

No meetings of the committee were scheduled for the first couple of months, which gave Heide a chance to read minutes and documents pertaining to previous meetings, many of which she photographed. She also photographed almost all of the documents being assembled for future meetings. One of these, a resumé of Soviet and Soviet Bloc espionage activities over a five year period, would, she knew, be of the greatest interest to the Centre. She had found the document fascinating. She was surprised both at the extent of the Centre's activities and the degree to which they were known to the RCMP Security Service. She hoped that their knowledge of 'illegals' was not as good as their knowledge of agents operating under diplomatic cover.

Her first meetings with the committee, on the other hand were disappointing. They never got beyond the first two items, dealing with the protection of diplomats in Canada and the classification of papers. They never discussed the paper on espionage activities or any of the other items. She had found it particularly difficult to render the rambling, often incoherent, discussion into a sensible account of what had taken place and what had been decided. By comparison, her social affairs committee was a model of precision and clarity. She was surprised when the Secretary to the Cabinet accepted her first draft of her first meeting, changing only a few words in the decision to make it even less precise.

"That's fine Heide. I suggest you circulate the decision after I get the P.M.'s okay."

Where formerly she had been denied access to some kinds of classified material she now found she was able to see almost everything pertaining to the work of the Cabinet Secretariat. In some ways she found this new situation frustrating since it called for the exercise of restraint in selecting material to photograph for the Centre. She would like to have continued photographing everything, as she had done at first, but that would have been impossible to handle and dangerous to attempt. She concentrated on the various products of the intelligence community which came into her hands and the material of a similar nature which derived from Canada's relationships abroad. She had been surprised at the enormous volume of material and the broad scope of the subject matter; military, economic, scientific and foreign relations in its many aspects. She told Brad that she had been on the point of asking Lavrov to provide her with a cutout who could supply her with cameras disguised as lighters when she had discovered the truth of her father's demise. After that her enthusiasm for the job waned. She continued to select material though now, she declared, she deliberately avoided anything that would benefit the KGB as an organization.

"O.K., Heide, that will have to do us. We won't be able to continue until after the President's visit."

"You know Marc has invited me to the State Dinner. Should I go? It won't be easy."

"We are aware he asked you. We see no objection."

"I need a break. The tension has been high in the house and I need to spend some time with Paul. Just a few days. Is it possible that he and I could go away after the dinner? We could visit his grandmother in Quebec City."

Brad played for time.

"I'll have to clear that with my superiors."

* * * * * * * * * * * * * * * * * * * *

By the time Heide and Patricia had returned home from the interrogation, Janet and Paul had eaten dinner. Heide suggested that Janet might like to take time off since she and Patricia would be staying in. Janet accepted the offer and decided to go to a movie. After she left Heide and Patricia ate and then went straight to bed. Heide pleading a headache.

Patricia read for a few hours, turning her light off about midnight. She awoke from a deep sleep and noted from the luminous dial of her wristwatch that it was twenty-five after three. She was uncertain what had caused her to awaken. Normally she was a light sleeper. As she lay in bed thinking over the day's events she heard a muffled sound from the opposite end of the house.

Light from a lamp in the street filtered through the curtained windows. With great care she made her way in her bare feet to the door, and opened it noiselessly. Her eyes became used to the increased darkness of the hallway. At the end of the long corridor a faint crack of light seeped from under the door leading to the stairway to the attic. She did not dare risk approaching closer. She waited, finding her vigil increasingly cold without slippers or dressing gown. Twenty minutes later the light was suddenly extinguished.

Patricia carefully closed her door and gratefully climbed back into her bed. It could only have been Heide in the attic. What could she have been doing there at four in the morning and how long had she been there? She could only speculate. It would be for Brad to decide on the meaning of the strange event and what to do about it. When she told him the next day, his reaction was immediate.

"Thanks Patricia. Do nothing at all. I'll let J.B. know at once. I'm sure he will agree to the boys going in for another look."

FOURTEEN

The TAP flight from Lisbon put down at Montreal's Mirabel airport three-quarters of an hour late, and disgorged a full load of sun-tanned travellers. Many were wearing rakish straw hats and brightly printed cotton shirts. Some were carrying carefully wrapped parcels of Portuguese pottery and most also were carrying plastic bags containing duty-free liquor.

The crowd of passengers pressed towards the customs areas, slowly forming lines before the dozen-odd booths where the immigration officers were examining passports. In the first of these lines was a tall, handsome, suntanned man wearing a light tan sports jacket, an open-neck yellow shirt and pale blue cotton trousers. He had a raincoat over his arm. It was difficult to judge his age; probably between fifty-five and sixty-five. Despite his holiday garb he had a military bearing about him.

When his turn came he stepped quickly forward, carying a brown paper parcel carefully tied with hemp and a plastic bag containing a bottle of Canadian rye whisky. He presented his Canadian passport. The immigration officer compared the photograph in the passport with its holder and leafed through the pages;

Name; Edwin Gustav Kern
Birthdate; Steinback, Man.
Sex; M
Height; 186 cm.
Hair; Grey
Eyes; Grey

"How long have you been out of Canada?"
"Two weeks. Had a great holiday but it's nice to be home."
He smiled, the sunburn accentuating the laugh lines about his eyes.
"Anything to declare?"
"Only these."
He held up the two parcels.
"Okay."
The immigration officer stamped the passport and handed it back.

"Next."

After surrendering the customs colour card which he had been given, the man picked up his suitcase from the luggage carousel and walked past the customs officers at the exit, unchallenged. He caught the next bus to Montreal, where he made his way to a large, downtown hotel.

"I'd like a room for one night, and I'd like to pre-pay in case you're busy when I want to check out tomorrow."

A bored reception clerk pushed a registration card across the desk.

"Okay. Leave us a forwarding address."

"Is there any mail for me?"

"What's the name?"

"Lewis, John Lewis. L-e-w-i-s."

After a moment the reception clerk returned with a brown manila envelope.

"Here you are, Mr. Lewis. It was left at the desk this morning."

In his room the man checked the contents of the envelope. Satisfied, he undressed quickly and took a shower. In the shower he carefully scrubbed off the suntan. When he was dry he deftly fitted a trim grey moustache to his upper lip with a special gum resin. From his suitcase he took a shirt and tie and a dark grey, business suit. When he had finished dressing he helped himself to a drink of the rye, placed the bottle in the suitcase and carefully re-packed it. He stripped the bed-spread off, turned down the sheets and lay on the bed to give the appearance that it had been slept in. He placed the paper parcel on the floor, and, putting a foot on it, pressed until the cheap glass vase inside collapsed with a muffled cracking sound. He threw the parcel into the wastebasket.

Putting on his raincoat he made his way to the lobby, and out of the hotel, carrying his suitcase. He walked to the railway station, stopping en route to put the keys to his hotel room into a post box. At the station he bought a ticket to Ottawa, catching the train three quarters of an hour later.

In Ottawa he took a bus from the railway station to the centre of the city. He checked into the Grand Hotel on Sussex Drive opposite the old railway station, registering as Clive E. Ardrey, a salesman with an American sporting goods manufacturer.

The next morning he made his way to the Avis agency and rented a Chevrolet sedan, which he parked at the rear of the hotel. In his room he studied a map of Ottawa with care and concentration. He re-folded the map and placed it in the pocket of his raincoat.

He removed a black fountain-pen from his jacket, which was hanging on the back of the kitchen type wooden chair beside the bed. With infinite care he unscrewed the thick cap, resembling that of a Montblanc pen, and examined the slender steel cylinder inside. With a jeweller's screwdriver he removed a small screw at the base of the cap, which released a tiny hollow plastic plug. From the plug he shook loose a small, red pill. He replaced the plug and tightened the screw holding it in place.

He ran the cold water tap at the small sink in the room and filled one of the cheap tumblers. He placed the pill in his mouth and washed it down with the water.

He replaced the cap on the pen as carefully as he had removed it, and put the pen back in his jacket pocket. From the brown suitcase on the bed he removed a small plastic inhaler and placed it in the left-hand pocket of his jacket.

He crossed himself in the Orthodox manner, not so much out of religious conviction, but rather, because of superstition. A feeling that it did no harm to take precautions. Had his daughter seen him, she would have been surprised and perplexed. Had Zagorin been present he would have been alarmed.

He checked the contract for the rented Chevrolet sedan, packed his suitcase with deliberation and descended to the front desk, where he paid his bill in cash.

* * * * * * * * * *   * * * * * * * * *

Air Force One put down at Ottawa international airport within a minute of its estimated time of arrival. The huge plane taxied to the military section of the airport, where the Governor-General, the Prime Minister and a gaggle of Cabinet Miniters and officials were on hand to greet their distinguished visitor. The area was swarming with plainclothesmen and uniformed police. A minimum amount of time was taken up with ceremony. Brief speeches were made for the benefit of the press and the television cameras. Within minutes after his speech ended and the appropriate replies had been made, the President and his party were en route to Government House, preceded and followed by motorcycle police. Overhead, an Armed Forces helicopter watched the progress of the cavalcade.

The line of cars swept through the grey stone and wrought-iron grille gates of Government House and up the winding driveway. On either side the extensive grounds were patrolled by police, some with dogs. Brad was riding in the second-last car with J.B., Silas and Marshall Teller. The four of them would be meeting together later in the day. J.B. intended using the occasion to make a pitch for some sophisticated new eavesdropping equipment he had seen during a briefing session at The National Security Agency laboratories at Langley, Virginia. On the second day of the meetings while J.B. and Silas were closeted, Brad and Teller would meet. The formal agenda topic at the second meeting was listed as 'Co-operation in counter-espionage'. Both J.B. and Brad knew what that meant. Their American colleagues would be pressing for fuller access to all Canadian intelligence material. They had no doubt that high on the list would be the Opal file. The trick would be to retain control of the file and selection of the material that would be passed to the Americans while still getting the new listening device with its pocket-size parabolic dish antenna.

The previous day while rehearsing the arguments they would raise and the ones they would have to counter, Brad had taken the opportunity to raise with J.B. Heide's request to take a few days in Quebec City. He also filled him in on Patricia's report of Heide's pre-dawn visit to the attic.

"I think we should let her go. It would give us the chance we've been looking for to conduct a Level II search of the house. And I really want that attic taken apart."

J.B. didn't answer at once.

"O.K. Let her visit the Latours. When?"

"As soon as possible. How about right after the state dinner?"

"Right. You arrange the Level II search. I'll look after surveillance for her trip. Perhaps Patricia Haley should accompany her. I don't like the idea of her travelling alone with the boy — aside from anything else she's very vulnerable."

Later that day Brad told Heide of the decision. She agreed to Patricia Haley going along, but raised a practical difficulty.

"The Latour house is small. They have only two bedrooms. Patricia would have to stay at an hotel, which wouldn't meet your point, would it? Moreover, the Latours might think it a bid odd."

"I see what you mean. I'll give you the final word at the dinner tomorrow night. In the meantime, you and Paul can plan on going in any event."

When Brad raised the problem with J.B., he called together a special meeting of the XX Committee. There was a wrangle. While J.B. wanted her followed from Ottawa by the Watcher Service, other members of the Committee felt that was unncecesary. The presidential visit was straining resources and J.B. could either withdraw his approval of the trip or let her go without an elaborate tail. Even the argument that a Level II search was urgently needed, could not dissuade them. In the end a compromise was worked out. It was agreed that the Quebec City office would cover the Latour house during the time Heide and Paul were there. J.B. didn't like the decision, and made no attempt to hide his feelings.

All through the following day attention was concentrated on the meetings that surrounded the President's visit. While J.B., Brad, Silas and Teller met in J.B.'s office, the President, the Prime Minister and their respective ministers and senior officials met in the Prime Minister's residence, a stone's throw from Government House.

Outside, the grounds were patrolled and inside the RCMP and the Secret Service were everywhere, except in the rooms where the meetings were taking place. A direct line from the Command Centre to J.B.'s office was kept open at all times but was never used. The day passed without event. In the late afternoon, after the President returned to Government House for a rest before the State Dinner, Silas and Teller were driven to their respective accomodation; Silas to the Ambassador's residence and Teller to the government guest house at 7 Rideau Gate.

The guests began arriving at 7.30, each one carefully screened by the male and female operatives spread throughout the regular household staff. Brad saw Galena as she arrived in the company of Marc Grandpre. She was stunningly beautiful in a white evening gown. She wore no jewelery other than an intricately wrought, heavy gold necklace. Brad had to admit that she knew how to accentuate her best points; her hair and her figure. Just ahead of her in the receiving line was Marshall Teller.

"How convenient," Brad thought, "both my charges in one place. Too bad Teller doesn't know who she is, he would have a field day."

As Heide neared the President, the Governor General and their ladies, she caught Brad's eye and bowed imperceptibly and almost smiled. Turning her attention back to the line, her expression suddenly darkened. Brad followed her line of sight and saw that she was looking straight at Marshall Teller.

By the time Brad looked back at Heide her expession had changed again. She had turned away from Teller and was talking to Marc Grandpre as they waited to be introduced to the Governor General. Brad looked back to Teller. He had just finished going down the line. As he turned, his gaze fell on Heide. Whether he recognized her or whether the life-long bachelor merely had an eye for beautiful women, Brad could not be sure. What he was sure of was that Teller hesistated in his step and stared at Heide.

Brad was desperate to know what was going on. There was no opportunity that night. Heide was with Grandpre and would be going home with him to pack for an early start to Quebec City the next morning. Teller was already deep in conversation with one of the White House aides. His curiosity would have to wait until he picked Teller up at 7 Rideau Gate in the morning.

To the intense relief of the protective staff everything was moving without a hitch. For the rest of the evening Brad shared his attention between his two charges. Neither seemed concerned with the other. Only at the very end, as guests were leaving, did Teller seem to pay any attention to Heide. While Grandpre fetched her silk wrap, Teller approached her. They only had a few seconds together. Brad wished he were closer or that he had one of Teller's pocket-sized listening devices. Instead he would have to content himself that he now had a way to broach the subject.

The following morning an elderly housemaid at 7 Rideau Gate let Brad in. He had waited outside in the car for twenty minutes and Teller had not appeared.

"No, I don't know if Mr. Teller left the building. He didn't come down for breakfast. He's in the suite at the top of the stairs."

Brad mounted the stairs and knocked. There was no response. The door was locked. He returned to the maid to get a spare key. She was not happy about his reappearance.

"Why doesn't he organize his life a little better. First, his secretary needs the key. Then the man from the Embassy needs the key. Now you need the key."

Brad mounted the thickly carpeted stairs three at a time. Inside the suite everything was as it should be — except for one thing. Teller was in the bathtub. Dead.

"Christ!"

He felt the water. It was cold. So was Teller — cold and stiff. His head was under the water and his fists were clenched. Downstairs again, Brad cut the complaining maid short and demanded a telephone. After a short wait on the line he was put through to George McCain at headquarters.

"What's up, Brad. I thought you were meeting with Teller."

"It's difficult to meet with a corpse. Get Doc Bradley over to 7 Rideau Gate with a couple of your best men right away — discreetly. Then get word to J.B. that Teller is dead. As soon as you've done that make your way over here and take charge of your men."

When he hung up the telephone, Brad summoned one of the Mounties standing guard on the street outside and posted him at the door to the suite with instructions to let no one in. Next he questioned the maid about the two earlier visitors she had admitted to Teller's suite.

"The woman was the same one that was waiting for him when he first arrived yesterday. I think he called her Hazel or Hazelton or some such name. She must have been his secretary. She came while he was at meetings yesterday afternoon and picked up a briefcase for him."

Brad remembered the interruption at the previous days meetings while Teller called for some additional material he had left behind.

"And the man?"

"He arrived about 9:30 last night. The policeman outside had let him through, so I assumed he had a right to be here. He showed me his diplomatic pass from the American Embassy and said he had some papers for Mr. Teller. I offered to take them from him, but he insisted on handing them to Mr. Teller himself, so I let him wait in the suite."

"Were you around when Mr. Teller returned last night?"

"Yes."

"Did you tell him he had a visitor?"

"Yes. He didn't seem to mind."

"Anything unusual when he went upstairs?"

"No. About fifteen minutes later the other man left."

"Did you see him go?"

"Only his back. I came into the hall as he closed the door behind him."

Brad's questioning was interrupted by the arrival of the RCMP doctor and the men McCain had sent. He took them to the suite and sent the young constable back out onto the street.

"What do you make of it, Doc?"

"I would guess he has been dead about twelve hours. Probably cardiac arrest followed by drowning. There appears to be some fluid in the lungs. Can't tell the exact cause of death until an autopsy is done."

Minutes later J.B. and Silas arrived. Brad briefed them on what he had found out. Silas took charge.

"I don't like it. I can think of no reason for a visitor from the Embassy last night, but that can be checked. I want his death kept quiet for the time being. The President has to be told — and I guess your Prime Minister — but no one else. I want the body out of here without being opened up. We'll do the autopsy in Washington."

J.B. agreed. While Brad was left to clean up the details, the two heads of security went off to interrupt their masters. As J.B. described it later, the President had barely paused when told of the sudden death of his counter-espionage chief.

"Marshall was a great guy. Worked his butt off. Probably what killed him. Not much of a politician up front but brilliant behind the scenes. I don't know what I'll ever do without him. Silas, you look after the details. Now then, where were we?"

It took Silas about an hour, and several pre-noon bourbons and branch waters to decide the different aspects of the matter. Teller's body would be flown home on Air Force One with the President that evening. Brad would have the body stored in the cooler until dinner time and then packed in dry ice and put on the plane while the President was addressing the joint session of the Canadian Parliament in the evening. To make the necessary arrangements required the cutting of much red tape and a lot of telephoning. A death certificate was provided by Doc Bradley, a friendly coroner agreed to waive an inquest and the Ottawa Chief of Police agreed to forgo an investigation. A local undertaker, selected by J.B., looked after the body.

The security arrangements surrounding the appearance of the President on Parliament Hill were even tighter than those that had preceded them. Crowd control became a real problem. The event had been widely advertised, and the fine weather had brought the sun worshippers from the Mall to the Hill. The day passed without incident. Air Force One took off within ten minutes of the estimated time of departure. All concerned were vastly relieved. The security arrangements had been flawless. Only Teller's death marred the visit, and few knew about that.

It was on the tarmac waiting for the President that Brad finally found an opportunity to inform J.B. of his suspicion that Heide and Teller had recognized each other. J.B. immediately informed Silas.

"Where is she now? In custody?"

"No she is en route to visit her mother-in-law."

Silas said nothing. His expression suggested that he thought his Canadian colleagues had lost possession of their senses.

"We had to," J.B. explained. "She's promised to work for us, so we have to handle her with kid gloves. In the meantime we have to go through her house again."

He looked at his watch.

"In fact, our boys have been in there for almost twelve hours. If you will now get your man on that plane and clear out we can check on how well they've been doing."

Silas smiled.

"Sorry, J.B.. You do what you have to do. I'm just a little on edge."

With the great silver bird in the air Brad went with J.B. to his car.

"Find out what's happening, Brad."

From the mobile phone in the back seat Brad was patched through to George McCain. Heide and Paul had left for Quebec City, by car, about ten o'clock that morning. The nursemaid, Janet Brown, had left to catch the noon bus to Kingston, where she was to stay with friends for the weekend. The house had not stood vacant for long. By one that afternoon the team of ten had begun a painstaking search. Starting with the basement they worked their way up. They were just about to move into the attic and would work through the night or until they had finished.

"I want that attic taken apart."

"It will be, Brad."

The new day began badly. At six Brad was called by the head of the surveillance team and asked to come to headquarters for a report on the results of the search. The lower floors had yielded nothing new. At first the attic, too, had proven negative. The only suspicious feature had been strong metal readings in the brick chimney, where it passed through to the roof. After taking the chimney apart, literally brick by brick, they had discovered only an old cast iron flu, which had been out of use for years. Further searches revealed nothing. They had even pried up the entire plywood flooring, under which had been laid batts of insulation. They were about to give the whole area a clean bill of health, when a pass by a metal detector over the body of a child's wooden hobby-horse registered a strong reading. One of the wooden runners of the toy horse had been splintered, and obviously it no longer could be used. It had been pushed into a corner of the attic with other toys, a sleigh, and several pairs of skis. Rather than damage the toy and leave evidence of their visit behind, the hobby-horse was removed to the R.C.M.P. laboratory. X-rays disclosed a concealed compartment in the horse's belly. Two hours later, they were ready to smash open the toy when at last they uncovered the locking mechanism. With each piece of the broken runner at right angles to the frame, pressure on the tail allowed the saddle to be swung open. Inside was a radio transmitting and receiving set. It was days later before the technical ingenuity of the set was fully appreciated, but even the preliminary findings were impressive. When set on 'automatic', the miniaturized equipment could send and receive high-grade cypher messages, in ultra-short burst transmissions. It was designed for use with batteries or from an 110/120 volt alternating current outlet. Observation demonstrated that the 'automatic' setting was synchronized to an orbiting communications satellite.

They also found a number of unused one-time cypher pads, lists of call signs, and tables set to twenty-four hour cycles, keyed to a five year calendar. On 'Manual', the equipment could be used to send and receive messages in morse code. It was calculated that by clipping the aerial lead to the metal clothes line, strung across the attic, it would be possible for short wave transmissions to be made and received over great distances.

Brad had no sooner passed on the bad news of the transmitter to J.B. when he received a telephone call from the surveillance team in Quebec City. They had the Latour house covered, but were uncertain whether Heide and Paul were there. There was no sign of her car, although she might have put it in a garage, since the street was too narrow for parking. They had made no direct inquiries in accordance with the instructions they had been given.

Brad cursed. He got the telephone number of the Latours. Posing as an External Affairs colleague, he quickly ascertained that, while Heide and Paul had been expected on Saturday night, they had not turned up. Madame Latour assumed that Heide had to postpone her trip for some reason. J.B.'s reaction to Brad's second report was explosive.

"Get an APB out on that car. Description, licence plate number, the works. Bloody Committee."

It was not until late that night that the Montreal office of the Security Service reported that the Montreal Harbour Police had located the car. It was found empty, with the keys still in the ignition, parked opposite Pier 11, on the docks. When Brad read the message to J.B. he reacted sharply.

"Pier 11?"

"That's what it says."

"Jesus. Isn't that the usual docking area for the *Pushkin*?"

A quick check with port authorities in Montreal established that the *M.S. Alexandr Pushkin* had sailed from Pier 11 at one o'clock on Saturday afternoon. They estimated the vessel by then was steaming in the Gulf of the St. Lawrence and would soon be in international waters. Next stop: Leningrad.

Technically the ship could be stopped and Heide seized. But to do so was certain to touch off an international row.

J.B. expelled his breath noisily.

"God Damn. The P.M. isn't going to like this one little bit. If that damn committee hadn't been so pig-headed perhaps this wouldn't have happened. I'd better tell him and try to get his agreement to tell our American and British friends. We're going to look like horse's asses to Silas."

J.B. saw the Prime Minister in his Centre Block office in the Houses of Parliament. To J.B.'s surprise, beyond an impatient shrug of his shoulders, the Prime Minister's reaction had been several minutes of silence. He rose from his chair to stand at the bay window, looking moodily across Parliament Hill to the lights of the U.S. Embassy. From experience J.B. knew better than to interrupt. Finally, the Prime Minister turned away from the window and faced him. His question caught J.B. by surprise.

"Where is the car?"

J.B. hesitated perceptibly, before answering.

"It was impounded by the RCMP and removed to one of our garages in Montreal. It was found on Federal property — in our jurisdiction."

"Good. Were she and Latour divorced or separated?"

"Separated, I believe, although I think she has started divorce proceedings."

"Check, will you. Before tomorrow morning."

The Prime Minister sat down and crossed his legs.

"I intend to call a special meeting of the Cabinet Committee on Security and Intelligence, early tomorrow morning. I would like you there. We will have a number of decisions to take. In the meantime arrange to have that car moved to Ottawa in a closed van, and stored in a secure garage. Good. By the way, you and the Secretary to the Cabinet will be the only officials present tomorrow. I do not want the meeting advertised. The secretary will let you know the time and the place, later tonight. Good night J.B."

The Prime Minister turned to the papers spread on the small table by his side. J.B. was familiar with this form of dismissal and withdrew quietly.

The meeting took place the next morning in one of the small conference rooms on the third floor of the Centre Block. A member of the House of Commons protective staff stood guard at the door.

J.B.'s arrival coincided with that of one of the two Ministers on the XX Committee. By the time the Prime Minister arrived seven of the eight Ministers on the committee were around the table. The two from the Double Cross committee sat together, and, to J.B.'s practiced eye, had an uneasy air about them. Of the others, three were reading newspapers, including J.B.'s own minister, one was working his way through an impressive pile of official papers requiring his signature, and the seventh, who reminded J.B. of Beau Brummel, was carefully re-tying a large, stylish, red bow tie. J.B. wondered how his minister would react when he learned about Opal and the fact that the whole affair had been kept from him. He was glad responsibility for the decision had been the Prime Minister's and not his.

A boyhood memory of coloured prints which hung in his uncle's law office flashed across J.B.'s mind. A dozen dogs, sitting about a table, playing poker. In one of the prints a Scottish sheep-dog was holding an ace of spades with a hind paw, passing it behind the back of his neighbour, an Alsatian, to an Irish terrier on the other side. Before J.B. could decide which Ministers resembled which dog, the Prime Minister, with the Secretary to the Cabinet on his right, tapped lightly on the table with his silver pen.

"Gentlemen. We have a quorum. I suggest we begin."

The minister signing papers kept on, without looking up. Two ministers kept reading their newspapers. J.B.'s minister folded his newspaper carefully. The others waited somewhat inattentively. J.B.'s eye caught three flies buzzing beneath the globe lamp hung from the high ceiling. He wondered idly which fly was Baron von Richtofen; probably the one with wings like a bi-plane. His day-dreaming was interrupted by the Prime Minister's voice.

"Gentlemen. I am sorry we have to meet on such short notice. As you will note the only officials present are the Secretary of the Cabinet and the Head of the Security Service. The reasons for that will become apparent. I have instructed that no minutes be kept of this meeting, and I do not intend to raise the matter in full Cabinet. I would ask that each of you refrain from discussing the subject matter of the meeting with anyone outside this group."

J.B. noted with amusement that the Prime Minister now had their full attention. With a slight smile the Prime Minister continued.

"Two of my colleagues here today are familiar with what I am about to tell you, since they have been serving on a small committee known as the Opal Double Cross Committee, which I established a short time ago. I have restricted attendance by officials since the decisions we may take are likely to be based, in part at least, on partisan considerations. I intend to speak personally to each of the officals not present who have been involved in the work of the committee. Among other things, I intend to remind them of the provisions of the Official Secrets Act and their oaths of office."

Before the Prime Minister could continue the door was opened by the member of the Commons protective staff guarding the door, to admit Magnus Kettle.

"Sorry to be late Prime Minister. We were thin on the ground on the joint Senate-Commons committee and I couldn't leave until I was replaced by a member of our party."

"I understand, Magnus. The others can fill you in on the details of what we have discussed so far. I might say though that the essence of what I have said is that if word of this meeting or what transpires at it leaks out, the person responsible will find himself unemployed — and unemployable."

J.B. was amused at the response. Magnus Kettle, representing a southern Ontario riding, was one of the youngest members of the Cabinet. He never seemed able to arrive on time for any meeting, and managed always to give a breathless, theatrical air to his late appearances. On this occasion, his role playing evaporated. He slid quietly into the empty chair and riveted his attention on his leader. He was not alone. Even the flies around the chandelier had stopped their dog-fight. The Prime Minister continued as if there had been no interruption.

"Gentlemen. We have a problem. The Secretary of this Committee, Mrs. Heide Latour, was discovered, not long ago, to be a spy — an agent of a foreign power — the Russians."

J.B. heard a low whistle to his left, followed by a single word, 'Christ', which echoed around the room. He was unable to identify the author. His own minister made no sound, but glowered at him from across the table. Appeasing him would not be easy.

The Prime Minister proceeded in his dry, matter-of-fact tone to lay before his colleagues the full story of Operation Opal; of Galena's discovery, her 'doubling' and her flight to the Soviet Union. No other noise could be heard in the room. The silences between the Prime Minister's measured words were deafening. He finished speaking and looked around.

"Comments gentlemen?"

Several ministers spoke at once. Beau Brummel, whose political acumen matched his sartorial splendor, won out.

"Why in hell didn't the RCMP keep her under surveillance?"

His question was met by silence. J.B. stirred.

"Prime Minister. Perhaps I could be permitted to answer?"

"Go ahead J.B."

"When it was agreed that Opal could visit her in-laws in Quebec with her son Paul, I suggested that she be accompanied by the woman operative who had been stationed in her house from the time we first picked her up. When this proved impossible, because of the lack of accommodation in the Latour house, I wanted Opal covered by a full surveillance team for the journey from Ottawa to Quebec City. I was over-ruled. The XX Committee felt that such surveillance was unnecessary. Instead, discreet coverage of the Latour house in Quebec city was arranged. It is not certain that a surveillance team would have prevented her escape. She was a very experienced agent and might have given us the slip. However, it would have made her plans more complicated and, even if surveillance had not prevented her escape, it would certainly have given us earlier notice that something was amiss."

There was a long silence. The two Ministers on the XX Committee looked uncomfortable, and managed to avoid the glances of their colleagues.

The Prime Minister broke the silence.

"Not much point in worrying about past mistakes. The fact is that the woman appears to have returned to Russia with her son, and their sudden dissappearance faces us with a serious problem. Given the sensitive nature of the jobs she has held, and particularly as Secretary of this Committee, and, her — ah — close relationship with one of our colleagues, public knowledge that she was a Russian spy could seriously damage the country and the government."

The Prime Minister paused and looked around the table. No one spoke, He continued.

"It appears to me there are two practical alternative ways of dealing with the problem; make a statement to the House of Commons, disclosing the facts of the case, or, provide some credible public explanation of her disappearance, which avoids disclosure of the true facts. Anyone care to comment?"

A Minister spoke.

"The first alternative would be political suicide, given our minority position in the House."

The PM did not wait for further discussion.

"Exactly my feelings, Harry. Instead, I propose that her disappearance be attributed to an accident to her car, the gas tank of which would have exploded, causing the vehicle to dissolve in a pillar of fire. The accident, of course, would have taken place on Saturday morning, the actual date of her departure for Russia."

"The car, and the remains of two bodies found in it, would be so badly burned that proper identification would take time, accounting for the interval between the accident and announcement of the tragic deaths of Mrs. Latour and her son."

The Prime Minister stopped and looked around the table. Several Ministers tried to speak at once. The Prime Minister held up his hands, palms outward.

"Gentleman. Hear me through. Mrs. Latour's car was discovered by the National Harbour Board Police in Montreal, a federal agency. The ignition keys were found in the car. However, except for the license plates there was no other means of identifying the owner immediately. Fortunately, and no doubt to confuse any would-be followers, before abandoning her car, Mrs. Latour removed the car registration and the insurance papers and everything else with her name on it. Shortly after its discovery the car was removed by the RCMP to one of their garages in Montreal. Neither the Montreal City Police nor the Sureté Quebec have been involved."

"Yesterday, I gave instructions to have Mrs. Latour's car removed to Ottawa in a closed van, for storage in a secure RCMP garage. This was done. Therefore, there is no reason for the Montreal Police, or anyone else, to connect the car discovered on the waterfront last Saturday with Mrs. Latour's car, destroyed in an accident in the Ottawa area, on the same day."

The Prime Minister turned to J.B.

"I assume your people can make the necessary arrangements?"

J.B. did not reply at once. When he did he spoke slowly and clearly.

"I believe something along the lines you have outlined could be arranged. However, it may be difficult to act without the help of others. I think our relations with the other police forces who might be involved, and the military are good enough that we can count on their cooperation. This would be especially true if I am authorized to indicate to everyone who might have to be involved that important matters of national security are at stake."

The Prime Minister said nothing. When nobody else sought to speak, he resumed.

"An account of the death of Mrs. Latour and her son, in the circumstances I have suggested, should satisfy even those who were closest to her: the Latours senior, her estranged husband, Armand, and the nursemaid, Janet Brown. None of these would venture to question the story.

"What I propose would result in mental anguish for the Latours senior, which is regrettable. However, it would be no greater than the mental anguish they would suffer from knowing the truth. Armand Latour does not seem much interested, these days, in either his wife or his son. None of the few friends who knew her well, and those who did not, are likely to doubt the story. It should be possible also to arrange matters so that her casual acquaintances among members of the Fourth Estate would have no cause for suspicion.

"As for the Russians, my guess is they would interpret an announcement of her 'accidental death' as being to their advantage, which, incidentally, might not be the case if we were to publicize the true story. Indeed if we were to publicize the truth as we know it, they might feel compelled to retaliate, possibly by revealing Marc Grandpre's involvement in a manner the government might find very embarrassing.

"As for Marc, I saw him earlier this morning. We discussed the situation very fully."

The Prime Minister placed the tips of the fingers of his hands together in an ecclesiastical gesture, to which he managed to impart a sense of mockery.

"Marc Grandpre is a staunch supporter of the Party. He offered to resign from the Cabinet. I told him that, in the circumstances, and with deep regret, I would accept the offer. He will be announcing his decison tomorrow, giving ill health as the reasons. He will say the ear infection, which some of you may remember he suffered some time ago, has resulted in a form of Ménières's disease; the symptoms being vertigo, and, — ah — a certain loss of balance."

J.B. sitting directly opposite the Prime Minister could detect not the slightest change of expression on his face or in his voice. Yet J.B. had the eerie impression he had smiled.

"The bloody hypocrite", thought J.B. "He wouldn't hesitate to slit his mother's throat, if it suited his purpose."

"Unofficially, he will let it be known amongst the press that without Heide he cannot carry on."

The Prime Minister fell silent. A Minister, not a member of the XX Committee, spoke.

"Prime Minister. What you are suggesting makes sense, at least in political terms. Perhaps it also makes sense in terms of national security. I would like to hear J.B.'s views on that score. However, I have been wondering why we didn't proceed against her as soon as it was discovered she was a spy? Surely, such a course of action might have avoided the fix in which we now find ourselves?"

"I'm glad you raised the question François. In fact, had we acted as you suggest, we would still have been faced with the same problem. That is to say, if we had arrested and charged Mrs. Latour for espionage, the matter inevitably would have become public. Moreover, in some ways it would have been worse, since her spying activities and her involvement with Marc Grandpre would have become public, bit by agonizing bit, through the slow process of the courts. By attempting to get her to work for us we sought to avoid publicity. At the same time we had hoped to lessen the damage which she undoubtedly did to us over many years. Perhaps J.B. can answer your question about the national security aspects of the matter."

J.B. cleared his throat.

"Well, Prime Minister, there is no doubt that if the affair becomes public, the damage done to our extensive and sensitive relationships with various foreign security and intelligence agencies, within and outside NATO would be considerable. We are very dependent upon these relations. Only the British and Americans are aware of Operation Opal. Their help has been invaluable.

"The fact that Opal was discovered by the Security Service, and our temporary success in 'doubling' her would give us some kudos with foreign agencies. However, the fact that she was able to operate against us for so long, undetected, would scare some of them off. They would not likely suspend their relations with us. Nothing quite so crude. They might however, withhold their more sensitive and valuable intelligence material. More important they might procrastinate when next we seek their active help in counter-espionage and other operations. Thus, years of effort spent in patiently building up their confidence in us would be dissipated.

"I should add that, while we have nothing more concrete to go on than disturbing increases in suspected agent communications traffic in the Eastern seaboard area, and a recent defector's report, there is the possibility that Opal may not have been the only 'sleeper' to successfully infiltrate the Canadian government. Anything which impedes our investigations on this score would be unfortunate. Public disclosure of the facts of Operation Opal could result in a drying up of the few promising leads we have begun to develop."

J.B. stopped.

"Sorry for being so long-winded, Prime Minister."

"Don't apologize J.B. I'm sure my colleagues found solace in the thought that there are other than purely political reasons for not making public the truth about Mrs. Latour's unfortunate disapperance."

The meeting reached a consensus in favour of the Prime Minister's approach. At the Prime Minister's suggestion, J.B. and Beau Brummel walked along the corridor to his Centre Block office.

"Well, J.B. The sooner the better."

"I understand Prime Minister. However, we did not discuss modalities. There are foreseeable risks. Everything will have to be done in a hell of a hurry. It could become messy."

Beau Brummel spoke.

"Yes, J.B. It could become messy. However, if it does, you will understand we would have to deny all knowledge of the affair."

The Prime Minister seemed not to have heard the comment. With difficulty J.B. suppressed a sigh, and the temptation to observe that the days of the heroes found in the turn of the century books by G.A. Hentey, were long since gone. Instead, he kept his mouth shut. They parted.

The story, carried by the wire services, did not make the front pages of the daily newspapers or any of the national radio or television newscasts.

"The badly charred remains of two bodies, believed by the RCMP to be those of Mrs. Heide Latour and her young son, Paul, were found in an automobile, subsequently established as belonging to her. The car, apparrently skidded on a patch of oil, crashed into a concrete abuttment close to the headquarters of RCMP 'N' Division last Saturday.

"Police believe the car had a fully loaded gas tank, which exploded when the rear end slammed into a concrete abutment. The car disintegrated and was completely demolished by fire. It took firefighters from 'N' Division, and the nearby Armed Forces base at Rockliffe over three-quarters of an hour to extinguish the blaze.

"It is known that Mrs. Latour and her son were enroute to visit her family in QuebecCity at the time of the tragic accident.

"An ecumenical memorial service is to be held for Mrs. Latour and her son, in the auditorium of the External Affairs building in Ottawa, at a date and time to be announced."

FIFTEEN

As the *MS Alexandr Pushkin* passed from Canadian territory into international waters it was joined by a Russian 'K' class destroyer. The Captain of the *Pushkin*, Vladimir Petrovitch Klimov and the senior political officer, Valeri Mikhailovitch Churilin, were in the Captain's quarters. Surprisingly spacious, and decorated in a style reminiscent of paddle-wheel steamers on the Mississippi in the 1800s, the room looked festive. A table, spread with a fine linen cloth, was laid for five. A waiter in a spotless white jacket, was making last minute preparations, adjusting the wine glasses and a magnificent bunch of red roses arranged in a silver bowl in the centre of the table. On a mahogany side-table were small glasses, an ice-cold bottle of Vodka, and a large open tin of Caspian caviar.

There was a knock on the door. The waiter opened it.

"Ah, my friends. Welcome to my cabin. Welcome to my ship. May I introduce Valeri Michailovitch Churilin. Galena Nadya Gribanov, General Anatoli Gribanov, and Paul Gribanov. Come, let us drink."

At the end of the dinner the Captain signalled the waiter to leave them.

"My friends. I have a surprise. I have been instructed by the Supreme Soviet to confer upon you, Galena Nadya, and you, General Gribanov, these decorations in recognition of your outstanding services to the State over a period of many years; the Red Banner Order, First degree."

Captain Klimov presented the decorations in the red velvet lined leather boxes in which they came. He embraced them heartily, as did the political officer, Churilin. The four of them stood, raised their glasses and tossed down the vodka.

"To the Motherland."

At the end of the table, Paul choked on the vodka. Galena looked at the child she had borne who was now becoming a man. He had followed her unquestioningly into this voyage to the unknown. She knew the questions that must be in his mind and hoped he would ask them and that she would be able to answer them. But not tonight. Tonight was for Galena and Anatoli.

Later, after they had taken a rather bibulous leave of Captain Klimov, father and daughter talked into the early hours of the morning. There was so much to say. Among many other things, Galena learned that she was to be transferred from the First Chief Directorate to the Fourth Department of the Second Chief Directorate. She was happy. In Moscow they would be together.

* * * * * * * * * * * * * * * * * * * *

The Prime Minister had made no objection to informing the British and the Americans about Galena's disappearance. To everyone's surprise, there was no reaction from Washington, and only a polite telegram of sympathy from J.B.'s opposite number in London. Two days later J.B. received a series of telegrams from the Security Service representative in Washington, which explained the lack of American reaction. The first was waiting for him when he arrived in the morning.

"FROM: SS REP WASH. TOP SECRET
TO: DIRECTOR-GENERAL U.S.-CAN EYES ONLY
PRIORITY

"CANNING, FBI REP ON INTERDEPTL. TEAM INVESTIGATING MARSHALL TELLER'S DEATH TOLD ME YESTERDAY IN 'STRICTEST CONFIDENCE', THERE ARE A NUMBER OF PUZZLING ASPECTS TO THE CASE.
"AUTOPSY SHOWS DEATH DUE CARDIAC ARREST, WITH DROWNING A SECONDARY CAUSE.
"TELLER, A BACHELOR, WITH APPARENTLY NO LIVING RELATIVES, HAD SMALL HOUSE GEORGETOWN. SEARCH HOUSE REVEALED THREE PUZZLING ANOMALIES: (A) FOLDER OF NEWSPAPER CLIPPINGS, SEVERAL MONTHS OLD, CONCERNING ALLEGED MURDER IN SOVIET PSYCHIATRIC HOSPITAL OF ANNA VASSILIEV SMIRNOV, NOTED RUSSIAN POET. STORIES DATE-LINED STOCKHOLM AND COPENHAGEN, QUOTED WELL KNOWN, RECENTLY EXILED SOVIET DISSIDENT WRITER AS SAYING THAT WHILE INCARCERATED IN PSYCHIATRIC HOSPITAL RUN BY KGB NEAR LENINGRAD, HE HAD LEARNED THAT ANNA SMIRNOV HAD DIED IN SAME HOSPITAL, WHILE UNDERGOING TREATMENT FOR ALLEGED SCHIZOPHRENIA, (B) SLIM VOLUME WRITTEN IN RUSSIAN, ANNA SMIRNOV'S POETRY, FROM WHICH FLY-LEAF HAD BEEN REMOVED, (C) KEY FOR YALE DEAD-BOLT LOCK WHICH FITS NONE OF THE LOCKS IN THE HOUSE OR TELLER'S OFFICE.
"USING SOPHISTICATED TECHNOLOGY THEY HAVE BEEN ABLE TO RECONSTRUCT INSCRIPTION ON FLY-LEAF OF SMIRNOV BOOK, BY LIFTING IT FROM SUCCEEDING PAGE. WRITTEN IN CYRILLIC SCRIPT, INSCRIPTION READ: '194(?) —MOEM(U) LYUBIM(OMU) SYN(U) Y(U)RY(U)' EXPERTS BELIEVE ENGLISH TRANSLATION TO BE, 'TO

MY BELOVED YURI'.

"CANNING WOULD NOT REPEAT NOT SPECULATE ON POSSIBLE
SIGNIFICANCE ANOMALIES. HE DID SAY THAT GIVEN TELLER'S
SENSITIVE POSITION, PRESIDENT HAS ORDERED FULL-SCALE TOP
PRIORITY INVESTIGATION HIS BACKGROUND AND BONA FIDES."

J.B. glanced at his list of appointments. The entire morning was
booked. He buzzed his secretary and told her to set up a meeting with
Brad Randall in the early afternoon. Before the meeting took place, a
second message had arrived from Washington.

"FROM: SS REP WASH. TOP SECRET
TO: DIRECTOR-GENERAL U.S. CAN EYES ONLY
FLASH
"CANNING INFORMED ME THIS MORNING THERE ARE DOUBTS
ABOUT IDENTITY OF MAN BEARING TELLER'S NAME.
"MARSHALL TELLER JOINED R.C.A.F. IN 1940, SERVING OVERSEAS
WITH R.A.F. BOMBER SQUADRON. HE TRANSFERRED IN BRITAIN, IN
1944, TO 8TH U.S.A.F. FLYING FORTRESS, OF WHICH HE WAS CREW
MEMBER, WAS SHOT DOWN OVER DRESDEN IN 1945. HE AND
SURVIVING CREW MEMBERS TAKEN PRISONER BY GERMANS. WHEN
RUSSIAN TROOPS OVERRAN PW CAMP, TELLER AND OTHER
PRISONERS REMOVED TO SOVIET UNION. REPATRIATION ARRANGED
ONLY AFTER PROLONGED NEGOTIATION AND DELAYS.
"UPON RETURN USA TELLER DISCHARGED RANK MAJOR. USING
VETERANS   BENEFITS TELLER COMPLETED UNIVERSITY
EDUCATION NYU, CORNELL AND HARVARD. AT LATTER HE BECAME
PROFESSOR, FACULTY POLITICAL SCIENCE. SUBSEQUENTLY HE
BECAME VERY ACTIVE POLITICALLY, REGISTERING AS A
DEMOCRAT. CANNING SAID VARIOUS THEORIES BEING EXAMINED.
IN HIS VIEW, MOST LIKELY ONE BEING THAT MAJOR TELLER, USAF,
WAS REPLACED BY KGB 'SLEEPER'. FILES FOR PERIOD SHOW MANY
US PW'S REMOVED TO SOVIET UNION WERE REPEATEDLY
INTERROGATED AND SOME WERE SEGREGATED ON GROUNDS THEY
REQUIRED MEDICAL TREATMENT. MAJOR TELLER WAS ONLY CHILD
OF PARENTS WHO EMIGRATED FROM EUROPE AFTER WORLD WAR I.
BOTH PARENTS KILLED AUTOMOBILE ACCIDENT, PASADENA,
CALIFORNIA, IN 1939. TELLER, THEREFORE, WOULD HAVE
PRESENTED NKVD WITH EXACTLY THE OPPORTUNITY THEY WERE
SEEKING. PRESUMABLY IF SUBSTITUTION WAS MADE, THE REAL
MARSHALL TELLER WAS LIQUIDATED."

This message was followed almost immediately by another.

"FROM: SS REP WASH. TOP SECRET
TO: DIRECTOR-GENERAL US-CAN EYES ONLY
FLASH
"CANNING HAS GIVEN ME ADDITIONAL FACTS TELLER CASE
(CODENAMED LOCKSTITCH), EXPLAINING BASIS THEIR JUDGEMENT
MAN KILLED OTTAWA NOT REPEAT NOT MARSHALL TELLER. WHEN
TELLER WAS FIRST GIVEN SECURITY CLEARANCE CANADIAN
AUTHORITIES PROVIDED FBI WITH HIS FINGERPRINTS, TAKEN FROM
RCAF RECORDS. SINCE THESE PRINTS MATCHED THOSE ON
TELLER'S SECURITY CLEARANCE APPLICATION, NO DOUBTS WERE
RAISED. CURRENT INVESTIGATION, BASED ON DENTAL RECORDS,
HAS ESTABLISHED BEYOND DOUBT, THAT MAN MURDERED OTTAWA
WAS NOT REPEAT NOT MARSHALL TELLER. IN CIRCUMSTANCES US
AUTHORITIES BELIEVE ORIGINAL TELLER FINGERPRINTS RECORDS
WERE REMOVED AND REPLACED WITH FINGERPRINTS DEAD MAN,
PROBABLY DURING 1950's.
"DURING AUTOPSY, DENTAL EXPERTS NOTICED UNUSUAL EARLY
DENTAL WORK. INTENSIVE INVESTIGATION LOCATED PASADENA
DENTIST WHO TREATED MARSHALL TELLER IMMEDIATELY PRIOR
TO WORLD WAR II. ALTHOUGH NO LONGER IN PRACTICE, HE HAD
RETAINED RELEVANT DENTAL RECORDS. COMPARISON
ESTABLISHED BEYOND DOUBT THAT JAW AND TEETH OF MAN
KILLED IN OTTAWA WERE NOT REPEAT NOT THOSE OF MARSHALL
TELLER. US AUTHORITIES NOW BELIEVE MAN WHO DIED IN OTTAWA
WAS YURI SMIRNOV, ONLY SON OF ANNA SMIRNOV, WHO HAD BEEN
INTRODUCED INTO US AS A KGB 'SLEEPER', USING MARSHALL
TELLER'S IDENTITY. THEY BELIEVE HE MAY HAVE BEEN ACTIVATED
AFTER JOINING THE OFFICE OF THE PRESIDENTIAL ADVISER ON
NATIONAL SECURITY AFFAIRS. THE US AUTHORITIES SPECULATE
KGB AGENT SMIRNOV, POSING AS TELLER MAY HAVE BEEN
PLANNING TO DEFECT AND KGB HAD GOT WIND OF HIS INTENTION.
THEY DECIDED TO LIQUIDATE HIM AND MAKE HIS DEATH APPEAR
DUE TO NATURAL CAUSES.
"THE THEORY BEING ADVANCED BY THE AMERICANS IS THAT THE
MAN POSING AS TELLER HAD BEEN MURDERED IN HIS SUITE AT 7
RIDEAU GATE, PROBABLY BY A PRUSSIC ACID PENCIL GUN. TO USE
SUCH A WEAPON THE ASSASSIN WOULD HAVE HAD TO INGEST A
PILL SHORTLY BEFORE USING THE WEAPON, AND TO HAVE
INHALED AN ANTIDOTE IMMEDIATELY AFTER ADMINISTERING THE
POISON. A SIMILAR WEAPON IS KNOWN TO HAVE BEEN USED BY
THE KGB FOR ASSASSINATION ON THREE OTHER OCCASIONS."

When Brad arrived, J.B. handed him the three telegrams and
said,
"In all our hurry to cover the tracks, we forgot the first rule of the
game — to ask the reason why."

Brad took the telegrams. Before reading them, he reached into his jacket pocket, removed an envelope, put it to his nose as though to sniff its perfume and handed it to J.B.

"This might help."

As Brad started to read the telegrams, J.B. examined the envelope. In a fine but firm scroll it was addressed to Inspector Randall at RCMP Headquarters and marked Private and Personal. The postmark showed it had been mailed in Montreal the previous Saturday.

"Well, I'll be damned! Heide?"

Brad neither confirmed J.B.'s exclamation nor responded to his interrogative. Afterwards he would not have been sure that J.B. had said anything at all. He was too engrossed in the series of telegrams.

"I'll be damned! Teller?"

J.B. was equally oblivious to Brad's comment. He had extracted a single sheet of notepaper from the envelope.

"Dear Inspector,

In half an hour I'll be aboard the *Pushkin* and heading home. I hope my actions don't cause you too much difficulty for, though I can't say it was a pleasure getting to know you, if one has to undergo such an ordeal I would rather it was with someone as humane as you have been than with some of the goons I have met in our business — on both sides.

You don't have to search too deeply for my motives. Lavrov lied. My father is alive. Indeed, he has just finished a mission to Canada of which you will no doubt become aware. Paul and I will be sailing with him aboard the *Pushkin*. It will be good, once more, to be myself.

Yours,
Galena Nadya Gribanov"

* * * * * * * * * *   * * * * * * * * *

INTERNAL MEMORANDUM

SECURITY
CLASSIFICATION:
Top Secret
DISTRIBUTION:
Opal Indoctrinated
Only

FROM: Special Analysis Group (Merrivale)
SUBJECT: Opal and Lockstitch

You asked SAG to examine possible links between the disappearance of Galena Nadya Gribanov and her son Paul, and the murder in Ottawa of Marshall Teller, alias Yuri Smirnov, and to assess the two events.

There are few verifiable facts, and much of our information must be considered as tainted, since it is derived from our interrogation of Galena Gribanov and her somewhat suspect letter to Inspector Randall. Moreover, the investigation by US authorities into the background of the man posing as Teller is far from completed. It has been necessary, therefore, to make a number of assumptions, based on general knowledge and experience, gained over a period of many years.

There is a strong case to be made for believing her story that her father was in fact alive and had completed an assignment in Canada. From what we know of the elder Gribanov, he was a veteran operative of V Directorate. A 'Victor' operation was definitely being mounted in Canada — witness one dead agent and one assassination. It would appear that Galena Gribanov, immediately following her apprehension, genuinely cooperated with the RCMP. Her identification of the 'V for Victor' agent with the missing finger, and the other information she supplied supports this belief. The undisclosed radio does not necessarily detract from the genuineness of her cooperation. We know from long experience that even genuine doubles often hold on to secret means of communication.

If she was genuinely cooperating with us, it would require some cataclysmic event to cause so sudden a change of heart as is evidenced by her subsequent escape aboard the *MS Alexandr Pushkin*.

To arrive at a credible explanation of what may have happened, we have reviewed Galena Gribanov's various statements during interrogation.

The transcripts clearly demonstrate that her father and her son are central to her motivation. There would appear to be nothing involving Paul which might have caused her a change of heart. Indeed, her son's welfare would be strong support for her staying in Canada and cooperating fully with us. However, discovering that her father was still alive, would certainly be sufficient for her to change her mind.

Analysis of available material shows that there is no proof that Gribanov was killed when he and a number of NKVD members were arrested on Stalin's orders. Indeed, there is some evidence that at least a few of those arrested were transported to slave camps in Siberia, instead of being shot. Gribanov may have been among them.

Assume that Gribanov was transported to Siberia, that he survived, and, following Khruschev's denunciation of Stalin, was rehabilitated. Assume, further, that Galena recently received proof that satisfied her that her father was still alive. She would have had a powerful motive for continuing to work for he KGB.

Based on this hypothesis, it is possible to construct the following scenario. Galena, believing that her father was murdered by the NKVD , and that Lavrov had lied to her, confronts him with her knowledge during their last meeting. Very likely, as she told us under interrogation, she and Lavrov had a fight, during which he pulled a pistol on her. However, instead of acknowledging that her father was killed, Lavrov tells her that although he was among those purged by Stalin, he was not among those shot. Instead, he was transported to Siberia, that he survived and that he is alive. No doubt Galena refused to believe him, and demanded proof of what he said. In the time left to them at that meeting, Lavrov was unable to do this, but promised to provide her with proof, and to communicate it to her in Canada.

When the Security Service apprehended Galena in Ottawa shortly after her last meeting with Lavrov, she was in a bitter mood. She probably told the truth when she said that she had been contemplating defection. Thus, her cooperation probably was genuine.

Although it is impossible now to know how Lavrov got proof to Galena that her father was alive, this could have been done through Maria. The telegram Galena received from Maria seemed innocuous enough. Analysis gave no indication of a hidden code. However, the plain text could have contained a meaning known only to Galena.

If she received some indication that her father was alive, either from Lavrov or her father, it is not hard to imagine that she would change her mind about cooperating with us. Upon learning of the death of the 'V for Victor' agent, she probably decided to pass this information to the Centre in Moscow and to seek instructions. The only obvious means by which she could have done this quickly, was the wireless set she had secreted in her attic.

Intercepted clandestine shortwave traffic during the period in question could be interpreted as supporting this assumption. Between midnight and six a.m. on the night she was observed in the attic by Mrs. Haley, fourteen radio messages, tentatively classified as 'agent traffic' were recorded. Eight of these involved call signs which are currently in use in the Eastern United States. The remaining six could have originated anywhere in the Eastern half of North America. None of these six transmissions could be pinpointed by direction finding techniques. Two of these latter messages, sent on the 31 meter band, used a similar call sign hitherto unknown to us. One message totalled 72 groups, the other 32 groups. It seems logical to suppose that these messages were sent by Galena. The longer message probably contained her report of the death of the 'V for Victor' agent and a request for instructions.

It is not unreasonable to assume the two messages were sent from her attic, and that they involved an exchange with the Centre, instructing her, among other things, about escape routes, with the preferred plan being departure on the *Pushkin*.

Although there is nothing more than the flimsiest circumstantial evidence upon which to support the theory, SAG believes it is not impossible that Anatoli Gribanov was the assassin. We have a fairly clear description of the mysterious visitor to 7 Rideau Gate which fit the descriptions we have of Galena's father. If Gribanov was the assassin, it would have been simple for him, on leaving 7 Rideau Gate, to drive directly to Montreal, presumably in a rented car. Once there, he would have returned the car, and holed up until he could board the *Alexandr Pushkin* to await the arrival of Galena and his grandson.

It is interesting to speculate whether the Centre would have informed her that her father was to be personally involved, when she exchanged radio messages with Moscow. Probably not. There remains the question of why the Centre decided to withdraw Galena at this time. We can find no evidence to suggest that the Centre was aware that she had been cooperating with us. It is possible that Anatoli Gribanov may have been able to strike a bargain with the Centre. In return for taking on the dangerous task of assassinating Teller, he obtained their agreement to instruct Galena to return to Russia, bringing his grandson with her.

From the standpoint of the KGB, the Canadian end of the operation must be considered a success. They achieved their immediate objective; the liquidation of Smirnov/Teller. In the process they lost a valuable agent in the man with the missing finger. However, they would have been consoled by the knowledge that his suicide denied the Canadian and American authorities a potentially valuable source of information about Smirnov, and KGB operations generally. They recovered Galena, and, presumably also, her father, and assured their continued control of them. No doubt the elaborate Canadian cover of Galena's disappearance will cause them and her a few anxious moments, about this we shall have more to say in the conclusion to this memo.

As to the American aspects of the case, the KGB probably feel equally confident. No doubt they had long since discounted the possibility that the real identity of the man posing as

Marshall Teller might be discovered. Smirnov's death will have assured them that the Americans will be incapable of assessing the full extent of the damage done to their interests by him. They also must have reckoned that in an election year, the U.S. Administration would be unable to take any advantage from the affair. Certainly the administration is unlikely to advertise the fact that one of the country's most senior security figures was a Soviet agent.

Until the U.S. investigation of Yuri Smirnov is further advanced it seems pointless to speculate about possible organic links between the two cases. On the basis of the present evidence the only links we can detect are the facts that Smirnov's assassination was planned to take place in Canada, and that Galena's father may have been the assassin. Inspector Randall's observation of the interaction between Galena Gribanov and Smirnov at the State dinner is too flimsy a basis on which to develop any hypotheses.

Finally, there remains the question of retaliation. A 'spoiling operation' could be mounted. We could arrange to let the KGB know that Galena cooperated with us. However, the benefits to us of such a vindictive course are not obvious, and, it could have an unwelcome boomerang effect in political and other terms. The KGB, if they are convinced of her treachery, are not above staging a trial, at which her activities in Canada, or some of them, at least, would be widely publicized. No doubt, among other things, they would contrive to bring out the nature of her relationship with Marc Grandpre. Such a result would have serious political and other disadvantages for a government holding a minority position in the House of Commons. In any event, when they learn of our elaborate cover of Opal's disappearance, they are bound to suspect that we had already turned her. That being so, we gain considerably from the resources they will have to divert to establish her true role. At this juncture any benefit we can derive by leaving doubts in Zagorov's mind should be encouraged.

* * * * * * * * * * * * * * * * * * *

About the time the *MS Alexandr Pushkin* was rounding Bornholm Island, on the last leg of the run to Leningrad, Igor Nikolaevich Zotov, Chief of Archives for the Illegals Department in the First Chief Directorate of the KGB, was unlocking the steel grill-door to the file vaults in the modern buildings on the outskirts of Moscow, to which the Directorate had moved, when the headquarters building on Djerzhinsky Square no longer could accommodate the rapidly proliferating Chief Directorates and Directorates. The two-ton circular steel door, which stood open beyond the grill, had been installed due to Zotov's perseverance. Manufactured in Dresden in 1908, the vault door, with its massive steel tumblers and spoke wheel handles, had once guarded the Czar's gold bullion. In 1922, it was acquired by the Cheka, and eventually incorporated into the headquarters complex on Djerzhinsky Square. The engineers responsible for the new KGB building, had wanted a spanking new, electronically operated door for the special file room. Zotov fought them, and eventually won, since it turned out that the construction and installation costs of a new door, would be nearly double the costs of installing the old one.

The truth of the matter was that Zotov had been in love with the old door, hated to part with it and thoroughly distrusted electronic gadgetry.

"How do we know these gadgets will work."

To the criticism that the old door took time to open, he had replied, that, while that might be the case, it remained more secure. This was difficult to refute, since it took three men to open it. One to open the top combination, another to open the bottom combination, and an overseer, who knew neither combination, and whose sole function was to ensure that neither of the first two ever learned the combination for both locks.

Inside the large vault were row upon row of steel filing cabinets, each fitted with a combination lock. Zotov went to the over-sized card index in the centre of the room, unlocked the case and, in the North American Section, found the tray he was seeking. He removed the tray and carried it to the row of filing cabinets marked NA(Kanada). Opening the combination lock, he carefully checked the numerous volume numbers of the file against the records in the card index for 'Agent NA(Kanada) 26-40'.

Working expertly, he packed as many volumes of the file as possible into each of the yellow canvas bags he had brought with him, making a note of the volumes in each package. He secured the top of each bag with special steel wire and lead seals, clamped on with a powerful steel hand-vise. Each bag was consecutively numbered. The front and back of the bags was stencilled with the words; 'NA(Kanada) 26-40. Inactive. To be opened only with the authority of Director.' With the files all accounted for and sealed, he replaced them in the filing cabinet, re-setting the lock.

Zotov carefully made a number of notations in ink on the card of Agent NA(Kanada) 26-40, including the fact that the agent had been temporarily de-activated and transferred to the Fourth Department of the Second Chief Directorate. Pausing to review what he had written, he reflected that it was better to be able to record a 'de-activated' than a 'deceased'. There had been too many, 'Deceased-Microfilm and destroy', notations lately. And too many of the agents involved had died due to unnatural causes. North American casualties had been high. As he replaced the card in the tray Zotov took satisfaction from the fact that the next card, Agent NA(Kanada) 34-44, not only was active, but that the number of volumes of that file far surpassed the number he had just sealed for Agent NA(Kanada) 26-40.